COW-COUNTRY

Buddy knew Indians as he knew cattle, horses, rattlesnakes and storms—by having them mixed in with his everyday life. Perhaps his first ideas on Indians were gleaned from the friendly tribes who lived along the Chisolm Trail.

He couldn't tell you where or when he had learned that Indians are tricky . . .

COW-COUNTRY

B. M. Bower

GUNSMOKE

First published by Hodder and Stoughton

This hardback edition 2002
by Chivers Press
by arrangement with
Golden West Literary Agency

ISBN 0 7540 8181 8

British Library Cataloguing in Publication Data available.

CONTENTS

COW–COUNTRY

CHAPTER ONE

An Ambitious Man-Child Was Buddy

In hot mid afternoon when the acrid, gray dust-cloud kicked up by the listless plodding of eight thousand cloven hoofs formed the only blot on the hard blue above the Staked Plains, an ox stumbled and fell awkwardly under his yoke, and refused to scramble up when his negro driver shouted and prodded him with the end of a willow gad.

"Call your master, Ezra," directed a quiet woman-voice gone weary and toneless with the heat and two restless children. "Don't beat the poor brute. He can't go any farther and carry the yoke, much less pull the wagon."

Ezra dropped the gad and stepped upon the wagon tongue where he might squint into the dust cloud and decide which gray, plodding horseman alongside the herd was Robert Birnie. Far across the sluggish river of grimy backs, a horse threw up its head with a peculiar sidelong motion, and Ezra's eyes lightened with recognition. That was the colt, Rattler, chafing against the slow pace he must keep. Hands cupped around big, chocolate-colored lips and big, yellow-white teeth, Ezra *whoo-ee-ed* the signal that called the nearest riders to the wagon that held the boss's family.

Bob Birnie and another man turned and came trotting back, and at the call a scrambling youngster peered over his mother's shoulder in the forward opening of the prairie schooner.

"O-oh, Dulcie! We gonna git a wile cow agin!"

Dulcie was asleep and did not answer, and the woman in the slat sun-bonnet pushed back with her elbow the eager, squirming body of her eldest. "Stay in the wagon, Buddy. Must n't get down amongst the oxen. One might kick you. Lie down and take a nap with sister. When you waken it will be nice and cool again."

"*Not* s'eepy!" objected Buddy for the twentieth time in the past two hours. But he crawled back, and his mother, relieved of his restless presence, leaned forward to watch the approach of her husband and the cowboy. This was the second time in the past two days that an ox had fallen exhausted, and her eyes showed a trace of anxiety. With the feed so poor and the water so scarce, it seemed as though the heavy wagon, loaded with a few household idols too dear to leave behind, a camp outfit and the necessary clothing and bedding for a woman and two children, was going to be a real handicap on the drive.

"Robert, if we had another wagon, I could drive it and make the load less for these four oxen," she suggested when her husband came up. "A lighter wagon, perhaps with one team of strong horses, or even with a yoke of oxen, I could drive well enough, and relieve these poor brutes." She pushed back her sun-bonnet and with it a mass of red-brown hair that curled damply on her forehead, and smiled disarmingly. "Buddy would be the happiest baby boy alive if I could let him drive now and then!" she added humorously.

"Can't make a wagon and an extra yoke of oxen out of this cactus patch," Bob Birnie grinned good-humoredly. "Not even to tickle Buddy. I'll see what I can do when we reach Olathe. But you won't have to take a man's place and drive, Lassie." He took the cup of water she drew from a keg and proffered — water was precious on the Staked Plains, that season — and his eyes dwelt on her fondly while he drank. Then, giving her hand a squeeze when he returned the cup, he rode back to scan the herd for an animal big enough and well-conditioned enough to supplant the worn-out ox.

"Aren't you thirsty, Frank Davis? I think a cup of water will do you good," she called out to the cowboy, who had dismounted to tighten his forward cinch in expectation of having to use his rope.

The cowboy dropped stirrup from saddle horn and came forward stiff-leggedly, leading his horse. His sun-baked face, grimed with the dust of the herd, was aglow with heat, and his eyes showed gratitude. A cup of water from the hand of the boss's wife was worth a gallon from the barrel slip-slopping along in the lurching chuck-wagon.

"How's the kids makin' out, Mis' Birnie?" Frank inquired politely when he had swallowed the last drop and had wiped his mouth with the back of his hand. "It's right warm and dusty t'day."

"They're asleep at last, thank goodness," she answered, glancing back at a huddle of pink calico that showed just over the crest of a pile of crumpled quilts. "Buddy has a hard time of it. He's all man in his disposition, and all baby in size. He's been teasing to walk with the niggers and help drive the drag. Is my husband calling?"

Her husband was, and Frank rode away at a leisurely trot. Haste had little to do with trailing a herd, where eight miles was called a good day's journey and six an average achievement. The fallen ox was unyoked by the mellow-voiced but exasperated Ezra, and since he would not rise, the three remaining oxen, urged by the gad and Ezra's upbraiding, swung the wagon to one side and moved it a little farther after the slow-moving herd, so that the exhausted animal could rest, and the raw recruit be yoked in where he could do the least harm and would the speediest learn a new lesson in discomfort. Mrs. Birnie glanced again at the huddle of pink in the nest of quilts behind a beloved chest of drawers in the wagon, and sighed with relief because Buddy slept.

An ambitious man-child already was Buddy, accustomed to certain phrases that, since he could toddle, had formed inevitable accompaniment to his investigative footsteps. "L'k-out-dah!" he had for a long time believed to be his name among the black folk of his world. White folk had varied it slightly. He knew that "Run-to-mother-now" meant that something he would delight in but must not watch was going to take place. Spankings more or less official and not often painful signified that big folks did not understand him and his activities, or were cross about something. Now, mother did not want him to watch the wild cow run and jump at the end of a rope until finally forced to submit to the ox-yoke and help pull the wagon. Buddy loved to watch them, but he understood that mother was afraid the wild cow might step on him. Why she should want him to sleep when he was not sleepy he had not yet discovered, and so disdained to give it serious consideration.

"*Not* s'eepy," Buddy stated again emphatically as a sort of mental dismissal of the command, and crawled carefully past Sister and lifted a flap of the canvas cover. A button — the last button — popped off his pink apron and the sleeves rumpled down over his hands. It felt all loose and useless, so Buddy stopped long enough to pull the apron off and throw it beside Sister before he crawled under the canvas flap and walked down the spokes of a rear wheel. He did not mean to get in the way of the wild cow, but he did want action for his restless legs. He thought that if he went away from the wagon and the herd and played while they were catching the wild cow, it would be just the same as if he took a nap. Mother had n't thought of it, or she might have suggested it.

So Buddy went away from the wagon and down into a shallow dry wash where the wild cow would not come, and played. The first thing he saw was a scorpion — nasty old bug that will bite *hard* — and he threw rocks at it until it scuttled under a ledge out of sight. The next thing he saw that interested him at all was a horned toad; a *hawn*-toe, he called it, after Ezra's manner of speaking. Ezra had caught a *hawn*-toe for him a few days ago, but it had mysteriously disappeared out of the wagon. Buddy did not connect his mother's lack of enthusiasm with the disappearance. Her sympathy with his loss had seemed to him real, and he wanted another, fully believing that in this also mother would be pleased. So he took after this particular *hawn*-toe, that crawled into various hiding places only to be spied and routed out with small rocks and a sharp stick.

The dry wash remained shallow, and after a while Buddy, still in hot pursuit of the horned toad, emerged upon the level where the herd had passed. The wagon was nowhere in sight, but this did not disturb Buddy. He was not lost. He knew perfectly that the brown cloud on his narrowed horizon was the dust over the herd, and that the wagon was just behind, because the wind that day was blowing from the southwest, and also because the oxen did not walk as fast as the herd. In the distance he saw the " drag " moving lazily along after the dust-cloud, with barefooted niggers driving the laggard cattle and singing dolefully as they walked. Emphatically Buddy was not lost.

He wanted that particular horned toad, however, and he kept after it until he had it safe in his two hands.

It happened that when he pounced at last upon the toad he disturbed with his presence a colony of red ants on moving day. The close ranks of them, coming and going in a straight line, caught and held Buddy's attention to the exclusion of everything else — save the horned toad he had been at such pains to acquire. He tucked the toad inside his underwaist and ignored its wriggling against his flesh while he squatted in the hot sunshine and watched the ants, his mind one great question. Where were they going, and what were they carrying, and why were they all in such a hurry?

Buddy had to know. To himself he called it a trail

herd — but father's cattle did not carry white lumps of stuff on their heads, and furthermore, they all walked together in the same direction; whereas the ant herd traveled both ways. Buddy made sure of this, and then started off, following what he had decided was the real trail of the ants. Most children would have stirred them up with a stick; Buddy let them alone so that he could see what they were doing all by themselves.

The ants led him to a tiny hole with a finely pulverized rim just at the edge of a sprawly cactus. This last Buddy carefully avoided, for even at four years old he had long ago learned the sting of cactus thorns. A rattlesnake buzzed warning when he backed away, and the shock to Buddy's nerves roused within him the fighting spirit. Rattlesnakes he knew also, as the common enemy of men and cattle. Once a steer had been bitten on the nose and his head had swollen up so he could n't eat. Buddy did not want that to happen to *him*.

He made sure that the horned toad was safe, chose a rock as large as he could lift and heave from him, and threw it at the buzzing, gray coil. He did not wait to see what happened, but picked up another rock, a terrific buzzing sounding stridently from the coil. He threw another and another with all the force of his healthy little muscles. For a four-year-old he aimed well; several of the rocks landed on the coil.

The snake wriggled feebly from under the rocks and tried to crawl away and hide, its rattles clicking listlessly. Buddy had another rock in his hands and in his eyes the blue fire of righteous conquest. He went close — close enough to have brought a protesting cry from a grownup — lifted the rock high as he could and brought it down fair on the battered head of the rattler. The loathsome length of it winced and thrashed ineffectively, and after a few minutes lay slack, the tail wriggling aimlessly.

Buddy stood with his feet far apart and his hands on his hips, as he had seen the cowboy do whom he had unconsciously imitated in the killing.

" Snakes like Injuns. Dead 'ns is good 'ns," he observed sententiously, still playing the part of the cowboy. Then, quite sure that the snake was dead, he took it by the tail, felt again of the horned toad on his chest and went back to see what the ants were doing.

When so responsible a person as a grownup stops to watch the orderly activities of an army of ants, minutes and hours slip away unnoticed. Buddy was absolutely fascinated, lost to everything else. When some instinct born in the very blood of him warned Buddy that time was passing, he stood up and saw that the sun hung just above the edge of the world, and that the sky was a glorious jumble of red and purple and soft rose.

The first thing Buddy did was to stoop and study attentively the dead snake, to see if the tail still wiggled. It did not, though he watched it for a full minute. He looked at the sun — it had not " set " but glowed big and yellow as far from the earth as his father was tall. Ezra had lied to him. Dead snakes did not wiggle their tails until sundown.

Buddy looked for the dust cloud of the herd, and was surprised to find it smaller than he had ever seen it, and farther away. Indeed, he could only guess that the faint smudge on the horizon was the dust he had followed for more days than he could count. He was not afraid, but he was hungry and he thought his mother would maybe wonder where he was, and he knew that the point-riders had already stopped pushing the herd ahead, and that the cattle were feeding now so that they would bed down at dusk. The chuck-wagon was camped somewhere close by, and old Step-and-a-Half, the lame cook, was stirring things in his Dutch ovens over the camp-fire. Buddy could almost smell the beans and the meat stew, he was so hungry. He turned and took one last, long look at the endless stream of ants still crawling along, picked up the dead snake by the tail, cupped the other hand over the horned toad inside his waist, and started for camp.

After a while he heard someone shouting, but beyond a faint relief that he was after all near his " outfit ", Buddy paid no attention. The boys were always shouting to one another, or yelling at their horses or at the herd or at the niggers. It did not occur to him that they might be shouting for him, until from another direction he heard Ezra's unmistakable, booming voice. Ezra sang a thunderous baritone when the niggers lifted up their voices in song around their camp-fire, and he could be heard for half a mile when he called in real earnest. He was calling now, and Buddy, stopping to listen, fancied that he heard his name. A little farther on, he was sure of it.

" Ooo-*ee!* Whah y' all, Buddy? Ooo-*eee!* "

" I 'm a-comin'," Buddy shrilled impatiently. " What y' all want? "

His piping voice did not carry to Ezra, who kept on shouting. The radiant purple and red and gold above him deepened, darkened. The whole wild expanse of half-barren land became suddenly a place of unearthly beauty that dulled to the shadows of dusk. Buddy trudged on, keeping to the deep-worn buffalo trails which the herd had followed and scored afresh with their hoofs. He could not miss his way — not Buddy, son of Bob Birnie, owner of the Tomahawk outfit — but his legs were growing pretty tired, and he was so hungry that he could have sat down on the ground and cried with the gnawing food-call of his empty little stomach.

He could hear other voices shouting at intervals now, but Ezra's voice was the loudest and the closest, and it seemed to Buddy that Ezra never once stopped calling. Twice Buddy called back that he was a-comin', but Ezra shouted just the same: " *Ooo-ee! Whah y' all, Buddy? Ooo-ee!* "

Imperceptibly dusk deepened to darkness. A gust of anger swept Buddy's soul because he was tired, because he was hungry and he was yet a long way from the camp, but chiefly because Ezra persisted in calling after Buddy had several times answered. He heard someone whom he recognized as Frank Davis, but by this time he was so angry that he would not say a word, though he was tempted to ask Frank to take him up on his horse and let him ride to camp. He heard others — and once the beat of hoofs came quite close. But there was a wide streak of Scotch stubbornness in Buddy — along with several other Scotch streaks — and he continued his stumbling progress, dragging the snake by the tail, his other hand holding fast the horned toad.

His heart jumped up and almost choked him when

he first saw the three twinkles on the ground which he knew were not stars but camp-fires.

Quite unexpectedly he trudged into the firelight where Step-and-a-Half was stirring delectable things in the iron pots and stopping every minute or so to stare anxiously into the gloom. Buddy stood blinking and sniffing, his eyes fixed upon the Dutch ovens.

"I'm *hungry!*" he announced accusingly, gripping the toad that had begun to squirm at the heat and light. "I kilt a snake an' I'm *hungry!*"

"Good gorry!" swore Step-and-a-Half, and whipped out his six-shooter and fired three shots into the air.

Footsteps came scurrying. Buddy's mother swept him into her arms, laughing with a little whimpering sound of tears in the laughter. Buddy wriggled protestingly in her arms.

"L'kout! Y'all *skush* 'im! I got a *hawn*-toe; wight here." He patted his chest gloatingly. "An' I got a snake. I kilt 'im. An' I'm *hungry.*"

Mother of Buddy though she was, Lassie set him down hurriedly and surveyed her man-child from a little distance.

"Buddy! Drop that snake instantly!"

Buddy obeyed, but he planted a foot close to his kill and pouted his lips. "'S *my* snake. I kilt 'im," he said firmly. He pulled the horned toad from his waist-front and held it tightly in his two hands. "An 's my *hawn*-toe. I ketched 'm. 'Way ova dere," he added, tilting his tow head toward the darkness behind him.

Bob Birnie rode up at a gallop, pulled up his horse in the edge of the fire glow and dismounted hastily.

Bob Birnie never needed more than one glance to furnish him the details of a scene. He saw the very small boy confronting his mother with a dead snake, a horned toad and a stubborn set to his lips. He saw that the mother looked rather helpless before the combination — and his brown mustache hid a smile. He walked up and looked his first-born over.

"Buddy," he demanded sternly, "where have you been?"

"Out dere. Kilt a snake. Ants was trailing a herd. I got a *hawn*-toe. An' I 'm hungry!"

"You know better than to leave the wagon, young man. Did n't you know we had to get out and hunt you, and mother was scared the wolves might eat you? Did n't you hear us calling you? Why did n't you answer?"

Buddy looked up from under his baby eyebrows at his father, who seemed very tall and very terrible. But his bare foot touched the dead snake and he took comfort. "I was comin'," he said. "I *was n't* los'. I bringed my snake and my *hawn*-toe. An' dey — *was n't* — any — woluffs!" The last word came muffled, buried in his mother's skirts.

CHAPTER TWO

THE TRAIL HERD

DAY after day the trail herd plodded slowly to the north, following the buffalo trails that would lead to water, and the crude map of one who had taken a herd north and had returned with a tale of vast plains and no rivals. Always through the day the dust cloud hung over the backs of the cattle, settled into the clothes of those who followed, grimed the pink aprons of Buddy and his small sister Dulcie so that they were no longer pink. Whenever a stream was reached, mother searched patiently for clear water and an untrampled bit of bank where she might do the family washing, leaving Ezra to mind the children. But even so the dust and the wear and tear of travel remained to harass her fastidious soul.

Buddy remembered that drive as he could not remember the comfortable ranch house of his earlier babyhood. To him afterward it seemed that life began with the great herd of cattle. He came to know just how low the sun must slide from the top of the sky before the " point " would spread out with noses to the ground, pausing wherever a mouthful of grass was to be found. When these leaders of the herd stopped, the cattle would scatter and begin feeding. If there was water they would crowd the banks of the stream or pool, pushing and prodding one another with their great, sharp horns. Later, when the sun was gone and dusk crept out of nowhere, the cowboys would ride slowly around the herd, pushing it quietly into a smaller compass. Then, if Buddy were not too sleepy, he would watch the cattle lie down to chew their cuds in deep, sighing content until they slept. It reminded Buddy vaguely of when mother popped corn in a wire popper, a long time ago — before they all lived in a wagon and went with the herd. First one and two — then there would be three, four, five, as many as Buddy could count — then the whole herd would be lying down.

Buddy loved the camp-fires. The cowboys would sit around the one where his father and mother sat — mother with Dulcie in her arms — and they would smoke and tell stories, until mother told him it was time little boys were in bed. Buddy always wanted to know what they said after he had climbed into the big wagon where mother had made a bed, but he never found out. He could remember lying there listening sometimes to the niggers singing at their own camp-fire within call, Ezra always singing the loudest, — just as a bull always could be heard above the bellowing of the herd.

All his life, Ezra's singing and the monotonous bellowing of a herd reminded Buddy of one mysteriously terrible time when there weren't any rivers or any ponds or anything along the trail, and they had to be careful of the water and save it, and he and Dulcie were not asked to wash their faces. I think that miracle helped to fix the incident indelibly in Buddy's mind; that, and the bellowing of the cattle. It seemed a month to Buddy, but as he grew older he learned that it was three days they went without water.

The first day he did not remember especially, except that mother had talked about clean aprons that night, and failed to produce any. The second he recalled quite clearly. Father came to the wagons sometime in the night to see if mother was asleep. Their murmured talk wakened Buddy and he heard father say: "We'll hold 'em, all right, Lassie. And there's water ahead. It's marked on the trail map. Don't you worry — I'll stay up and help the boys. The cattle are uneasy — but we'll hold 'em."

The third day Buddy never forgot. That was the day when mother forgot that q stands for Quagga, and permitted Buddy to call it p, just for fun, because it looked so much like p. And when he said "w is water", mother made a funny sound and said right out loud, "Oh God, please!" and told Buddy to creep back and play with Sister — when Sister was asleep, and there were still x, y and z to say, let alone that mysterious And-so-forth which seemed to mean so much and so little and never was called upon to help spell a word. Never since he began to have lessons had mother omitted a single letter or cut the study hour down the teeniest little bit.

Buddy was afraid of something, but he could not think what it was that frightened him. He began to think seriously about water, and to listen uneasily to the constant lowing of the herd. The increased shouting of the niggers driving the lagging ones held a sudden significance. It occurred to him that the niggers had their hands full, and that they had never driven so big a "drag." It was hotter than ever, too, and they had twice stopped to yoke in fresh oxen. Ezra had boasted all along that ole Bawley would keep his end up till they got clah to Wyoming. But ole Bawley had stopped, and stopped, and at last had to be taken out of the yoke. Buddy began to wish they would hurry up and find a river.

None of the cowboys would take him on the saddle and let him ride, that day. They looked harassed — Buddy called it cross — when they rode up to the wagon to give their horses a few mouthfuls of water from the barrel. Step-and-a-Half could n't spare any more, they told mother. He had declared at noon that he needed every drop he had for the cooking, and there would be no washing of dishes whatever. Later, mother had studied a map and afterwards had sat for a long while staring out over the backs of the cattle, her face white. Buddy thought perhaps mother was sick.

That day lasted hours and hours longer than any other day that Buddy could remember. His father looked cross, too, when he rode back to them. Once it was to look at the map which mother had studied. They talked together afterwards, and Buddy heard his father say that she must not worry; the cattle had good bottom, and could stand thirst better than a poor herd, and another dry camp would not really hurt anyone.

He had uncovered the water barrel and looked in, and had ridden straight over to the chuck-wagon, his horse walking alongside the high seat where Step-and-a-Half sat perched listlessly with a long-lashed ox-whip in his hand. Father had talked for a few minutes, and had ridden back scowling.

"That old scoundrel has got two ten-gallon kegs that have n't been touched!" he told mother. "Yo' all must n't water any more horses out of your barrel. Send the boys to Step-and-a-Half. Yo' all keep what you 've got. The horses have got to have water — to-night it 's going to be hell to hold the herd, and if anybody goes thirsty it 'll be the men, not the horses. But yo' all send them to the other wagon, Lassie. Mind, now! Not a drop to anyone."

After father rode away, Buddy crept up and put his two short arms around mother. "Don't cry. I don't have to drink any water," he soothed her. He waited a minute and added optimistically, "Dere 's a *bi-ig* wiver comin' pitty soon. Oxes smells water a hunerd miles. Ezra says so. An' las' night Crumpy was snuffin' an' snuffin'. I saw 'im do it. He smelt a *big* wiver. *That* bi-ig!" He spread his short arms as wide apart as they would reach, and smiled tremulously.

Mother squeezed Buddy so hard that he grunted.

"Dear little man, of course there is. *We* don't mind, do we? I — was feeling sorry for the poor cattle."

"De 're firsty," Buddy stated solemnly, his eyes big. "De 're bawlin' fer a drink of water. I guess de 're *awful* firsty. Dere 's a big wiver comin' now. Crumpy smelt a big wiver."

Buddy's mother stared across the arid plain parched into greater barrenness by the heat that had been unremitting for the past week. Buddy's faith in the big river she could not share. Somehow they had drifted off the trail marked on the map drawn by George Williams.

Williams had warned them to carry as much water as possible in barrels, as a precaution against suffering if they failed to strike water each night. He had told them that water was scarce, but that his cowboy scouts and the deep-worn buffalo trails had been able to bring him through with water at every camp save two or three. The Staked Plains, he said, would be the hardest drive. And this was the Staked Plains — and it was hard driving!

Buddy did not know all that until afterwards, when he heard father talk of the drive north. But he would have remembered that day and the night that followed, even though he had never heard a word about it. The bawling of the herd became a doleful chant of misery. Even the phlegmatic oxen that drew the wagons bawled and slavered while they strained forward, twisting their heads under the heavy yokes. They stopped oftener than usual to rest, and when Buddy was permitted to walk with the perspiring Ezra by the leaders, he wondered why the oxen's eyes were red, like Dulcie's when she had one of her crying spells.

At night the cowboys did not tie their horses and sit down while they ate, but stood by their mounts and bolted food hurriedly, one eye always on the restless cattle, that walked around and around, and would neither eat nor lie down, but lowed incessantly. Once a few animals came close enough to smell the water in a bucket where Frank Davis was watering his sweat-streaked horse, and Step-and-a-Half's wagon was almost upset before the maddened cattle could be driven back to the main herd.

"No use camping," Bob Birnie told the boys gath-

ered around Step-and-a-Half's Dutch ovens. "The
cattle won't stand. We'll wear ourselves and them
out trying to hold 'em — they may as well be hunting
water as running in circles. Step-and-a-Half, keep
your cooked grub handy for the boys, and yo' all pack
up and pull out. We'll turn the cattle loose and follow. If there's any water in this damned country
they'll find it."

Years afterwards, Buddy learned that his father
had sent men out to hunt water, and that they had not
found any. He was ten when this was discussed
around a spring roundup fire, and he had studied the
matter for a few minutes and then had spoken boldly
his mind.

"You oughta kept your horses as thirsty as the
cattle was, and I bet they'd a' found that water," he
criticized, and was sent to bed for his tactlessness.
Bob Birnie himself had thought of that afterwards,
and had excused the oversight by saying that he had
depended on the map, and had not foreseen a three-
day dry drive.

However that may be, that night was a night of
panicky desperation. Ezra walked beside the oxen
and shouted and swung his lash, and the oxen strained
forward bellowing so that not even Dulcie could
sleep, but whimpered fretfully in her mother's arms.
Buddy sat up wide-eyed and watched for the big
river, and tried not to be a 'fraid-cat and cry like
Dulcie.

It was long past starry midnight when a little wind
puffed out of the darkness and the oxen threw up their
heads and sniffed, and put a new note into their
" M-*baw-aw-aw*-mm!" They swung sharply so that

the wind blew straight into the front of the wagon, which lurched forward with a new impetus.

"Glo-ory t' Gawd, Missy! Dey smells watah, sho 's yo' bawn!" sobbed Ezra as he broke into a trot beside the wheelers. "'Tain't fur — lookit dat-ah huhd a-goin' it! No 'm, Missy, *dey* ain't woah out — dey smellin' watah an' dey 'm gittin' *to* it! 'Tain't fur, Missy."

Buddy clung to the back of the seat and stared round-eyed into the gloom. He never forgot that lumpy shadow which was the herd, traveling fast in dust that obscured the nearest stars. The shadow humped here and there as the cattle crowded forward at a shuffling half trot, the *click*-swash of their shambling feet treading close on one another. The rapping tattoo of wide-spread horns clashing against wide-spread horns filled him with a formless terror, so that he let go the seat to clutch at mother's dress. He was not afraid of cattle — they were as much a part of his world as were Ezra and the wagon and the camp-fires — but he trembled with the dread which no man could name for him.

These were not the normal, everyday sounds of the herd. The herd had somehow changed from plodding animals to one overwhelming purpose that would sweep away anything that came in its path. Two thousand parched throats and dust-dry tongues — and suddenly the smell of water that would go gurgling down two thousand eager gullets, and every intervening second a cursed delay against which the cattle surged blindly. It was the mob spirit, when the mob was fighting for its very existence.

Over the bellowing of the cattle a yelling cowboy

now and then made himself heard. The four oxen straining under their yokes broke into a lumbering gallop lest they be outdistanced by the herd, and Dulcie screamed when the wagon lurched across a dry wash and almost upset, while Ezra plied the ox-whip and yelled frantically at first one ox and then another, inventing names for the new ones. Buddy drew in his breath and held it until the wagon rolled on four wheels instead of two, — but he did not scream.

Still the big river did not come. It seemed to Buddy that the cattle would never stop running. Tangled in the terror was Ezra's shouting as he ran alongside the wagon and called to Missy that it was " dat ole Crumpy actin' the fool ", and that the wagon would n't upset. " No 'm, dey 's jest in a hurry to git dere fool haids sunk to de eyes in dat watah. Dey ain't aimin' to run away — no 'm, dish yer ain't no stampede ! "

Perhaps Buddy dozed. The next thing he remembered, day was breaking, with the sun all red, seen through the dust. The herd was still going, but now it was running and somehow the yoked oxen were keeping close behind, lumbering along with heads held low and the sweat reeking from their spent bodies. Buddy heard dimly his mother's sharp command to Ezra :

" Stand back, Ezra ! We 're not going to be caught in that terrible trap. They 're piling over the bank ahead of us. Get away from the leaders. I am going to shoot."

Buddy crawled up a little higher on the blankets behind the seat, and saw mother steady herself and aim the rifle straight at Crumpy. There was the familiar, deafening roar, the acrid smell of black powder smoke, and Crumpy went down loosely, his nose rooting the trampled ground for a space before the gun belched black smoke again and Crumpy's yoke-mate pitched forward. The wagon stopped so abruptly that Buddy sprawled helplessly on his back like an overturned beetle.

He saw mother stand looking down at the wheelers, that backed and twisted their necks under their yokes. Her lips were set firmly together, and her eyes were bright with purple hollows beneath. She held the rifle for a moment, then set the butt of it on the "jockey box" just in front of the dashboard. The wheelers, helpless between the weight of the wagon behind and the dead oxen in front, might twist their necks off but they could do no damage.

"Unyoke the wheelers, Ezra, and let the poor creatures have their chance at the water," she cried sharply, and Ezra, dodging the horns of the frantic brutes, made shift to obey.

Fairly on the bank of the sluggish stream with its flood-worn channel and its treacherous patches of quicksand, the wagon thus halted by the sheer nerve and quick-thinking of mother became a very small island in a troubled sea of weltering backs and tossing horns and staring eyeballs. Riders shouted and lashed unavailingly with their quirts, trying to hold back the full bulk of the herd until the foremost had slaked their thirst and gone on. But the herd was crazy for the water, and the foremost were plunged headlong into the soft mud where they mired, trampled under the hoofs of those who came crowding from behind.

Someone shouted, close to the wagon yet down the

bank at the edge of the water. The words were in-distinguishable, but a warning was in the voice. On the echo of that cry, a man screamed twice.

"Ezra!" cried mother fiercely. "It's Frank Davis — they've got him down, somehow. Climb over the backs of the cattle — there's no other way — and *get him!*"

"Yas'm, Missy!" Ezra called back, and then Buddy saw him go over the herd, scrambling, jumping from back to back.

Buddy remembered that always, and the funeral they had later in the day, when the herd was again just trail-weary cattle feeding hungrily on the scanty grass. Down at the edge of the creek the carcasses of many dead animals lay half-buried in the mud. Up on a little knoll where a few stunted trees grew, the negroes dug a long, deep hole. Mother's eyes were often filled with tears that day, and the cowboys scarcely talked at all when they gathered at the chuck-wagon.

After a while they all went to the hole which the negroes had dug, and there was a long Something wrapped up in canvas. Mother wore her best dress, which was black, and father and all the boys had shaved their faces and looked very sober. The negroes stood back in a group by themselves, and every few minutes Buddy saw them draw their tattered shirt-sleeves across their faces. And father — Buddy looked once and saw two tears running down father's cheeks. Buddy was shocked into a stony calm. He had never dreamed that fathers ever cried.

Mother read out of her Bible, and all the boys held their hats in front of them, with their hands clasped, and looked at the ground while she read. Then mother sang. She sang, " We shall meet beyond the river ", which Buddy thought was a very queer song, because they were all there but Frank Davis; then she sang " Nearer, My God, to Thee." Buddy sang too, piping the notes accurately, with a vague pronunciation of the words and a feeling that somehow he was helping mother.

After that they put the long, canvas-wrapped Something down in the hole, and mother said " Our Father Who Art in Heaven ", with Buddy repeating it uncertainly after her and pausing to say " *treth*patheth " very carefully. Then mother picked up Dulcie in her arms, took Buddy by the hand and walked slowly back to the wagon, and would not let him turn to see what the boys were doing.

It was from that day that Buddy missed Frank Davis, who had mysteriously gone to Heaven, according to mother. Buddy's interest in Heaven was extremely keen for a time, and he asked questions which not even mother could answer. Then his memory of Frank Davis blurred. But never his memory of that terrible time when the Tomahawk outfit lost five hundred cattle in the dry drive and the stampede for water.

CHAPTER THREE

Some Indian Lore

Buddy knew Indians as he knew cattle, horses, rattlesnakes and storms — by having them mixed in with his everyday life. He could n't tell you where or when he had learned that Indians are tricky. Perhaps his first ideas on that subject were gleaned from the friendly tribes who lived along the Chisolm Trail and used to visit the chuck-wagon, their blankets held close around them and their eyes glancing everywhere while they grinned and talked and pointed — and ate. Buddy used to sit in the chuck-wagon, out of harm's way, and watch them eat.

Step-and-a-Half had a way of entertaining Indians which never failed to interest Buddy, however often he witnessed it. When Step-and-a-Half glimpsed Indians coming afar off, he would take his dishpan and dump into it whatever scraps of food were left over from the preceding meal. He used to say that Indians could smell grub as far as a buzzard can smell a dead carcase, and Buddy believed it, for they always arrived at meal time or shortly afterwards. Step-and-a-Half would make a stew, if there were scraps enough. If the gleanings were small, he would use the dishwater — he was a frugal man — and with that for the start-off he would make soup, which the Indians gulped down with great relish and many gurgly sounds.

Buddy watched them eat what he called pig-dinner. When Step-and-a-Half was not looking he saw them steal whatever their dirty brown hands could readily snatch and hide under their blankets. So he knew from very early experience that Indians were not to be trusted.

Once, when he had again strayed too far from camp, some Indians riding that way saw him, and one leaned and lifted him from the ground and rode off with him. Buddy did not struggle much. He saved his breath for the long, shrill yell of cow-country. Twice he yodled before the Indian clapped a hand over his mouth.

Father and some of the cowboys heard and came after, riding hard and shooting as they came. Buddy's pink apron fluttered a signal flag in the arms of his captor, and so it happened that the bullets whistled close to that particular Indian. He gathered a handful of calico between Buddy's shoulders, held him aloft like a puppy, leaned far over and deposited him on the ground.

Buddy rolled over twice and got up, a little dizzy and very indignant, and shouted to father, " Shoot a sunsyguns! "

From that time Buddy added hatred to his distrust of Indians.

From the time when he was four until he was thirteen Buddy's life contained enough thrills to keep a movie-mad boy of to-day sitting on the edge of his seat gasping enviously through many a reel, but to Buddy it was all rather humdrum and monotonous.

What he wanted to do was to get out and hunt buffalo. Just herding horses, and watching out for Indians, and killing rattlesnakes was what any boy in the country would be doing. Still, Buddy himself achieved now and then a thrill.

There was one day, when he stood heedlessly on a ridge looking for a dozen head of lost horses in the draws below. It was all very well to explain missing horses by the conjecture that the Injuns must have got them, but Buddy happened to miss old Rattler with the others. Rattler had come north with the trail herd, and he was wise beyond the wisdom of most horses. He would drive cattle out of the brush without a rider to guide him, if only you put a saddle on him. He had helped Buddy to mount his back — when Buddy was much smaller than now — by lowering his head until Buddy straddled it, and then lifting it so that Buddy slid down his neck and over his withers to his back. Even now Buddy sometimes mounted that way when no one was looking. Many other lovable traits had Rattler, and to lose him would be a tragedy to the family.

So Buddy was on the ridge, scanning all the deep little washes and draws, when a bullet *ping-g-ged* over his head. Buddy caught the bridle reins and pulled his horse into the shelter of rocks, untied his rifle from the saddle and crept back to reconnoitre. It was the first time he had ever been shot at — except in the army posts, when the Indians had "broken out",— and the aim then was generally directed toward his vicinity rather than his person.

An Indian on a horse presently appeared cautiously from cover, and Buddy, trembling with excitement, shot wild; but not so wild that the Indian could afford to scoff and ride closer. After another ineffectual shot at Buddy, he whipped his horse down the ridge, and made for Bannock creek.

Buddy at thirteen knew more of the wiles of Indians than does the hardiest Indian fighter on the screen to-day. Father had warned him never to chase an Indian into cover, where others would probably be waiting for him. So he stayed where he was, pretty well hidden in the rocks, and let the bullets he himself had " run " in father's bullet-mold follow the enemy to the fringe of bushes. His last shot knocked the Indian off his horse — or so it looked to Buddy. He waited for a long time, watching the brush and thinking what a fool that Indian was to imagine Buddy would follow him down there. After a while he saw the Indian's horse climbing the slope across the creek. There was no rider.

Buddy rode home without the missing horses, and did not tell anyone about the Indian, though his thoughts would not leave the subject.

He wondered what mother would think of it. Mother's interests seemed mostly confined to teaching Buddy and Dulcie what they were deprived of learning in schools, and to play the piano — a wonderful old square piano that had come all the way from Scotland to the Tomahawk ranch, the very frontier of the West.

Mother was a wonderful woman, with a soft voice and a slight Scotch accent, and wit; and a knowledge of things which were little known in the wilderness. Buddy never dreamed then how strangely culture was mixed with pure savagery in his life. To him the secret regret that he had not dared ride into the bushes to scalp the Indian he believed he had shot, and the fact that his hands were straining at the full chords of the *Anvil Chorus* on that very evening, was not even to be considered unusual. Still, certain strains of that classic were always afterward associated in his mind with the shooting of the Indian — if he had really shot him.

While he counted the time with a conscientious regard for the rests, he debated the wisdom of telling mother, and decided that perhaps he had better keep that matter to himself, like a man.

CHAPTER FOUR

BUDDY GIVES WARNING

BUDDY swung down from his horse, unsaddled it and went staggering to the stable wall with the burden of a stock-saddle much too big for him. He had to stand on his boot-toes to reach and pull the bridle down over the ears of Whitefoot, which turned with an air of immense relief into the corral gate and the hay piled at the further end. Buddy gave him one pre-occupied glance and started for the cabin, walking with the cowpuncher's peculiar, bowlegged gait which comes of wearing chaps and throwing out the knees to overcome the stiffness of the leather. At thirteen Buddy was a cowboy from hat-crown to spurs — and at thirteen Buddy gloried in the fact. To-day, how-ever, his mind was weighted with matters of more importance than himself.

"The Utes are having a war-dance, mother," he announced when he had closed the stout door of the kitchen behind him. "They mean it this time. I lay in the brush and watched them last night." He stood looking at his mother speculatively, a little grin on his face. "I told you you can't change an Injun by learning him to eat with a knife and fork," he added. "Colorou ain't any whiter than he was be-fore you set out to learn him manners. He was hoppin' higher than any of 'em."

"Teach, Buddy, not learn. You know better than to say ' learn him manners.' "

"Teach him manners," Buddy corrected himself obediently. " I was thinking more about what I saw than about grammar. Where's father? I guess I'd better tell him. He'll want to get the stock out of the mountains, I should think."

"Colorou will send me word before they take the warpath," mother observed reassuringly. " He always has. I gave him a whole pound of tea and a blue ribbon the last time he was here."

"Yes, and the last time they broke out they got away with more 'n a hundred head of cattle. You got to Laramie, all right, but he did n't tell father in time to make a roundup back in the foothills. They're *dancing,* mother! "

"Well, I suppose we're due for an outbreak," sighed mother. " Colorou says he can't hold his young men off when some of the tribe have been killed. He himself does n't countenance the stealing and the occasional killing of white men. There are bad Indians and good ones."

"I know a couple of good ones," Buddy murmured as he made for the wash basin. " It's the bad ones that were doing the dancing, mother," he flung over his shoulder. " And if I was you I'd take Dulcie and the cats and hit for Laramie. Colorou might get busy and forget to send word! "

"If I *was* you? " Mother came up and nipped his ear between thumb and finger. " Robert, I am discouraged over you. All that I teach you in the winter seems to evaporate from your mind during the summer when you go out riding with the boys."

Buddy wiped his face with an up-and-down motion on the roller, towel and clanked across to the cupboard which he opened investigatively. "Any pie?" he questioned as he peered into the corners. "Say, if I had the handling of those Utes, mother, I'd fix 'em so they would n't be breaking out every few months and making folks leave their homes to be pawed over and burnt, maybe." He found a jar of fresh dough-nuts and took three.

"They 'll tromp around on your flower-beds — it just makes me *sick* when I think how they 'll muss things up around here! I wish now," he blurted un-thinkingly, "that I had n't killed the Injun that stole Rattler."

"Buddy! Not *you?*" His mother made a swift little run across the kitchen and caught him on his lean, hard-muscled young shoulders. "You — you *baby!* What did you do? You did n't harm an Indian, did you, laddie?"

Buddy tilted his head downward so that she could not look into his eyes. "I dunno as I harmed him — much," he said, wiping doughnut crumbs from his mouth with one hasty sweep of his forearm. "But his horse came outa the brush, and he never. I guess I killed him, all right. Anyway, mother, I had to. He took a shot at me first. It was the day we lost Rattler and the bronks," he added accurately.

Mother did not say anything for a minute, and Buddy hung his head lower, dreading to see the hurt look which he felt was in her eyes.

"I have to pack a gun when I ride anywhere," he reminded her defensively. "It ain't to balance me on the horse, either. If Injuns take in after me, the gun's so I can shoot. And a feller don't shoot up in the air — and if an Injun is hunting trouble he oughta expect that maybe he might get shot sometime. You — you would n't want me to just run and let them catch me, would you?"

Mother's hand slipped up to his head and pressed it against her breast so that Buddy heard her heart beating steady and sweet and true. Mother was n't afraid — never, never!

"I know — it's the dreadful necessity of defending our lives. But you're so young — just mother's baby man!"

Buddy looked up at her then, a laugh twinkling in his eyes. After all, mother understood.

"I'm going to be your baby man always if you want me to, mother," he whispered, closing his arms around her neck in a sturdy hug. "But I'm father's horse-wrangler, too. And a horse-wrangler has got to hold up his end. I — I did n't want to kill anybody, honest. But Injuns are different. You kill rattlers, and they ain't as mean as Injuns. That one I shot at was shooting at me before I even so much as knew there was one around. I just shot back. Father would, or anybody else."

"I know — I know," she conceded, the tender womanliness of her sighing over the need. In the next moment she was all mother, ready to fight for her young. "Buddy, never, never ride *anywhere* without your rifle! And a revolver, too — be sure that it is in perfect condition. And — have you a knife? You're so *little!*" she wailed. "But father will need you, and he'll take care of you — and Colorou would not let you be hurt if he knew. But — Buddy, you **must** be careful, and always watching — never let them catch you off your guard. I shall be in Laramie before you and father and the boys, I suppose, if the Indians really do break out. And you must promise me — "

" I 'll promise, mother. And don't you go and trust old Colorou an inch. He was jumping higher than any of 'em, and shaking his tomahawk and yelling — he 'd have scalped me right there if he 'd seen me watching 'em. Mother, I 'm going to find father and tell him. And you may as well be packing up, and — don't leave my guitar for them to smash, will you, mother? "

His mother laughed then and pushed him toward the door. She had an idea of her own and she did not want to be hindered now in putting it into action. Up the creek, in the bank behind a clump of willows, was a small cave — or a large niche, one might call it — where many household treasures might be safely hidden, if one went carefully, wading in the creek to hide the tracks. She followed Buddy out, and called to Ezra who was chopping wood with a grunt for every fall of the axe and many rest-periods in the shade of the cottonwood tree.

At the stable, Buddy looked back and saw her talking earnestly to Ezra, who stood nodding his head in complete approval. Buddy's knowledge of women began and ended with his mother. Therefore, to him all women were wonderful creatures whom men worshipped ardently because they were created for the adoration of lesser souls. Buddy did not know what his mother was going to do, but he was sure that whatever she did would be right; so he hoisted his saddle on the handiest fresh horse, and loped off to drive in the *remuda,* feeling certain that his father would move swiftly to save his cattle that ranged back in the foothills, and that the saddle horses would be wanted at a moment's notice.

Also, he reasoned, the range horses (mares and colts and the unbroken geldings) would not be left to the mercy of the Indians. He did not quite know how his father would manage it, but he decided that he would corral the *remuda* first, and then drive in the other horses, that fed scattered in undisturbed possession of a favorite grassy creek-bottom farther up the Platte.

The saddle horses, accustomed to Buddy's driving, were easily corralled. The other horses were fat and "sassy" and resented his coming among them with the shrill whoop of authority. They gave him a hot hour's riding before they finally bunched and went tearing down the river bottom toward the ranch. Even so, Buddy left two of the wildest careening up a narrow gulch. He had not attempted to ride after them; not because he was afraid of Indians, for he was not. The war-dance held every young buck and every old one in camp beyond the Pass. But the margin of safety might be narrow, and Buddy was taking no chances that day.

When he was convinced that it was impossible for one boy to be in half a dozen places at once, and that the cowboys would be needed to corral the range bunch, Buddy whooped them all down the creek below the home ranch and let them go just as his father came riding up to the corral.

"They're war-dancing, father," Buddy shouted ea-

gerly, slipping off his horse and wiping away the trickles
of perspiration with a handkerchief not much redder
than his face. " I drove all the horses down, so they 'd
be handy. Them range horses are pretty wild. There
was two I could n't get. What 'll I do now? "

Bob Birnie looked at his youngest rider and
smoothed his beard with one hand. " You 're an ambitious lad, Buddy. It 's the Utes you 're meaning —
or is it the horses? "

Buddy lifted his head and stared at his father dis-
approvingly.

" Colorou is going to break out. I know. They 've
got their war paint all on and they 're dancing. I saw
them myself. I was going after the gloves Colorou's
squaw was making for me, — but I did n't get 'em. I
laid in the brush and watched 'em dance." He stopped
and looked again doubtfully at his father. " I thought
you might want to get the cattle outa the way," he
added. " I thought I could save some time — "

" You 're sure about the paint? "

" Yes, I 'm sure. And Colorou was just a-going it
with his war bonnet on and shaking his tomahawk and
yelling — "

" Ye did well, lad. We 'll be leaving for Big Creek
to-night, so run away now and rest yourself."

" Oh, and can I go? " Buddy's voice was shrill
with eagerness.

" I 'll need you, lad, to look after the horses. It
will give me one more hand with the cattle. Now go
tell Step-and-a-Half to make ready for a week on the
trail, and to have supper early so he can make his
start with the rest."

Buddy walked stiffly away to the cook's cabin where

Step-and-a-Half sat leisurely gouging the worst blemishes out of soft, old potatoes with a chronic tendency to grow sprouts, before he peeled them for supper. His crippled leg was thrust out straight, his hat was perched precariously over one ear because of the slanting sun rays through the window, and a half-smoked cigarette waggled uncertainly in the corner of his mouth while he sang dolefully a most optimistic ditty of the West:

> " O give me a home where the buff-alo roam,
>   Where the deer and the antelope play,
>   Where never is heard a discouraging word
>   And the sky is not cloudy all day."

" You 're going to hear a discouraging word right now," Buddy broke in ruthlessly upon the song. Whereupon, with a bit of importance in his voice and in his manner, he proceeded to spoil Step-and-a-Half's disposition and to deepen, if that were possible, his loathing of Indians. Too often had he made dubious soup of his dishwater and the leavings from a roundup crew's dinner, and watched blanketed bucks smack lips over the mess, to run from them now without feeling utterly disgusted with life. Step-and-a-Half's vituperations could be heard above the clatter of pots and pans as he made ready for the journey.

That night's ride up the pass through the narrow range of high-peaked hills to the Tomahawk's farthest range on Big Creek was a tedious affair to Buddy. A man had been sent on a fast horse to warn the nearest neighbor, who in turn would warn the next, — until no settler would be left in ignorance of his danger. Ezra was already on the trail to Laramie, with mother and

Dulcie and the cats and a slat box full of chickens, and a young sow with little pigs.

Buddy, whose word no one had questioned, who might pardonably have considered himself a hero, was concerned chiefly with his mother's flower garden which he had helped to plant and had watered more or less faithfully with creek water carried in buckets. He was afraid the Indians would step on the poppies and the phlox, and trample down the four o'clocks which were just beginning to branch out and look nice and bushy, and to blossom. The scent of the four o'clocks had been in his nostrils when he came out at dusk with his fur overcoat which mother had told him must not be left behind. Buddy himself merely liked flowers: but mother talked to them and kissed them just for love, and pitied them if Buddy forgot and let them go thirsty. He would have stayed to fight for mother's flower garden, if it would have done any good.

He was thinking sleepily that next year he would plant flowers in boxes that could be carried to the cave if the Indians broke out again, when Tex Farley poked him in the ribs and told him to wake up or he'd fall off his horse. It was a weary climb to the top of the range that divided the valley of Big Creek from the North Platte, and a wearier climb down. Twice Buddy caught himself on the verge of toppling out of the saddle. For after all he was only a thirteen-year-old boy, growing like any other healthy young animal. He had been riding hard that day and half of the preceding night when he had raced back from the Reservation to give warning of the impending outbreak. He needed sleep, and nature was determined that he should have it.

CHAPTER FIVE

Buddy Runs True to Type

One never could predict with any certainty how long Indians would dance before they actually took the trail of murder and pillage. So much depended upon the Medicine, so much on signs and portents. It was even possible that they might, for some mysterious reason unknown to their white neighbors, decide at the last moment to bide their time. The Tomahawk outfit worked from dawn until dark, and combed the foothills of the Snowies hurriedly, riding into the most frequented, grassy basins and wide canyons where the grass was lush and sweet and the mountain streams rushed noisily over rocks. As fast as the cattle were gathered they were pushed hastily toward the Platte. And though the men rode warily with rifles as handy as their ropes, they rode in peace.

Buddy, proud of his job, counting himself as good a man as any of them, became a small riding demon after rebellious saddle horses, herding them away from thick undergrowth that might, for all he knew, hold Indians waiting a chance to scalp him, driving the *remuda* close to the cabins when night fell, because no man could be spared for night herding, sleeping lightly as a cat beside a mouse hole. He did not say much, perhaps because everyone was too busy to talk, himself included.

Men rode in at night dog-weary, pulled their saddles and hurried stiffly to the cabin where Step-and-a-Half was showing his true worth as a cook who could keep the coffee-pot boiling and yet be ready to pack up and go at the first rifle-shot. They would bolt down enormous quantities of bannock and boiled beef, swallow their coffee hot enough to scald a hog, and stretch themselves out immediately to sleep.

Buddy would be up and on his horse in the clear starlight before dawn, with a cup of coffee swallowed to hearten him for the chilly ride after the *remuda*. Even with the warmth of the coffee his teeth would chatter just at first, and he would ride with his thin shoulders lifted and a hand in a pocket. He could not sing or whistle to keep himself company. He must ride in silence until he had counted every dark, moving shape and knew that the herd was complete, then ease them quietly to camp.

On the fourth morning he rode anxiously up the valley, fearing that the horses had been stolen in the night, yet hoping they had merely strayed up the creek to find fresh pastures. A light breeze that carried the keen edge of frost made his nose tingle. His horse trotted steadily forward, as keen on the trail as Buddy himself; keener, for he would be sure to give warning of danger. So they rounded a bend in the creek and came upon the scattered fringe of the *remuda* cropping steadily at the meadow grass there.

Buddy circled them, glancing now and then at the ridge beyond the valley. It seemed somehow unnatural — lower, with the stars showing along its wooded crest in a row, as if there were no peaks. Then quite suddenly he knew that the ridge was the same, and that the stars he saw were little, breakfast camp-fires. His heart gave a jump when he realized how many little fires there were, and knew that the dance was over. The Indians had left the reservation and had crossed the ridge yesterday, and had camped there to wait for the dawn.

While he gathered his horses together he guessed how old Colorou had planned to catch the Tomahawk riders when they left camp and scattered, two by two, on " circle." He had held his band well out of sight and sound of the Big Creek cabin, and if the horses had not strayed up the creek in the night he would have caught the white men off their guard.

Buddy looked often over his shoulder while he drove the horses down the creek. It seemed stranger than luck, that he had been compelled to ride so far on this particular morning; as if mother's steadfast faith in prayer and the guardianship of angels was justified by actual facts. Still, Buddy was too hard-headed to assume easily that angels had driven the horses up the creek so that he would have to ride up there and discover the Indian fires. If angels could do that, why had n't they stopped Colorou from going on the warpath? It would have been simpler, in Buddy's opinion.

He did not mention the angel problem to his father, however. Bob Birnie was eating breakfast with his men when Buddy rode up to the cabin and told the news. The boys did not say anything much, but they may have taken bigger bites by way of filling their stomachs in less time than usual.

" I 'll go see for myself," said Bob Birnie. " You

boys saddle up and be ready to start. If it's Indians, we'll head for Laramie and drive everything before us as we go. But the lad may be wrong." He took the reins from Buddy, mounted, and rode away, his booted feet hanging far below Buddy's short stirrups.

Speedily he was back, and the scowl on his face told plainly enough that Buddy had not been mistaken.

"They're coming off the ridge already," he announced grimly. "I heard their horses among the rocks up there. They think to come down on us at sunrise. There'll be too many for us to hold off, I'm thinking. Get ye a fresh horse, Buddy, and drive the horses down the creek fast as ye can."

Buddy uncoiled his rope and ran with his mouth full to do as he was told. He did not think he was scared, exactly, but he made three throws to get the horse he wanted, blaming the poor light for his ill luck; and then found himself in possession of a tall, uneasy brown that Dick Grimes had broken and sometimes rode. Buddy would have turned him loose and caught another, but the horses had sensed the suppressed excitement of the men and were circling and snorting in the half light of dawn; so Buddy led out the brown, pulled the saddle from the sweaty horse that had twice made the trip up the creek, and heaved it hastily on the brown's back. Dick Grimes called to him, to know if he wanted any help, and Buddy yelled, "No!"

"Here they come — damn 'em — turn the bunch loose and ride!" called Bob Birnie as a shrill, yelling war-whoop, like the yapping of many coyotes, sounded from the cottonwoods that bordered the creek. "Yuh all right, Buddy?"

"Yeah — I'm a-comin'," shrilled Buddy, hastily

looping the latigo. Just then the sharp staccato of rifle-shots mingled with the whooping of the Indians. Buddy was reaching for the saddle horn when the brown horse ducked and jerked loose. Before Buddy realized what was happening the brown horse, the herd and all the riders were pounding away down the valley, the men firing back at the cottonwoods.

In the dust and clamor of their departure Buddy stood perfectly still for a minute, trying to grasp the full significance of his calamity. Step-and-a-Half had packed hastily and departed ahead of them all. His father and the cowboys were watching the cottonwood grove many rods to Buddy's right and well in the background, and they would not glance his way. Even if they did they would not see him, and if they saw him it would be madness to ride back — though there was not a man among them who would not have wheeled in his tracks and returned for Buddy in the very face of Colorou and his band.

From the cottonwoods came the pound of galloping hoofs. " Angels *nothing!* " cried Buddy in deep disgust and scuttled for the cabin.

The cabin, he knew as he ran, was just then the worst place in the world for a boy who wanted very much to go on living. Through its gaping doorway he saw a few odds and ends of food lying on the table, but he dared not stop long enough to get them. The Indians were thundering down to the corral, and as he rounded the cabin's corner he glanced back and saw the foremost riders whipping their horses on the trail of the fleeing white men. But some, he knew, would stop. Even the prospect of fresh scalps could not hold the greedy ones from prowling around a white man's dwelling place. There might be tobacco or whiskey left behind, or something with color or a shine to it. Buddy knew well the ways of Indians.

He made for the creek, thinking at first to hide somewhere in the brush along the bank. Then, fearing the brightening light of day and the wide space he must cross to reach the first fringe of brush, he stopped at a dugout cellar that had been built into the creek bank above high-water mark. There was a pole-and-dirt roof, and because the dirt sifted down between the poles whenever the wind blew — which was always — the place had been crudely ceiled inside with split poles overlapping one another. The ceiling was more or less flat; the roof had a slight slope. In the middle of the tiny attic thus formed Buddy managed to worm his body through a hole in the gable next to the creek.

He wriggled back to the end next the cabin and lay there very flat and very quiet, peeping out through a half-inch crack, too wise in the ways of silence to hold his breath until he must heave a sigh to relieve his lungs. It was hard to breathe naturally and easily after that swift dash, but somehow he did it. An Indian had swerved and ridden behind the cabin, and was leaning and peering in all directions to see if anyone had remained. Perhaps he suspected an ambush; Buddy was absolutely certain that the fellow was looking for him, personally, and that he had seen Buddy run toward the creek.

It was not a pleasant thought, and the fact that he knew that buck Indian by name, and had once traded him a jackknife for a beautifully tanned wolf skin for his mother, did not make it pleasanter. Hides-the-face would not let past friendliness stand in the way of a killing.

Presently Hides-the-face dismounted and tied his horse to a corner log of the cabin, and went inside with the others to see what he could find that could be eaten or carried off. Buddy saw fresh smoke issue from the stone chimney, and guessed that Step-and-a-Half had left something that could be cooked. It became evident, in the course of an hour or so, that his presence was absolutely unsuspected, and Buddy began to watch them more composedly, silently promising especial forms of punishment to this one and that one whom he knew. Most of them had been to the ranch many times, and he could have called to a dozen of them by name. They had sat in his father's cabin or stood immobile just within the door, and had listened while his mother played and sang for them. She had fed them cakes — Buddy remembered the good things which mother had given these despicable ones who were looting and gobbling and destroying like a drove of hogs turned loose in a garden, and the thought of her wasted kindness turned him sick with rage. Mother had believed in their friendliness. Buddy wished that mother could see them setting fire to the low, log stable and the corral, and swarming in and out of the cabin.

Painted for war they were, with red stripes across their foreheads, ribs outlined in red which, when they loosened their blankets as the sun warmed them, gave them a fantastic likeness to the skeletons Buddy wished they were; red stripes on their arms, the number showing their rank in the tribe; open-seated, buckskin breeches to their knees where they met the tightly wrapped leggings; moccasins laced snugly at the ankle —they were picturesque enough to any eyes but Buddy's. He saw the ghoulish greed in their eyes, heard it in their voices when they shouted to one another; and he hated them even more than he feared them.

Much that they said he understood. They were cursing the Tomahawk outfit, chiefly because the men had not waited there to be surprised and killed. They cursed his father in particular, and were half sorry that they had not ridden on in pursuit with the others. They hoped no white man would ride alive to Laramie. It made cheerful listening to Buddy, flat on his stomach in the roof of the dugout!

After a while, when the cabin had been gutted of everything it contained save the crude table and benches, a few Indians brought burning brands from the stable and set it afire. They were very busy inside and out, making sure that the flames took hold properly. Then, when the dry logs began to blaze and flames licked the edges of the roof, they stood back and watched it.

Buddy saw Hides-the-face glance speculatively toward the dugout, and slipped his hand back where he could reach his six-shooter. He felt pretty certain that they meant to demolish the dugout next, and he knew exactly what he meant to do. He had heard men at the posts talk of "selling their lives dearly", and that is what he intended to do.

He was not going to be in too much of a hurry; he would wait until they actually began on the dugout — and when they were on the bank within a few feet of him, and he saw that there was no getting away from death, he meant to shoot five Indians, and himself last of all.

Tentatively he felt of his temple where he meant to place the muzzle of the gun when there was just one bullet left. It was so nice and smooth — he wondered if God would really help him out, if he said Our Father with a pure heart and with faith, as his mother said one must pray. He was slightly doubtful of both conditions, when he came to think of it seriously. This spring he had felt grown-up enough to swear a little at the horses, sometimes — and he was not sure that shooting the Indian that time would not be counted a crime by God, who loved all His creatures. Mother always stuck to it that Injuns were God's creatures — which brought Buddy squarely against the incredible assumption that God must love them. He did not in the least mean to be irreverent, but when he watched those painted bucks his opinion of God changed slightly. He decided that he himself was neither pure nor full of faith, and that he would not pray just yet. He would let God go ahead and do as He pleased about it; except that Buddy would never let those Indians get him alive, no matter what God expected.

Hides-the-face walked over toward the dugout. Buddy crooked his left arm and laid the gun barrel across it to get a "dead rest" and leave nothing to chance. Hides-the-face stared at the dugout, moved to one side — and the muzzle of the gun followed, keeping its aim directly at the left edge of his breastbone as outlined with the red paint. Hides-the-face craned, stepped into the path down the bank and passed out of range. Buddy gritted his teeth malevolently and waited, his ears strained to catch and interpret the meaning of every soft sound made by Hides-the-face's moccasins.

Hides-the-face cautiously pushed open the door of the cellar and looked in, standing for interminable minutes, as is the leisurely way of Indians when there is no great need of haste. Buddy cautiously lowered his face and peered down like a mouse from the thatch, but he could not handily bring his gun to bear upon Hides-the-face, who presently turned back and went up the path, his shoulder-muscles moving snakishly under his brown skin as he climbed the bank.

Hides-the-face returned to the others and announced that there was a place where they could camp. Buddy could not hear all that he said, and Hides-the-face had his back turned so that not all of his signs were intelligible; but he gathered that these particular Indians had chosen or had been ordered to wait here for three suns, and that the cellar appealed to Hides-the-face as a shelter in case it stormed.

Buddy did not know whether to rejoice at the news or to mourn. They would not destroy the dugout, so he need not shoot himself, which was of course a relief. Still, three suns meant three days and nights, and the prospect of lying there on his stomach, afraid to move for that length of time, almost amounted to the same thing in the end. He did not believe that he could hold out that long, though of course he would try pretty hard.

All that day Buddy lay watching through the crack, determined to take any chance that came his way. None came. The Indians loitered in the shade, and some slept. But always two or three remained awake;

and although they sat apparently ready to doze off at any minute, Buddy knew them too well to hope for such good luck. Two Indians rode in toward evening dragging a calf that had been overlooked in the roundup; and having improvidently burned the cabin, the meat was cooked over the embers which still smouldered in places where knots in the logs made slow fuel.

Buddy watched them hungrily, wondering how long it took to starve.

When it was growing dark he tried to keep in mind the exact positions of the Indians, and to discover whether a guard would be placed over the camp, or whether they felt safe enough to sleep without a sentinel. Hides-the-face he had long ago decided was in charge of the party, and Hides-the-face was seemingly concerned only with gorging himself on the half-roasted meat. Buddy hoped he would choke himself, but Hides-the-face was very good at gulping half-chewed hunks and finished without disaster.

Then he grunted something to someone in the dark, and there was movement in the group. Buddy ground his growing " second " teeth together, clenched his fist and said " Damn it! " three times in a silent crescendo of rage because he could neither see nor hear what took place; and immediately he repented his profanity, remembering that God could hear him. In Buddy's opinion, you never could be sure about God; He bestowed mysterious mercies and strange punishments, and His ways were past finding out. Buddy tipped his palms together and repeated all the prayers his mother had taught him and then, with a flash of memory, finished with " Oh, God, *please!* " just as mother had done long ago on the dry drive. After that he meditated uncomfortably for a few minutes and added in a faint whisper, " Oh, shucks! You don't want to pay any attention to a fellow cussing a little when he's mad. I could easy make that up if you helped me out some way."

Buddy believed afterwards that God yielded to persuasion and decided to give him a chance. For not more than five minutes passed when a far-off murmur grew to an indefinable roar, and the wind whooped down off the Snowies so fiercely that even the dugout quivered a little and rattled dirt down on Buddy through the poles just over his head.

At first this seemed an unlucky circumstance, for the Indians came down into the dugout for shelter, and now Buddy was afraid to breathe in the quiet intervals between the gusts. Just below him he could hear the occasional mutters of laconic sentences and grunted answers as the bucks settled themselves for the night, and he had a short, panicky spell of fearing that the poles would give way beneath him and drop him in upon them.

After a while — it seemed hours to Buddy — the wind settled down to a steady gale. The Indians, so far as he could determine, were all asleep in the cellar. And Buddy, setting his teeth hard together, began to slide slowly backward toward the opening through which he had crawled into the roof. When he had crawled in he had not noticed the springiness of the poles, but now his imagination tormented him with the sensation of sagging and swaying. When his feet pushed through the opening he had to grit his teeth to hold himself steady. It seemed as if someone were reaching up in the dark to catch him by the legs and pull him out. Nothing happened, however, and after a little he inched backward until he hung with his elbows hooked desperately inside the opening, his head and shoulders within and protesting with every nerve against leaving the shelter.

Buddy said afterwards that he guessed he'd have hung there until daylight, only he was afraid it was about time to change guard, and somebody might catch him. But he said he was scared to let go and drop, because it must have been pretty crowded in the cellar, and he knew the door was open, and some buck might be roosting outside handy to be stepped on. But he knew he had to do something, because if he ever went to sleep up in that place he'd snore, maybe; and anyway, he said, he'd rather run himself to death than starve to death. So he dropped.

It was two days after that when Buddy shuffled into a mining camp on the ridge just north of Douglas Pass. He was still on his feet, but they dragged like an old man's. He had walked twenty-five miles in two nights, going carefully, in fear of Indians. The first five miles he had waded along the shore of the creek, he said, in case they might pick up his tracks at the dugout and try to follow him. He had hidden himself like a rabbit in the brush through the day, and he had not dared shoot any meat, wherefore he had not eaten anything.

"I ain't as hungry as I was at first," he grinned tremulously. "But I guess I better — eat. I don't want — to lose the — habit — " Then he went slack, and a man swearing to hide his pity picked him up in his arms and carried him into the tent.

CHAPTER SIX

The Young Eagle Must Fly

"You 're of age," said Bob Birnie, sucking hard at his pipe. "You 've had your schooling as your mother wished that you should have it. You 've got the music in your head and your fingers and your toes, and that 's as your mother wished that you should have.

"Your mother would have you be all for music, and make tunes out of your own head. She tells me that you have made tunes and written them down on paper, and that there are those who would buy them and print copies to sell, with your name at the top of the page. I 'll not say what I think of that — your mother is an angel among women, and she has taught you the things she loves hersel'.

"But my business is with the cattle, and I 've had you out with me since you could climb on the back of a horse. I 've watched you, with the rope and the irons and in the saddle and all. You 've been in tight places that would try the mettle of a man grown — I mind the time ye escaped Colorou's band, and we thought ye dead 'til ye came to us in Laramie. You 've showed that you 're able to hold your own on the range, lad. Your mother 's all for the music — but I leave it to you.

"Ten thousand dollars I 'll give ye, if that 's your

wish, and you can go to Europe as she wishes and study and make tunes for others to play. Or if ye prefer it, I 'll brand you a herd of she stock and let ye go your ways. No son of mine can take orders from his father after he 's a man grown, and I 'm not to the age where I can sit with the pipe from morning to night and let another run my outfit. I 've talked it over with your mother, and she 'll bide by your decision, as I shall do.

"So I put it in a nutshell, Robert. You 're twenty-one to-day; a man grown, and husky as they 're made. 'Tis time you faced the world and lived your life. You 've been a good lad — as lads go." He stopped there to rub his jaw thoughtfully, perhaps remembering certain incidents in Buddy's full-flavored past. Buddy — grown to plain Bud among his fellows — turned red without losing the line of hardness that had come to his lips.

"You 're of legal age to be called a man, and the future 's before ye. I 'll give ye five hundred cows with their calves beside them — you can choose them yourself, for you 've a sharp eye for stock — and you can go where ye will. Or I 'll give ye ten thousand dollars and ye can go to Europe and make tunes if you 're a mind to. And whatever ye choose it 'll be make or break with ye. Ye can sleep on the decision, for I 've no wish that ye should choose hastily and be sorry after."

Buddy — grown to Bud — lifted a booted foot and laid it across his other knee and with his forefinger absently whirled the long-pointed rowel on his spur. The hardness at his lips somehow spread to his eyes, that were bent on the whirring rowel. It was the look that had come into the face of the baby down on the Staked Plains when Ezra called and called after he had been answered twice; the look that had held firm the lips of the boy who had lain very flat on his stomach in the roof of the dugout and had watched the Utes burning the cabin.

"There's no need to sleep on it," he said after a minute. "You've raised me, and spent some money on me — but I've saved you a man's wages ever since I was ten. If you think I've evened things up, all right. If you don't, make out your bill and I'll pay it when I can. There's no reason why you should give me anything I haven't earned, just because you're my father. You earned all you've got, and I guess I can do the same. As you say, I'm a man. I'll go at the future man fashion. And," he added with a slight flare of the nostrils, "I'll start in the morning."

"And is it to make tunes for other folks to play?" Bob Birnie asked after a silence, covertly eyeing him.

"No, sir. There's more money in cattle. I'll make my stake in the cow-country, same as you've done." He looked up and grinned a little. "To the devil with your money and your she-stock! I'll get out all right — but I'll make my own way."

"You're a stubborn fool, Robert. The Scotch now and then shows itself like that in a man. I got my start from my father and I'm not ashamed of it. A thousand pounds — and I brought it to America and to Texas, and got cattle."

Bud laughed and got up, hiding how the talk had struck deep into the soul of him. "Then I'll go you one better, dad. I'll get my own start."

"You'll be back home in six months, lad, saying

you've changed your mind," Bob Birnie predicted sharply, stung by the tone of young Bud. "That," he added grimly, "or for a full belly and a clean bed to crawl into."

Bud stood licking the cigarette he had rolled to hide an unaccountable trembling of his fingers. "When I come back I'll be in a position to buy you out! I'll borrow Skate and Maverick, if you don't mind, till I get located somewhere." He paused while he lighted the cigarette. "It's the custom," he reminded his father unnecessarily, "to furnish a man a horse to ride and one to pack his bed, when he's fired."

"Ye've horses of yer own," Bob Birnie retorted, "and you've no need to borrow."

Bud stood looking down at his father, plainly undecided. "I don't know whether they're mine or not," he said after a minute. "I don't know what it cost you to raise me. Figure it up, if you have n't already, and count the time I've worked for you. Since you've put me on a business basis, like raising a calf to shipping age, let's be businesslike about it. You are good at figuring your profits — I'll leave it to you. And if you find I've anything coming to me besides my riding outfit and the clothes I've got, all right; I'll take horses for the balance."

He walked off with the swing to his shoulders that had always betrayed him when he was angry, and Bob Birnie gathered his beard into a handful and held it while he stared after him. It had been no part of his plan to set his son adrift on the range without a dollar, but since Bud's temper was up, it might be a good thing to let him go.

So Bob Birnie went away to confer with his wife, and Bud was left alone to nurse his hurt while he packed his few belongings. It did hurt him to be told in that calm, cold-blooded manner that, now he was of legal age, he would not be expected to stay on at the Tomahawk. Until his father had spoken to him about it, Bud had not thought much about what he would do when his school days were over. He had taken life as it was presented to him week by week, month by month. He had fulfilled his mother's hopes and had learned to make music. He had lived up to his father's unspoken standards of a cowman. He had made a "hand" ever since his legs were long enough to reach the stirrups of a saddle. There was not a better rider, not a better roper on the range than Bud Birnie. Morally he was cleaner than most young fellows of his age. He hated trickery, he reverenced all good women; the bad ones he pitied because he believed that they sorrowed secretly because they were not good, because they had missed somehow their real purpose in life, which was to be wife and mother. He had, in fact, grown up clean and true to type. He was Buddy, grown to be Bud.

And Buddy, now that he was a man, had been told that he was not expected to stay at home and help his father, and be a comfort to his mother. He was like a young eagle which, having grown wing-feathers that will bear the strain of high air currents, has been pecked out of the nest. No doubt the young eagle resents his unexpected banishment, although in time he would have felt within himself the urge to go. Leave Bud alone, and soon or late he would have gone — perhaps with compunctions against leaving home, and the feeling that he was somehow a disappointment to his parents. He would have explained to his father, apologized to his mother. As it was, he resented the alacrity with which his father was pushing him out.

So he packed his clothes that night, and pushed his guitar into its case and buckled the strap with a vicious yank, and went off to the bunkhouse to eat supper with the boys instead of sitting down to the table where his mother had placed certain dishes which Buddy loved best — wanting to show in true woman fashion her love and sympathy for him.

Later — it was after Bud had gone to bed — mother came and had a long talk with him. She was very sweet and sensible, and Bud was very tender with her. But she could not budge him from his determination to go and make his way without a Birnie dollar to ease the beginning. Other men had started with nothing and had made a stake, and there was no reason why he could not do so.

"Dad put it straight enough, and it's no good arguing. I'd starve before I'd take anything from him. I'm entitled to my clothes, and maybe a horse or two for the work I've done for him while I was growing up. I've figured out pretty close what it cost to put me through the University, and what I was worth to him during the summers. Father's Scotch — but he isn't a darned bit more Scotch than I am, mother. Putting it all in dollars and cents, I think I've earned more than I cost him. In the winters, I know I earned my board doing chores and riding line. Many a little bunch of stock I've saved for him by getting out in the foothills and driving them down below heavy snowline before a storm. You remember the bunch of horses I found by watching the magpies — the time we tied hay in canvas and took it up to them 'til they got strength enough to follow the trail I trampled in the snow? I earned my board and more, every winter since I was ten. So I don't believe I owe dad a cent, when it's all figured out.

"But you've done for me what money can't repay, mother. I'll always be in debt to you — and I'll square it by being the kind of a man you've tried to teach me to be. I will, mother. Dad and the dollars are a different matter. The debt I owe you will never be paid, but I'm going to make you glad I know there's a debt. I believe there's a God, because I know there must have been one to make you! And no matter how far away I may drift in miles, your Buddy is going to be here with you always, mother, learning from you all there is of goodness and sweetness." He held her two hands against his face, and she felt his cheeks wet beneath her palms. Then he took them away and kissed them many times, like a lover.

"If I ever have a wife, she's going to have her work cut out for her," he laughed unsteadily. "She'll have to live up to you, mother, if she wants me to love her."

"If you have a wife she'll be well-spoiled, young man! Perhaps it is wise that you should go — but don't you forget your music, Buddy — and be a good boy, and remember, mother's going to follow you with her love and her faith in you, and her prayers."

It may have been that Buddy's baby memory of going north whenever the trail herd started remained to send Bud instinctively northward when he left the Tomahawk next morning. It had been a case of stubborn father and stubborn son dickering politely over the net earnings of the son from the time when he was old enough to leave his mother's lap and climb into a saddle to ride with his father. Three horses and his personal belongings had been agreed upon between them as the balance in Bud's favor; and at that, Bob Birnie dryly remarked, he had been a better investment as a son than most young fellows, who cost more than they were worth to raise.

Bud did not answer the implied praise, but roped the Tomahawk's best three horses out of the *remuda* corralled for him by his father's riders. You should have seen the sidelong glances among the boys when they learned that Bud, just home from the University, was going somewhere with all his earthly possessions and a look in his face that meant trouble!

Two big valises and his blankets he packed on Sunfish, a deceptively raw-boned young buckskin with much white showing in his eyes — an ornery looking brute if ever there was one. Bud's guitar and a mandolin in their cases he tied securely on top of the pack. Smoky, the second horse, a deep-chested "mouse" with a face almost human in its expression, he saddled, and put a lead rope on the third, a bay four-year-old called Stopper, which was the Tomahawk's best rope-horse and one that would be missed when fast work was wanted in branding.

"He sure as hell picked himself three top hawses," a tall puncher murmured to another. "Wonder where he's headed for? Not repping — this late in the season."

Bud overheard them, and gave no sign. Had they asked him directly he could not have told them, for he did not know, except that somehow he felt that he was going to head north. Why north, he could not have explained, since cow-country lay all around him; nor how far north, — for cow-country extended to the upper boundary of the States, and beyond into Canada.

He left his horses standing by the corral while he went to the house to tell his mother good-by, and to send a farewell message to Dulcie, who had been married a year and lived in Laramie. He did not expect to strike Laramie, he told his mother when she asked him.

" I 'm going till I stop," he explained, with a squeeze of her shoulders to reassure her. " I guess it 's the way you felt, mother, when you left Texas behind. You could n't tell where you folks would wind up. Neither can I. My trail herd is kinda small, right now; a lot smaller than it will be later on. But such as it is, it 's going to hit the right range before it stops for good. And I 'll write."

He took a doughnut in his hand and a package of lunch to slip in his pocket, kissed her with much cheerfulness in his manner and hurried out, his big-rowelled spurs burring on the porch just twice before he stepped off on the gravel. Telling mother good-by had been the one ordeal he dreaded, and he was glad to have it over with.

Old Step-and-a-Half hailed him as he went past the chuck-house, and came limping out, wiping his hands on his apron before he shook hands and wished him good luck. Ezra, pottering around the tool shed, ambled up with the eyes of a dog that has been sent back home by his master. " Ah shoah do wish yo' all good fawtune an' health, Marse Buddy," Ezra quavered. "Ah shoah do. It ain' goin' seem lak de same place — and Ah shoah do hopes yo' all writes frequent lettahs to yo' mothah, boy!"

Bud promised that he would, and managed to break away from Ezra without betraying himself. How, he wondered, did everyone seem to know that he was going for good, this time? He had believed that no one knew of it save himself, his father and his mother; yet everyone else behaved as if they never expected to see him again. It was disconcerting, and Bud hastily untied the two led horses and mounted Smoky, the mouse-colored horse he himself had broken two years before.

His father came slowly up to him, straight-backed and with the gait of the man who has ridden astride a horse more than he has walked on his own feet. He put up his hand, gloved for riding, and Bud changed the lead-ropes from his right hand to his left, and shook hands rather formally.

"Ye 've good weather for travelling," said Bob Birnie tentatively. "I have not said it before, lad, but when ye own yourself a fool to take this way of making your fortune, ten thousand dollars will still be ready to start ye right. I 've no wish to shirk a duty to my family."

Bud pressed his lips together while he listened. "If you keep your ten thousand till it 's called for, you 'll be drawing interest a long time on it," he said. "It 's going to be hot to-day. I 'll be getting along."

He lifted the reins, glanced back to see that the two horses were showing the proper disposition to follow, and rode off down the deep-rutted road that followed up the creek to the pass where he had watched the

Utes dancing the war dance one night that he remembered well. If he winced a little at the familiar landmarks he passed, he still held fast to the determination to go, and to find fortune somewhere along the trail of his own making; and to ask help from no man, least of all his father who had told him to go.

CHAPTER SEVEN

BUD FLIPS A COIN WITH FATE

" I DON'T think it matters so much where we light, it's what we do when we get there," said Bud to Smoky, his horse, one day as they stopped where two roads forked at the base of a great, outstanding peak that was but the point of a mountain range. " This trail straddles the butte and takes on up two different valleys. It's all cow-country — so what do yuh say, Smoke? Which trail looks the best to you?"

Smoky flopped one ear forward and the other one back, and switched at a pestering fly. Behind him Sunfish and Stopper waited with the patience they had learned in three weeks of continuous travel over country that was rough in spots, barren in places, with wind and sun and occasional, sudden thunderstorms to punctuate the daily grind of travel.

Bud drew a half dollar from his pocket and regarded it meditatively. " They're going fast — we'll just naturally have to stop pretty soon, or we don't eat," he observed. " Smoke, you're a quitter. What you want to do is go back — but you won't get the chance. Heads, we take the right hand trail. I like it better, anyway — it angles more to the north."

Heads it was, and Bud leaned from the saddle and recovered the coin, Smoky turning his head to regard his rider tolerantly. " Right hand goes — and we camp at the first good water and grass. I can grain the three of you once more before we hit a town, and that goes for me, too. G'wan, Smoke, and don't act so mournful."

Smoky went on, following the trail that wound in and out around the butte, hugging close its sheer sides to avoid a fifty-foot drop into the creek below. It was new country — Bud had never so much as seen a map of it to give him a clue to what was coming. The last turn of the deep-rutted, sandy road where it left the river's bank and led straight between two humpy shoulders of rock to the foot of a platter-shaped valley brought him to a halt again in sheer astonishment.

From behind a low hill still farther to the right, where the road forked again, a bluish haze of smoke indicated that there was a town of some sort, perhaps. Farther up the valley a brownish cloud hung low — a roundup, Bud knew at a glance. He hesitated. The town, if it were a town, could wait; the roundup might not. And a job he must have soon, or go hungry. He turned and rode toward the dust-cloud, came shortly to a small stream and a green grass-plot, and stopped there long enough to throw the pack off Sunfish, unsaddle Smoky and stake them both out to graze. Stopper he saddled, then knelt and washed his face, beat the travel dust off his hat, untied his rope and coiled it carefully, untied his handkerchief and shook it as clean as he could and knotted it closely again. One might have thought he was preparing to meet a girl; but the habit of neatness dated back to his pink-apron days and beyond, the dirt and dust meant discomfort.

When he mounted Stopper and loped away toward the dust-cloud, he rode hopefully, sure of himself, carrying his range credentials in his eyes, in his perfect saddle-poise, in the tan on his face to his eyebrows, and the womanish softness of his gloved hands, which had all the sensitive flexibility of a musician.

His main hope was that the outfit was working short-handed; and when he rode near enough to distinguish the herd and the riders, he grinned his satisfaction.

"Good cow-country, by the look of that bunch of cattle," he observed to himself. "And eight men is a small crew to work a herd that size. I guess I'll tie onto this outfit. Stopper, you'll maybe get a chance to turn a cow this afternoon."

Just how soon the chance would come, Bud had not realized. He had no more than come within shouting distance of the herd when a big, rollicky steer broke from the milling cattle and headed straight out past him, running like a deer. Stopper, famed and named for his prowess with just such cattle, wheeled in his tracks and lengthened his stride to a run.

"Tie 'im down!" someone yelled behind Bud. And "Catch 'im and tie 'im down!" shouted another.

For answer Bud waved his hand, and reached in his pocket for his knife. Stopper was artfully circling the steer, forcing it back toward the herd, and in another hundred yards or so Bud must throw his loop. He sliced off a saddle-string and took it between his teeth, jerked his rope loose, flipped open the loop as Stopper raced up alongside, dropped the noose neatly, and took his turns while Stopper planted his forefeet

and braced himself for the shock. Bud's right leg
was over the cantle, all his weight on the left stirrup
when the jerk came and the steer fell with a thump.
By good luck — so Bud afterwards asserted — he was
off and had the steer tied before it had recovered its
breath to scramble up. He remounted, flipped off the
loop and recoiled his rope while he went jogging up to
meet a rider coming out to him.

If he expected thanks for what he had done, he
must have received a shock. Other riders had left
their posts and were edging up to hear what happened,
and Bud reined up in astonishment before the most
amazing string of unseemly epithets he had ever heard.
It began with: " What 'd you throw that critter for? "
—which of course is putting it mildly — and ended in
a choked phrase which one man may not use to another's face and expect anything but trouble afterwards.

Bud unbuckled his gun and hung the belt on his
saddle horn, and dismounted. " Get off your horse
and take the damnedest licking you ever had in your
life, for that! " he invited vengefully. " You told me
to tie down that steer, and I tied him down. You 've
got no call to complain — and there is n't a man· on
earth I 'll take that kinda talk from. Crawl down,
you parrot-faced cow-eater — and leave your gun on
the saddle."

The man remained where he was and looked Bud
over uncertainly. " Who are you, and where 'd yuh
come from? " he demanded more calmly. " I never saw
yuh before."

" Well, I never grew up with *your* face before me,
either! " Bud snapped. " If I had I 'd probably be

cross-eyed by now. You called me something! Get off that horse or I 'll pull you off!"

"Aw, yuh don't want to mind —" began a tall, lean man pacifically; but he of the high nose stopped him with a wave of the hand, his eyes still measuring the face, the form and the fighting spirit of one Bud Birnie, standing with his coat off, quivering with rage.

"I guess I 'm in the wrong, young fellow — I *did* holler ' Tie 'im down.' But if you 'd ever been around this outfit any you 'd have known I did n't mean it literal." He stopped and suddenly he laughed. "I 've been yellin' ' Tie 'im down ' for two years and more, when a critter breaks outa the bunch, and nobody was ever fool enough to tackle it before. It 's just a sayin' we 've got, young man. We —"

"What about the name you called me?" Bud was still advancing slowly, not much appeased by the explanation. "I don't give a darn about the steer. You said tie him, and he 's tied. But when you call me —"

"My mistake, young feller. When I get riled up I don't pick my words." He eyed Bud sharply. "You 're mighty quick to obey orders," he added tentatively.

"I was brought up to do as I 'm told," Bud retorted stiffly. "Any objections to make?"

"Not one in the world. Wish there was more like yuh. You ain't been in these parts long?" His tone made a question of the statement.

"Not right here." Bud had no reason save his temper for not giving more explicit information, but Bart Nelson — as Bud knew him afterwards — continued to study him as if he suspected a blotched past.

" Hunh. That your horse? "

" I 've got a bill of sale for him."

" You don't happen to be wanting a job, I s'pose? "

" I would n't refuse to take one." And then the twinkle came back to Bud's eyes, because all at once the whole incident struck him as being rather funny. " I 'd want a boss that expected to have his orders carried out, though. I lack imagination, and I never did try to read a man's mind. What he says he 'd better mean — when he says it to me."

Bart Nelson gave a short laugh, turned and sent his riders back to their work with oaths tingling their ears. Bud judged that cursing was his natural form of speech.

" Go let up that steer, and I 'll put you to work," he said to Bud afterwards. " That 's a good rope horse you 're riding. If you want to use him, and if you can hold up to that little sample of roping yuh gave us, I 'll pay yuh sixty a month. And that 's partly for doing what you 're told," he added with a quick look into Bud's eyes. " You did n't say where you 're from — "

" I was born and raised in cow-country, and nobody 's looking for me," Bud informed him over his shoulder while he remounted, and let it go at that. From southern Wyoming to Idaho was too far, he reasoned, to make it worth while stating his exact place of residence. If they had never heard of the Tomahawk outfit it would do no good to name it. If they had heard of it, they would wonder why the son of so rich a cowman as Bob Birnie should be hiring out as a common cowpuncher so far from home. He had studied the matter on his way north, and had decided to let people form their own conclusions. If he could not make good without the name of Bob Birnie behind him, the sooner he found it out the better.

He untied the steer, drove it back into the herd and rode over to where the high-nosed man was helping hold the " cut."

" Can you read brands? We 're cuttin' out AJ and AJBar stuff; left ear-crop on the AJ, and undercut on the AJBar."

Bud nodded and eased into the herd, spied an AJ two-year-old and urged it toward the outer edge, smiling to himself when he saw how Stopper kept his nose close to the animal's rump. Once in the milling fringe of the herd, Stopper nipped it into the open, rushed it to the cut herd, wheeled and went back of his own accord. From the corner of his eye, as he went, Bud saw that Bart Nelson and one or two others were watching him. They continued to eye him covertly while he worked the herd with two other men. He was glad that he had not travelled far that day, and that he had ridden Smoky and left Stopper fresh and eager for his favorite pastime, which was making cattle do what they particularly did not want to do. In that he was adept, and it pleased Bud mightily to see how much attention Stopper was attracting.

Not once did it occur to him that it might be himself who occupied the thoughts of his boss. Buddy — afterwards Bud — had lived his whole life among friends, his only enemies the Indians who preyed upon the cowmen. White men he had never learned to distrust, and to be distrusted had never been his portion. He had always been Bud Birnie, son and heir of Bob Birnie, as clean-handed a cattle king as ever recorded a brand. Even at the University his position had been accepted without question. That the man he mentally called Parrotface was puzzled and even worried about him was the last thing he would think of.

But it was true. Bart Nelson watched Bud, that afternoon. A man might ride up to Bart and assert that he was an old hand with cattle, and Bart would say nothing, but set him to work, as he had Bud. Then he would know just how old a "hand" the fellow was. Fifteen minutes convinced him that Bud had "growed up in the saddle", as he would have put it. But that only mystified him the more. Bart knew the range, and he knew every man in the country, from Burroback Valley, which was this great valley's name, to the Black Rim, beyond the mountain range, and beyond the Black Rim to the Sawtooth country. He knew their ways and he knew their past records.

He knew that this young fellow came from farther ranges, and he would have been at a loss to explain just how he knew it. He would have said that Bud did not have the "earmarks" of an Idaho rider. Furthermore, the small Tomahawk brand on the left flank of the horse Bud rode was totally unknown to Bart. Yet the horse did not bear the marks of long riding. Bud himself looked as if he had just ridden out from some nearby ranch — and he had refused to say where he was from.

Bart swore under his breath and beckoned to him a droopy-mustached, droopy-shouldered rider who was circling the herd in a droopy, spiritless manner and chewing tobacco with much industry.

"Dirk, you know brands from the Panhandle to Cypress Hills. What d' yuh make of that horse?

Where does he come from?" Bart stopped abruptly and rode forward then to receive and drive farther back a galloping AJBar cow which Bud and Stopper had just hazed out of the herd. Dirk squinted at Stopper's brand which showed cleanly in the glossy, new hair of early summer. He spat carefully with the wind and swung over to meet his boss when the cow was safely in the cut herd.

"New one on me, Bart. They's a hatchet brand over close to Jackson's Hole, somewhere. Where'd the kid say he was from?"

"He wouldn't say, but he's a sure-enough cowhand."

"That there horse ain't been rode down on no long journey," Dirk volunteered after further scrutiny. And he added with the unconscious impertinence of an old and trusted employee, "Yuh goin' to put him on?"

"Already done it — sixty a month," Bart confided. "That'll bring out what's in him; he's liable to turn out good for the outfit. Showed he'll do what he's told first, and think it over afterwards. I like that there trait in a man."

Dirk pulled his droopy mustache away from his lips as if he wanted to make sure that his smile would show; though it was not a pretty smile, on account of his tobacco-stained teeth.

"'S your fun'ral, Bart. I'd say he's from Jackson's Hole, on a rough guess — but I wouldn't presume to guess what he's here fur. Mebby he come across from Black Rim. I can find out, if you say so."

Bud was weaving in and out through the herd, scanning the animals closely. While the two talked he singled out a yearling heifer, let Stopper nose it out beyond the bunch and drove it close to the boss.

"Better look that one over," he called out. "One way, it looks like AJ, and another way I could n't name it. And the ear looks as if about half of it had been frozen off. Did n't want to run it into the cut until you passed on it."

Bart looked first at Bud, and he looked hard. Then he rode over and inspected the yearling, Dirk close at his heels.

"Throw 'er back with the bunch," he ordered.

"That finishes the cut, then," Bud announced, rubbing his hand along Stopper's sweaty neck. "I kept passing this critter up, and I guess the other boys did the same. But it 's the last one, and I thought I 'd run her out for you to look over."

Bart grunted. "Dirk, you take a look and see if they 've got 'em all. And you, Kid, can help haze the cut up the Flat — the boys 'll show you what to do."

Bud, remembering Smoky and Sunfish and his camp, hesitated. "I 've got a camp down here by the creek," he said. "If it 's all the same to you, I 'll report for work in the morning, if you 'll tell me where to head for. And I 'll have to arrange somehow to pasture my horses; I 've got a couple more at camp."

Bart studied him for a minute, and Bud thought he was going to change his mind about the job, or the sixty dollars a month. But Bart merely told him to ride on up the Flat next morning, and take the first trail that turned to the left. "The Muleshoe ranch is up there agin that pine mountain," he explained. "Bring along your outfit. I guess we can take care of a couple of horses, all right."

That suited Bud very well, and he rode away thinking how lucky he was to have taken the right fork in the road, that day. He had ridden straight into a job, and while he was not very enthusiastic over the boss, the other boys seemed all right, and the wages were a third more than he had expected to get just at first. It was the first time, he reminded himself, that he had been really tempted to locate, and he certainly had struck it lucky.

He did not know that when he left the roundup his going had been carefully noted, and that he was no sooner out of sight than Dirk Tracy was riding cautiously on his trail. While he fed his horses the last bit of grain he had, and cooked his supper over what promised to be his last camp-fire, he did not dream that the man with the droopy mustache was lying amongst the bushes on the other bank of the creek, watching every move he made.

He meant to be up before daylight so that he could strike the ranch of the Muleshoe outfit in time for breakfast, wherefore he went to bed before the afterglow had left the mountain-tops around him. And being young and carefree and healthfully weary, he was asleep and snoring gently within five minutes of his last wriggle into his blankets. But Dirk Tracy watched him for fully two hours before he decided that the kid was not artfully pretending, but was really asleep and likely to remain so for the night.

Dirk was an extremely cautious man, but he was also tired, and the cold food he had eaten in place of a hot supper had not been satisfying to his stomach. He crawled carefully out of the brush, stole up the creek to where he had left his horse, and rode away.

He was not altogether sure that he had done his full duty to the Muleshoe, but it was against human nature for a man nearing forty to lie uncovered in the brush, and let a numerous family of mosquitoes feed upon him while he listened to a young man snoring comfortably in a good camp bed a hundred feet away.

Dirk, because his conscience was not quite clear, slept in the stable that night and told his boss a lie next morning.

CHAPTER EIGHT

The Muleshoe

THE riders of the Muleshoe outfit were eating breakfast when Bud rode past the long, low-roofed log cabin to the corral which stood nearest the clutter of stables and sheds. He stopped there and waited to see if his new boss was anywhere in sight and would come to tell him where to unpack his belongings. A sandy complexioned young man with red eyelids and no lashes presently emerged from the stable and came toward him, his mouth sagging loosely open, his eyes vacuous. He was clad in faded overalls turned up a foot at the bottom and showing frayed, shoddy trousers beneath and rusty, run-down shoes that proved he was not a rider. His hat was peppered with little holes, as if someone had fired a charge of birdshot at him and had all but bagged him.

The youth's eyes became fixed upon the guitar and mandolin cases roped on top of Sunfish's pack, and he pointed and gobbled something which had the sound of speech without being intelligible. Bud cocked an ear toward him inquiringly, made nothing of the jumble and rode off to the cabin, leading Sunfish after him. The fellow might or might not be the idiot he looked, and he might or might not keep his hands off the pack; Bud was not going to take any chance.

He heard sounds within the cabin, but no one appeared until he shouted, " Hello! " twice. The door opened then and Bart Nelson put out his head, his jaws working over a mouthful of food that seemed tough.

" Oh, it 's you. C'm awn in an' eat," he invited, and Bud dismounted, never guessing that his slightest motion had been carefully observed from the time he had forded the creek at the foot of the slope beyond the cabin.

Bart introduced him to the men by the simple method of waving his hand at the group around the table and saying, " Guess you know the boys. What 'd yuh say we could call yuh? "

" Bud — ah — Birnie," Bud answered, swiftly weighing the romantic idea of using some makeshift name until he had made his fortune, and deciding against it. A false name might mean future embarrassment, and he was so far from home that his father would never hear of him anyway. But his hesitation served to convince every man there that Birnie was not his name, and that he probably had good cause for concealing his own. Adding that to Dirk Tracy's guess that he was from Jackson's Hole, the sum spelled outlaw.

The Muleshoe boys were careful not to seem curious about Bud's past. They even refrained from manifesting too much interest in the musical instruments until Bud himself took them out of their cases that evening and began tuning them. Then the half-baked, tongue-tied fellow came over and gobbled at him eagerly.

" Hen wants yuh to play something," a man they

called Day interpreted. "Hen's loco on music. If
you can sing and play both, Hen'll set and listen till
plumb daylight and never move an eyewinker."

Bud looked up, smiled a little because Hen had no
eyewinkers to move, and suddenly felt pity because a
man could be so altogether unlikeable as Hen. Also
because his mother's face stood vividly before him for
an instant, leaving him with a queer tightening of the
throat and the feeling that he had been rebuked. He
nodded to Hen, laid down the mandolin and picked up
the guitar, turned up the *a* string a bit, laid a booted-
and-spurred foot across the other knee, plucked a minor
chord sonorously and began abruptly:

"Yo' kin talk about you coons a-havin' trouble —
  Well, Ah think Ah have enough-a of mah
  oh-own — "

Hen's high-pointed Adam's apple slipped up and
down in one great gulp of ecstasy. He eased slowly
down upon the edge of the bunk beside Bud and gazed
at him fascinatedly, his lashless eyes never winking,
his jaw dropped so that his mouth hung half open.
Day nudged Dirk Tracy, who parted his droopy mustache and smiled his unlovely smile, lowering his left
eyelid unnecessarily at Bud. The dimple in Bud's
chin wrinkled as he bent his head and plunked the in-
terlude with a swing that set spurred boots tapping the
floor rhythmically.

"Bart, he's went and hired a show-actor, looks
like," Dirk confided behind his hand to Shorty
McGuire. "That's real *singin'*, if yuh ask me!"

"Shut up!" grunted Shorty, and prodded Dirk into
silence so that he would miss none of the song.

Since Buddy had left the pink-apron stage of his adventurous life behind him, singing songs to please other people had been as much a part of his life as riding and roping and eating and sleeping. He had always sung or played or danced when he was asked to do so — accepting without question his mother's doctrine that it was unkind and ill-bred to refuse when he really could do those things well, because on the cattle ranges indoor amusements were few, and those who could furnish real entertainment were fewer. Even at the University, coon songs and Irish songs and love songs had been his portion; wherefore his repertoire seemed endless, and if folks insisted upon it he could sing from dark to dawn, providing his voice held out.

Hen sat with his big-jointed hands hanging loosely over his knees and listened, stared at Bud and grinned vacuously when one song was done, gulped his Adam's apple and listened again as raptly to the next one. The others forgot all about having fun watching Hen, and named old favorites and new ones, heard them sung inimitably and called for more. At midnight Bud blew on his blistered fingertips and shook the guitar gently, bottomside up.

" I guess that 's all the music there is in the darned thing to-night," he lamented. " She 's made to keep time, and she always strikes, along about midnight."

" Huh-huh!" chortled Hen convulsively, as if he understood the joke. He closed his mouth and sighed deeply, as one who has just wakened from a trance.

After that, Hen followed Bud around like a pet dog, and found time between stable chores to groom those astonished horses, Stopper and Smoky and Sunfish, as if they were stall-kept thoroughbreds. He had them coming up to the pasture gate every day for the few handfuls of grain he purloined for them, and their sleekness was a joy to behold.

"Hen, he's adopted yuh, horses and all, looks like," Dirk observed one day to Bud when they were riding together. And he tempered the statement by adding that Hen was trusty enough, even if he didn't have as much sense as the law allows. "He sure is takin' care of them cayuses of yourn. D'you tell him to?"

Bud came out of a homesick revery and looked at him inquiringly. "No, I didn't tell him anything."

"I believe that, all right," Dirk retorted. "You don't go around tellin' all yuh know. I like that in a feller. A man never got into trouble yet by keepin' his mouth shut; but there's plenty that have talked themselves into the pen. Me, I've got no use for a talker."

Bud sent him a sidelong glance of inquiry, and Dirk caught him at it and grinned.

"Yuh been here a month, and you ain't said a damn word about where you come from or anything further back than throwin' and tyin' that critter. You said cow-country, and that has had to do some folks that might be curious. Well, she's a tearin' big place — cow-country. She runs from Canady to Mexico, and from the corn belt to the Pacific Ocean, mighty near. Takes in Jackson's Hole, and a lot uh country I know." He parted his mustache and spat carefully into the sand. "I'm willin' to tie to a man, specially a young feller, that can play the game the way you been playin' it, Bud. Most always," he complained vaguely, "they carry their brand too damn plain. They either pull

their hats down past their eyebrows and give everybody the bad eye, or else they're too damn ready to
lie about themselves. You throw in with the boys
just fine — but you ain't told a one of 'em where you
come from, ner why, ner nothin'."

"I'm here because I'm here," Bud chanted softly,
his eyes stubborn even while he smiled at Dirk.

"I know — yuh sung that the first night yuh come,
and yuh looked straight at the boss all the while you was
singin' it," Dirk interrupted, and laughed slyly. "The
boys, they took that all in, too. And Bart, he wasn't
asleep, neither. You sure are smooth as they make
'em, Bud. I guess," he leaned closer to predict confidentially, "you've just about passed the probation
time, young feller. If I know the signs, the boss is
gittin' ready to raise yuh."

He looked at Bud rather sharply. Instantly the
training of Buddy rose within Bud. His memory
flashed back unerringly to the day when he had
watched that Indian gallop toward the river, and had
sneered because the Indian evidently expected him to
follow into the undergrowth.

Dirk Tracy did not in the least resemble an Indian,
nor did his rambling flattery bear any likeness to a
fleeing enemy; yet it was plain enough that he was
trying in a bungling way to force Bud's confidence,
and for that reason Bud stared straight ahead and
said nothing.

He did not remember having sung that particular
ditty during his first evening at the Muleshoe, nor of
staring at the boss while he sung. He might have done
both, he reflected; he had sung one song after another
for about four hours that night, and unless he sang

with his eyes shut he would have to look somewhere. That it should be taken by the whole outfit as a broad hint to ask no questions seemed to him rather far-fetched.

Nor did he see why Dirk should compliment him on keeping his mouth shut, or call him smooth. He did not know that he had been on probation, except perhaps as that applied to his ability as a cow-hand. And he could see no valid reason why the boss should contemplate "raising" him. So far, he had been doing no more than the rest of the boys, except when there was roping to be done and he and Stopper were called upon to distinguish themselves by fast rope-work, with never a miss. Sixty dollars a month was as good pay as he had any right to expect.

Dirk, he decided, had given him one good tip which he would follow at once. Dirk had said that no man ever got into trouble by keeping his mouth shut. Bud closed his for a good half hour, and when he opened it again he undid all the good he had accomplished by his silence.

"Where does that trail go, that climbs up over the mountains back of that peak?" he asked. "Seems to be a stock trail. Have you got grazing land beyond the mountains?"

Dirk took time to pry off a fresh chew of tobacco before he replied. "You mean Thunder Pass? That there crosses over into the Black Rim country. Yeah —there's a big wide range country over there, but we don't run any stock on it. Burroback Valley's big enough for the Muleshoe."

Bud rolled a cigarette. "I didn't mean that main trail; that's a wagon road, and Thunder Pass cuts through between Sheepeater peak and this one ahead of us — Gospel, you call it. What I referred to is that blind trail that takes off up the canyon behind the corrals, and crosses into the mountains the other side of Gospel."

Dirk eyed him. "I dunno 's I could say, right offhand, what trail yuh mean," he parried. "Every canyon's got a trail that runs up a ways, and there's canyons all through the mountains; they all lead up to water, or feed, or something like that, and then quit, most gen-'rally; jest peter out, like." And he added with heavy sarcasm, "A feller that's lived on the range oughta know what trails is for, and how they're made. Cow-critters are curious — same as humans."

To this Bud did not reply. He was smoking and staring at the brushy lower slopes of the mountain ridge before them. He had explained quite fully which trail he meant. It was, as he had said, a "blind" trail; that is, the trail lost itself in the creek which watered a string of corrals. Moreover, Bud had very keen eyes, and he had seen how a panel of the corral directly across the shale-rock bed of a small stream was really a set of bars. The round pole corral lent itself easily to hidden gateways, without any deliberate attempt at disguising their presence.

The string of four corrals running from this upper one — which, he remembered, was not seen from nearer the stables — was perhaps a convenient arrangement in the handling of stock, although it was unusual. The upper corral had been built to fit snugly into a rocky recess in the base of the peak called Gospel. It was larger than some of the others, since it followed the contour of the basin-like recess. Access to it was had from the fourth corral (which from the ranch appeared to be the last) and from the creek-bed that filled the narrow mouth of the canyon behind.

Dirk might not have understood him, Bud thought. He certainly should have recognized at once the trail Bud meant, for there was no other canyon back of the corrals, and even that one was not apparent to one looking at the face of the steep slope. Stock had been over that canyon trail within the last month or so, however; and Bud's inference that the Muleshoe must have grazing ground across the mountains was natural; the obvious explanation of its existence.

"How'd you come to be explorin' around Gospel, anyway?" Dirk quizzed finally. "A person'd think, short-handed as the Muleshoe is this spring, 't you'd git all the ridin' yuh want without prognosticatin' around aimless."

Now Bud was not a suspicious young man, and he had been no more than mildly inquisitive about that trail. But neither was he a fool; he caught the emphasis which Dirk had placed on the word aimless, and his thoughts paused and took another look at Dirk's whole conversation. There was something queer about it, something which made Bud sheer off from his usual unthinking assurance that things were just what they seemed.

Immediately, however, he laughed — at himself as well as at Dirk.

"We've been feeding on sour bread and warmed-over coffee ever since the cook disappeared and Bart put Hen in the kitchen," he said. "If I were you, Dirk, I wouldn't blister my hands shovelling that grub into myself for a while. You're bilious, old-timer.

No man on earth would talk the way you 've been talking to-day unless his whole digestive apparatus were out of order."

Dirk spat angrily at a dead sage bush. "They shore as hell would n't talk the kinda talk you 've been talkin' unless they was a born fool or else huntin' trouble," he retorted venomously.

"The doctor said I 'd be that way if I lived," Bud grinned amiably, although his face had flushed at Dirk's tone. "He said it would n't hurt me for work."

"Yeah — and what kinda work?" Dirk rode so close that his horse shouldered Bud's leg discomfortingly. "I been edgin' yuh along to see what-f'r brand yuh carried. And I 've got ye now, you damned snoopin' kioty. Bart, he hired yuh to work — and not to go prowling around lookin' up trails that ain't there — "

"You 're a dim-brand reader, I don't think! Why you — !"

Oh, well — remember that Bud was only Buddy grown bigger, and he had never lacked the spirit to look out for himself. Remember, too, that he must have acquired something of a vocabulary, in the course of twenty-one years of absorbing everything that came within his experience.

Dirk reached for his gun, but Bud was expecting that. Dirk was not quite quick enough, and his hand therefore came forward with a jerk when he saw that he was "covered." Bud leaned, pulled Dirk's six-shooter from its holster and sent it spinning into a clump of bushes. He snatched a wicked-looking knife from Dirk's boot where he had once seen Dirk slip it sheathed when he dressed in the bunk-house, and sent that after the gun.

"Now, you long-eared walrus, you're in a position to play fair. What are you going to do about it?" He reined away, out of Dirk's reach, took his handkerchief and wrapped his own gun tightly to protect it from sand, and threw it after Dirk's gun and the knife. "Am I a snooping coyote?" he demanded, watching Dirk.

"You air. More'n all that, you're a damned spy! And I kin lick yuh an' lass' yuh an' lead yuh to Bart like a sheep!"

They dismounted, left their horses to stand with reins dropped, threw off their coats and fought until they were too tired to land another blow. There were no fatalities. Bud did not come out of the fray unscathed and proudly conscious of his strength and his skill and the unquestionable righteousness of his cause. Instead he had three bruised knuckles and a rapidly swelling ear, and when his anger had cooled a little he felt rather foolish and wondered what had started them off that way. They had ridden away from the ranch in a very good humor, and he had harbored no conscious dislike of Dirk Tracy, who had been one individual of a type of rangemen which he had known all his life and had accepted as a matter of course.

Dirk, on his part, had some trouble in stopping the bleeding of his nose, and by the time he reached the ranch his left eye was closed completely. He was taller and heavier than Bud, and he had not expected such a slugging strength behind Bud's blows.

He was badly shaken, and when Bud recovered the two guns and the knife and returned his weapons to him, Dirk was half tempted to shoot. But he did not — perhaps because Bud had unwrapped his own six-shooter and was looking it over with the muzzle slanting a wicked eye in Dirk's direction.

Late that afternoon, when the boys were loafing around the cabin waiting for their early supper, Bud packed his worldly goods on Sunfish and departed from the Muleshoe — " by special request ", he admitted to himself ruefully — with his wages in gold and silver in his pocket and no definite idea of what he would do next.

He wished he knew exactly why Bart had fired him. He did not believe that it was for fighting, as Bart had declared. He thought that perhaps Dirk Tracy had some hold on the Muleshoe not apparent to the outsider, and that he had lied about him to Bart as a sneaking kind of revenge for being whipped. But that explanation did not altogether satisfy him, either.

In his month at the Muleshoe he had gained a very fair general idea of the extent and resources of Burroback Valley, but he had not made any acquaintances and he did not know just where to go for his next job. So for want of something better, he rode down to the little stream which he now knew was called One Creek, and prepared to spend the night there. In the morning he would make a fresh start — and because of the streak of stubbornness he had, he meant to make it in Burroback Valley, under the very nose of the Mule-shoe outfit.

CHAPTER NINE

LITTLE LOST

LITTLE LOST — somehow the name appealed to Bud, whose instinct for harmony extended to words and phrases and, for that matter, to everything in the world that was beautiful. From the time when he first heard Little Lost mentioned, he had felt a vague regret that chance had not led him there instead of to the Muleshoe. Brands he had heard all his life as the familiar, colloquial names for ranch headquarters. The Muleshoe was merely a brand name. Little Lost was something else, and because Buddy had been taught to "wait and find out" and to ask questions only as a last resort, Bud was still in ignorance of the meaning of Little Lost. He knew, from careless remarks made in his presence, that the mail came to Little Lost, and that there was some sort of store where certain everyday necessities were kept, for which the store-keeper charged "two prices." But there was also a ranch, for he sometimes heard the boys mention the Little Lost cattle, and speak of some man as a rider for the Little Lost.

So to Little Lost Bud rode blithely next morning, riding Stopper and leading Smoky, Sunfish and the pack following as a matter of course. Again his trained instinct served him faithfully. He had a very good general idea of Burroback Valley, he knew that the Muleshoe occupied a fair part of the south side, and guessed that he must ride north, toward the Gold Gap Mountains, to find the place he wanted.

The trail was easy, his horses were as fat as was good for them. In two hours of riding at his usual trail pace he came upon another stream which he knew must be Sunk Creek grown a little wider and deeper in its journey down the valley. He forded that with a great splashing, climbed the farther bank, followed a stubby, rocky bit of road that wound through dense willow and cottonwood growth, came out into a humpy meadow full of ant hills, gopher holes and soggy wet places where the water grass grew, crossed that and followed the road around a brushy ridge and found himself squarely confronting Little Lost.

There could be no mistake, for " Little Lost Post-Office " was unevenly painted on the high cross-bar of the gate that stood wide open and permanently warped with long sagging. There was a hitch-rail outside the gate, and Bud took the hint and left his horses there. From the wisps of fresh hay strewn along the road, Bud knew that haying had begun at Little Lost. There were at least four cabins and a somewhat pretentious, story-and-a-half log house with vines reaching vainly to the high window sills, and coarse lace curtains. One of these curtains moved slightly, and Bud's sharp eyes detected the movement and knew that his arrival was observed in spite of the emptiness of the yard.

The beaten path led to a screen door which sagged with much slamming, leaving a wide space at the top through which flies passed in and out quite comfortably. Bud saw that, also, and his fingers itched to reset that door, just as he would have done for his mother — supposing his mother would have tolerated the slamming which had brought the need. Bud lifted his gloved knuckles to knock, saw that the room within was grimy and bare and meant for public use, very much like the office of a country hotel, with a counter and a set of pigeon-holes at the farther end. He walked in.

No one appeared, and after ten minutes or so Bud guessed why, and went back to the door, pushed it wide open and permitted it to fly shut with a bang. Whereupon a girl opened the door behind the counter and came in, glancing at Bud with frank curiosity.

Bud took off his hat and clanked over to the counter and asked if there was any mail for Bud Birnie — Robert Wallace Birnie.

The girl looked at him again and smiled, and turned to shuffle a handful of letters. Bud employed the time in trying to guess just what she meant by that smile.

It was not really a smile, he decided, but the beginning of one. And if that were the beginning, he would very much like to know what the whole smile would mean. The beginning hinted at things. It was as if she doubted the reality of the name he gave, and meant to conceal her doubt, or had heard something amusing about him, or wished to be friends with him, or was secretly timorous and trying to appear merely indifferent. Or perhaps —

She replaced the letters and turned, and rested her hands on the counter. She looked at him and again her lips turned at the corners in that faint, enigmatical beginning of a smile.

"There is n't a thing," she said. "The mail comes this noon again. Do you want yours sent out to any of the outfits? Or shall I just hold it?"

"Just hold it, when there is any. At least, until I see whether I land a job here. I wonder where I could find the boss?" Bud was glancing often at her hands. For a ranch girl her hands were soft and white, but her fingers were a bit too stubby and her nails were too round and flat.

"Uncle Dave will be home at noon. He's out in the meadow with the boys. You might sit down and wait."

Bud looked at his watch. Sitting down and waiting for four hours did not appeal to him, even supposing the girl would keep him company. But he lingered awhile, leaning with his elbows on the counter near her; and by those obscure little conversational trails known to youth, he progressed considerably in his acquaintance with the girl and made her smile often without once feeling quite certain that he knew what was in her mind.

He discovered that her name was Honora Krause, and that she was called Honey "for short." Her father had been Dutch and her mother a Yankee, and she lived with her uncle, Dave Truman, who owned Little Lost ranch, and took care of the mail for him, and attended to the store — which was nothing more than a supply depot kept for the accommodation of the neighbors. The store, she said, was in the next room.

Bud asked her what Little Lost meant, and she replied that she did not know, but that it might have something to do with Sunk Creek losing itself in The Sinks. There was a Little Lost river, farther across the mountains, she said, but it did not run through Little Lost ranch, nor come anywhere near it.

After that she questioned him adroitly. Perversely Bud declined to become confidential, and Honey Krause changed the subject abruptly.

"There's going to be a dance here next Friday night. It'll be a good chance to get acquainted with everybody — if you go. There'll be good music, I guess. Uncle Dave wrote to Crater for the Saunders boys to come down and play. Do you know anybody in Crater?"

The question was innocent enough, but perverseness still held Bud. He smiled and said he did not know anybody anywhere, any more. He said that if Bobbie Burns had asked him "Should auld acquaintance be forgot," he'd have told him yes, and he'd have made it good and strong. But he added that he was just as willing to make new acquaintance, and thought the dance would be a good place to begin.

Honey gave him a provocative glance from under her lashes, and Bud straightened and stepped back.

"You let folks stop here, I take it. I've a pack outfit and a couple of saddle horses with me. Will it be all right to turn them in the corral? I hate to have them eat post hay all day. Or I could perhaps go back to the creek and camp."

"Oh, just turn your horses in the corral and make yourself at home till uncle comes," she told him with that tantalizing half-smile. "We keep people here — just for accommodation. There has to be some place in the valley where folks can stop. I can't promise that uncle will give you a job, but there's going to be chicken and dumplings for dinner. And the mail will be in, about noon — you'll want to wait for that."

She was standing just within the screen door, frankly watching him as he came past the house with the horses, and she came out and halted him when she spied the top of the pack.

"You'd better leave those things here," she advised him eagerly. "I'll put them in the sitting-room by the piano. My goodness, you must be a whole orchestra! If you can play, maybe you and I can furnish the music for the dance, and save Uncle Dave hiring the Saunders boys. Anyway, we can play together, and have real good times."

Bud had an odd feeling that Honey was talking one thing with her lips, and thinking an entirely different set of thoughts. He eyed her covertly while he untied the cases, and he could have sworn that he saw her signal someone behind the lace curtains of the nearest window. He glanced carelessly that way, but the curtains were motionless. Honey was holding out her hands for the guitar and the mandolin when he turned, so Bud surrendered them and went on to the corrals.

He did not return to the house. An old man was pottering around a machine shed that stood backed against a thick fringe of brush, and when Bud rode by he left his work and came after him, taking short steps and walking with his back bent stiffly forward and his hands swinging limply at his sides.

He had a long black beard streaked with gray, and sharp blue eyes set deep under tufted white eyebrows. He seemed a friendly old man whose interest in life remained keen as in his youth, despite the feebleness of his body. He showed Bud where to turn the horses, and went to work on the pack rope, his crooked old fingers moving with the sureness of lifelong habit. He was eager to know all the news that Bud could tell him, and when he discovered that Bud had just left the Muleshoe, and that he had been fired because of a fight with Dirk Tracy, the old fellow cackled gleefully.

"Well, now, I guess you just about had yore hands full, young man," he commented shrewdly. "Dirk ain't so easy to lick."

Bud immediately wanted to know why it was taken for granted that he had whipped Dirk, and grandpa chortled again. "Now if you hadn't of *licked* Dirk, you wouldn't of got fired," he retorted, and proceeded to relate a good deal of harmless gossip which seemed to bear out the statement. Dirk Tracy, according to grandpa, was the real boss of the Muleshoe, and Bart was merely a figure-head.

All of this did not matter to Bud, but grandpa was garrulous. A good deal of information Bud received while the two attended to the horses and loitered at the corral gate.

Grandpa admired Smoky, and looked him over carefully, with those caressing smoothings of mane and forelock which betray the lover of good horseflesh.

"I reckon he's purty fast," he said, peering shrewdly into Bud's face. "The boys has been talking about pulling off some horse races here next Sunday — we got a good, straight, hard-packed creek-bed up here a piece that has been cleaned of rocks fer a mile track, and they're goin' to run a horse er two. Most generally they do, on Sunday, if work's slack. You might git in on it, if you're around in these parts." He pushed his back straight with his palms, turned his head sidewise and squinted at Smoky through half-closed lids while he fumbled for cigarette material.

"I dunno but what I might be willin' to put up a few dollars on that horse myself," he observed, "if you say he kin run. You would n't go an' lie to an old feller like me, would yuh, son?"

Bud offered him the cigarette he had just rolled. "No, I won't lie to you, dad," he grinned. "You know horses too well."

"Well, but *kin* he run? I want yore word on it."

"Well — yes, he 's always been able to turn a cow," Bud admitted cautiously.

"Ever run him fer money?" The old man began teetering from his toes to his heels, and to hitch his shoulders forward and back.

"Well, no, not for money. I 've run him once or twice for fun, just trying to beat some of the boys to camp, maybe."

"Sho! That 's no way to do! No way at all!" The old man spat angrily into the dust of the corral. Then he thought of something. "Did yuh *beat* 'em?" he demanded sharply.

"Why, sure, I beat them!" Bud looked at him surprised, seemed about to say more, and let the statement stand unqualified.

Grandpa stared at him for a minute, his blue eyes blinking with some secret excitement. "Young feller," he began abruptly, "lemme tell yuh something. Yuh never want to do a thing like that agin. If you got a horse that can outrun the other feller's horse, figure to make him bring yuh in something — if it ain't no more 'n a quarter! Make him *bring* yuh a little something. That's the way to do with everything yuh turn a hand to; make it bring yuh *in* something! It ain't what goes out that'll do yuh any good — it's what comes in. You mind that. If you let a horse run agin another feller's horse, bet on him to come in ahead — and then," he cried fiercely, pounding one fist into the other palm, "by Christmas, make 'im *come* in ahead!" His voice cracked and went flat with emotion.

He stopped suddenly and let his arms fall slack, his shoulders sag forward. He waggled his head and muttered into his beard, and glanced at Bud with a crafty look.

"If I'd a took that to m'self, I wouldn't be chorin' around here now for my own son," he lamented. "I'd of saved the quarters, an' I'd of had a few dollars now of my own. Uh course," he made haste to add, "I git holt of a little, now and agin. Too old to ride — too old to work — jest manage to pick up a dollar er two now and agin — on a horse that kin run."

He went over to Smoky again and ran his hand down over the leg muscles to the hocks, felt for imperfections and straightened painfully, slapped the horse approvingly between the forelegs and laid a hand on his shoulder while he turned slowly to Bud.

"Young feller, there ain't a man on the place right now but you an' me. What say you throw yore saddle on this horse and take 'im up to the track? I'd like to see him run. Seems to me he'd ought to be a purty good quarter-horse."

Bud hesitated. "I wouldn't mind running him, grandpa, if I thought I could make something on him. I've got my stake to make, and I want to make it before all my teeth fall out so I can't chew anything but the cud of reflection on my lost opportunities. If Smoky can run a few dollars into my pocket, I'm with you."

Grandpa teetered forward and put out his hand. "Shake on that, boy!" he cackled. "Pop Truman ain't too old to have his little joke — and make it bring him *in* something, by Christmas! You saddle up and we'll go try him out on a quarter-mile — mebby a half, if he holds up good."

He poked a cigarette-stained forefinger against Bud's chest and whispered slyly: "My son Dave, he's got a horse in the stable that's been cleanin' everything in the valley. I'll slip him out and up the creek-trail to the track, and you run that horse of yourn agin him. Dave, he can't git a race outa nobody around here, no more, so he won't run next Sunday. We'll jest see how yore horse runs alongside Boise. I kin tell purty well how you kin run agin the rest — Pop, he ain't s' thick-headed they kin fool him much. What say we try it?"

Bud stood back and looked him over. "You shook hands with me on it," he said gravely. "Where I came from, that holds a man like taking oath on a Bible in court. I'm a stranger here, but I'm going to expect the same standard of honor, grandpa. You can back out now, and I'll run Smoky without any tryout, and you can take your chance. I couldn't expect you to stand by a stranger against your own folks — "

"Sho! Shucks a'mighty!" Grandpa spat and wagged his head furiously. "My own folks 'd beat *me* in a horse race if they could, and I wouldn't hold it agin 'em! Runnin' horses is like playin' poker. Every feller fer himself an' mercy to-ward none! I knowed what it meant when I shook with yuh, young feller, and I hold ye to it. I hold ye to it! You lay low if I *tell* ye to lay low, and we 'll make us a few dollars, mebby. C'm on and git that horse outa here b'fore somebuddy comes. It 's mail day."

He waved Bud toward his saddle and took himself off in a shuffling kind of trot. By the time Bud had saddled Smoky grandpa hailed him cautiously from the brush-fringe beyond the corral. He motioned toward a small gate and Bud led Smoky that way, closing the gate after him.

The old man was mounted on a clean-built bay whose coat shone with little glints of gold in the dark red. With one sweeping look Bud observed the points that told of speed, and his eyes went inquiringly to meet the sharp blue ones, that sparkled under the tufted white eyebrows of grandpa.

"Do you expect Smoky to show up the same day that horse arrives?" he inquired mildly. "Pop, you'll have to prove to me that he won't run Sunday—"

Pop snorted. "Seems to me like you do know a speedy horse when you see one, young feller. Beats me 't you been overlookin' what you got under yore saddle right now. Boise, he 's the best runnin' horse in the valley — and that 's why he won't run next Sunday, ner no other Sunday till somebuddy brings in a strange horse to put agin him. Dave, he won't crowd ye fur a race, boy. You kin refuse to run yore horse agin him, like the rest has done. I 'll jest lope along t'day and see what yours kin do."

"Well, all right, then." Bud waited for the old man to ride ahead down the obscure trail that wound through the brush for half a mile or so before they emerged into the rough border of the creek bed. Pop reined in close and explained garrulously to Bud how this particular stream disappeared into the ground two miles above Little Lost, leaving the wide, level river bottom bone dry.

Pop was cautious. He rode up to a rise of ground and scanned the country suspiciously before he led the way into the creek bed. Even then he kept close under the bank until they had passed two of the quarter-mile posts that had been planted in the hard sand.

Evidently he had been doing a good deal of thinking during the ride; certainly he had watched Smoky. When he stopped under the bank opposite the half-mile post he dismounted more spryly than one would have expected. His eyes were bright, his voice sharp. Pop was forgetting his age.

"I guess I'll ride yore horse m'self," he announced, and they exchanged horses under the shelter of the bank. "You kin take an' ride Boise — an' I want you should beat me if you kin." He looked at Bud appraisingly. "I'll bet a dollar," he cried suddenly, "that I kin outrun ye, young feller! An' you got the fastest horse in Burroback Valley and I don't know what I got under me. I'm seventy years old come September — when I'm afoot. Are ye afraid to bet?"

"I'm scared a dollar's worth that I'll never see you again to-day unless I ride back to find you," Bud grinned.

"Any time you lose ole Pop Truman — shucks

a'mighty! Come on, then — I 'll show ye the way to
the quarter-post!"

"I 'm right with you, Pop. You say so, and I 'm
gone!"

They reined in with the shadow of the post falling
square across the necks of both horses. Pop gathered
up the reins, set his feet in the stirrups and shrilled,
"Go, gol darn ye!"

They went, like two scared rabbits down the smooth,
yellow stretch of packed sand. Pop's elbows stuck
straight out, he held the reins high and leaned far over
Smoky's neck, his eyes glaring. Bud — oh, never
worry about Bud! In the years that lay between
thirteen and twenty-one Bud had learned a good many
things, and one of them was how to get out of a horse
all the speed there was in him.

They went past the quarter-post and a furlong beyond before either could pull up. Pop was pale and
triumphant, and breathing harder than his mount.

"Here 's your dollar, Pop — and don't you talk in
your sleep!" Bud admonished, smiling as he held out
the dollar, but with an anxious tone in his voice. "If
this is the best running horse you 've got in the valley,
I may get some action, next Sunday!"

Pop dismounted, took the dollar with a grin and
mounted Boise — and that in spite of the fact that
Boise was keyed up and stepping around and snorting
for another race. Bud watched Pop queerly, remembering how feeble had been the old man whom he had
met at the corral.

"Say, Pop, you ought to race a little every day,"
he bantered. "You 're fifteen years younger than
you were an hour ago."

For answer Pop felt of his back and groaned. "Oh, I'll pay fer it, young feller! I don't look fer much peace with my back fer a week, after this. But you kin make sure of one thing, and that is, I ain't goin' to talk in my sleep none. By Christmas, we'll make this horse of yours bring us *in* something! I guess you better turn yore horses all out in the pasture. Dave, he'll give yuh work all right. I'll fix it with Dave. And you listen to Pop, young feller. I'll show ye a thing or two about runnin' horses. You 'n me 'll clean up a nice little bunch of money — *he-he!* — beat Boise in a quarter dash! Tell that to Dave, an' he would n't b'lieve ye!"

When Pop got off at the back of the stable he could scarcely move, he was so stiff. But his mind was working well enough to see that Bud rubbed the saddle print off Boise and turned his own horses loose in the pasture, before he let him go on to the house. The last Bud heard from Pop that forenoon was a senile chuckle and a cackling, "Outrun Boise in a quarter dash! Shucks a'mighty! But I knew it — I knew he had the speed — sho! Ye can't fool ole Pop — shucks!"

CHAPTER TEN

Bud Meets the Woman

A WOMAN was stooping at the woodpile, filling her arms with crooked sticks of rough-barked sage. From the color of her hair Bud knew that she was not Honey, and that she was therefore a stranger to him. But he swung off the path and went over to her as naturally as he would go to pick up a baby that had fallen.

"I 'll carry that in for you," he said, and put out his hand to help her to her feet.

Before he touched her she was on her feet and looking at him. Bud could not remember afterwards that she had done anything else; he seemed to have seen only her eyes, and into them and beyond them to a soul that somehow made his heart tremble.

What she said, what he answered, was of no moment. He could not have told afterwards what it was. He stooped and filled his arms with wood, and walked ahead of her up the pathway to the kitchen door, and stopped when she flitted past him to show him where the wood-box stood. He was conscious then of her slenderness and of the lightness of her steps. He dropped the wood into the box behind the stove on which kettles were steaming. There was the smell of chicken stewing, and the odor of fresh-baked pies.

She smiled up at him and offered him a crisp, warm

cookie with sugared top, and he saw her eyes again and felt the same tremor at his heart. He pulled himself together and smiled back at her, thanked her and went out, stumbling a little on the doorstep, the cookie untasted in his fingers.

He walked down to the corral and began fumbling at his pack, his thoughts hushed before the revelation that had come to him.

" Her hands — her poor, little, red hands! " he said in a whisper as the memory of them came suddenly. But it was her eyes that he was seeing with his mind; her eyes, and what lay deep within. They troubled him, shook him, made him want to use his man-strength against something that was hurting her. He did not know what it could be; he did not know that there was anything — but oddly the memory of his mother's white face back in the long ago, and of her tone when she said, " Oh, God, *please!* " came back and fitted themselves to the look in this woman's eyes.

Bud sat down on his canvas-wrapped bed and lifted his hat to rumple his hair and then smooth it again, as was his habit when worried. He looked at the cookie, and because he was hungry he ate it with a foolish feeling that he was being sentimental as the very devil, thinking how her hands had touched it. He rolled and smoked a cigarette afterwards, and wondered who she was and whether she was married, and what her first name was.

A quiet smoke will bring a fellow to his senses sometimes when nothing else will, and Bud managed, by smoking two cigarettes in rapid succession, to restore himself to some degree of sanity.

" Funny how she made me think of mother, back

when I was a kid coming up from Texas," he mused.
" Mother 'd like her." It was the first time he had
ever thought just that about a girl. " She 's no rela-
tion to Honey," he added. " I 'd bet a horse on that."
He recalled how white and soft were Honey's hands,
and he swore a little. " Would n't hurt her to get
out there in the kitchen and help with the cooking,"
he criticised. Then suddenly he laughed. " Shucks
a'mighty, as Pop says! with those two girls on the
ranch I 'll gamble Dave Truman has a full crew of
men that are plumb willing to work for their board! "

The stage came, and Bud turned to it relievedly.
After that, here came Dave Truman on a deep-chested
roan. Bud knew him by his resemblance to the old
man, who came shuffling bent-backed from the ma-
chine-shed as Dave passed.

Pop beckoned, and Dave reined his horse that way
and stopped at the shed door. The two talked for a
minute and Dave rode on, passing Bud with a curt
nod. Pop came over to where Bud stood leaning
against the corral.

" How are you feeling, dad? " Bud grinned absently.

" Purty stiff an' sore, boy — my rheumatics is bad
to-day." Pop winked solemnly. " I spoke to Dave
about you wantin' a job, and I guess likely Dave 'll
put you on. They 's plenty to do — hayin' comin' on
and all that." He lowered his voice mysteriously,
though there was no man save Bud within a hundred
feet of him. "Don't ye go 'n talk horses — not yet.
Don't let on like yore interested much. I 'll tell yuh
when to take 'em up."

The men came riding in from the hayfield, some in
wagons, two astride harnessed work-horses, and one

long-legged fellow in chaps on a mower, driving a sweaty team that still had life enough to jump side-wise when they spied Bud's pack by the corral. The stage driver sauntered up and spoke to the men. Bud went over and began to help unhitch the team from the mower, and the driver eyed him sharply while he grinned his greeting across the backs of the horses.

"Pop says you're looking for work," Dave Truman observed, coming up. "Well, if you ain't scared of it, I'll stake yuh to a hayfork after dinner. Where yuh from?"

"Just right now, I'm from the Muleshoe. Bud Birnie's my name. I was telling dad why I quit."

"Tell me," Dave directed briefly. "Pop ain't as reliable as he used to be. He'd never get it out straight."

"I quit," said Bud, "by special request." He pulled off his gloves carefully and held up his puffed knuckles. "I got that on Dirk Tracy."

The driver of the mower shot a quick, meaning glance at Dave, and laughed shortly. Dave grinned a little, but he did not ask what had been the trouble, as Bud had half expected him to do. Apparently Dave felt that he had received all the information he needed, for his next remark had to do with the heat. The day was a "weather breeder", he declared, and he was glad to have another man to put at the hauling.

An iron triangle beside the kitchen door clamored then, and Bud, looking quickly, saw the slim little woman with the big, troubled eyes striking the iron bar vigorously. Dave glanced at his watch and led the way to the house, the hay crew hurrying after him.

Fourteen men sat down to a long table with a great shuffling of feet and scraping of benches, and immediately began a voracious attack upon the heaped platters of chicken and dumplings and the bowls of vegetables. Bud found a place at the end where he could look into the kitchen, and his eyes went that way as often as they dared, following the swift motions of the little woman who poured coffee and filled empty dishes and said never a word to anyone.

He was on the point of believing her a daughter of the house when a square-jawed man of thirty, or thereabout, who sat at Bud's right hand, called her to him as he might have called his dog, by snapping his fingers.

She came and stood beside Bud while the man spoke to her in an arrogant undertone.

"Marian, I told yuh I wanted tea for dinner after this. D'you bring me coffee on purpose, just to be onery? I thought I told yuh to straighten up and quit that sulkin'. I ain't going to have folks think—"

"Oh, be quiet! Shame on you, before everyone!" she whispered fiercely while she lifted the cup and saucer.

Bud went hot all over. He did not look up when she returned presently with a cup of tea, but he felt her presence poignantly, as he had never before sensed the presence of a woman. When he was able to swallow his wrath and meet calmly the glances of these strangers he turned his head casually and looked the man over.

Her husband, he guessed the fellow to be. No other relationship could account for that tone of proprietorship, and there was no physical resemblance between the two. A mean devil, Bud called him mentally, with a narrow forehead, eyes set too far apart and the mouth of a brute. Someone spoke to the man, calling him Lew, and he answered with rough good humor, repeating a stale witticism and laughing at it just as though he had not heard others say it a hundred times.

Bud looked at him again and hated him, but he did not glance again at the little woman named Marian; for his own peace of mind he did not dare. He thought that he knew now what it was he had seen in the depth of her eyes, but there seemed to be nothing that he could do to help.

That evening after supper Honey Krause called to him when he was starting down to the bunk-house with the other men. What she said was that she still had his guitar and mandolin, and that they needed exercise. What she looked was the challenge of a born coquette. In the kitchen dishes were rattling, but after they were washed there would be a little leisure, perhaps, for the kitchen drudge. Bud's impulse to make his sore hands an excuse for refusing evaporated. It might not be wise to place himself deliberately in the way of getting a hurt — but youth never did stop to consult a sage before following the lure of a woman's eyes.

He called back to Honey that those instruments ought to have been put in the hayfield, where there was more exercise than the men could use. "You boys ought to come and see me safe through with it," he added to the loitering group around him. "I'm afraid of women."

They laughed and two or three went with him. Lew went on to the corral and presently appeared on horseback, riding up to the kitchen and leaving his horse standing at the corner while he went inside and talked to the woman he had called Marian.

Bud was carrying his guitar outside, where it was cooler, when he heard the fellow's arrogant voice. The dishes ceased rattling for a minute, and there was a sharp exclamation, stifled but unmistakable. Involuntarily Bud made a movement in that direction, when Honey's voice stopped him with a subdued laugh.

"That's only Lew and Mary Ann," she explained carelessly. "They have a spat every time they come within gunshot of each other."

The lean fellow who had driven the mower, and whose name was Jerry Myers, edged carelessly close to Bud and gave him a nudge with his elbow, and a glance from under his eyebrows by way of emphasis. He turned his head slightly, saw that Honey had gone into the house, and muttered just above a whisper, "Don't see or hear anything. It's all the help you can give her. And for Lord's sake don't let on to Honey like you — give a cuss whether it rains or not, so long 's it don't pour too hard the night of the dance."

Bud looked up at the darkening sky speculatively, and tried not to hear the voices in the kitchen, one of which was brutally harsh while the other told of hate and fear suppressed under gentle forbearance. The harsh voice was almost continuous, the other infrequent, reluctant to speak at all. Bud wanted to go in and smash his guitar over the fellow's head, but Jerry's warning held him. There were other ways, however, to help; if he must not drive off the tormentor, then he would call him away. He ignored his bruised knuckles and plucked the guitar strings as if he held a grudge against them, and then began to sing the first song that came into his mind — one that started in a rollicky fashion.

Men came straggling up from the bunk-house before he had finished the first chorus, and squatted on their heels to listen, their cigarettes glowing like red finger-tips in the dusk. But the voice in the kitchen talked on. Bud tried another — one of those old-time favorites, a " laughing coon " song, though he felt little enough in the mood for it. In the middle of the first laugh he heard the kitchen door slam, and Lew's footsteps coming around the corner. He listened until the song was done, then mounted and rode away, Bud's laugh following him triumphantly — though Lew could not have guessed its meaning.

Bud sang for two hours expectantly, but Marian did not appear, and Bud went off to the bunk-house feeling that his attempt to hearten her had been a failure. Of Honey he did not think at all, except to wonder if the two women were related in any way, and to feel that if they were Marian was to be pitied. At that point Jerry overtook him and asked for a match, which gave him an excuse to hold Bud behind the others.

" Honey like to have caught me, to-night," Jerry observed guardedly. " I had to think quick. I 'll tell you the lay of the land, Bud, seeing you 're a stranger here. Marian's man, Lew, he 's a damned bully and somebody is going to draw a fine bead on him some day when he ain't looking. But he stands in, so the less yuh take notice the better. Marian, she 's a fine little woman that minds her own business, but she 's getting a cold deck slipped into the game right along. Honey 's jealous of her and afraid somebody 'll give her a pleasant look. Lew 's jealous, and he watches her like a cat watches a mouse it 's caught and wants to play with. Between the two of 'em Marian has a real nice time of it. I 'm wising you up so you won't hand her any more misery by trying to take her part. Us boys have learned to keep our mouths shut."

"Glad you told me," Bud muttered. "Otherwise — "

"Exactly," Jerry agreed understandingly. "Otherwise any of us would."

He stopped and then spoke in a different tone. "If Lew stays off the ranch long enough, maybe you 'll get to hear her sing. Wow-ee, but that lady has sure got the meadow-larks whipped! But look out for Honey, old-timer."

Bud laughed unmirthfully. "Looks to me as if you are n't crazy over Honey," he ventured. "What has she done to you?"

"Her?" Jerry inspected his cigarette, listened to the whisper of prudence in his ear, and turned away. "Forget it. I never said a word." He swept the whole subject from him with a comprehensive gesture, and snorted. "I 'm gettin' as bad as Pop," he grinned. "But lemme tell yuh something. Honey Krause runs more 'n the post-office."

CHAPTER ELEVEN

GUILE AGAINST THE WILY

BUD liked to have his life run along accustomed lines with a more or less perfect balance of work and play, friendships and enmities. He had grown up with the belief that any mystery is merely a synonym for menace. He had learned to be wary of known enemies such as Indians and outlaws, and to trust implicitly his friends. To feel now, without apparent cause, that his friends might be enemies in disguise, was a new experience that harried him.

He had come to Little Lost on Tuesday, straight from the Muleshoe where his presence was no longer desired for some reason not yet satisfactorily explained to him. You know what happened on Tuesday. That night the land crouched under a terrific electric storm, with crackling swords of white death dazzling from inky black clouds, and ear-splitting thunder close on the heels of it. Bud had known such storms all his life, yet on this night he was uneasy, vaguely disturbed. He caught himself wondering if Lew Morris's wife was frightened, and the realization that he was worrying about her fear worried him more than ever and held him awake long after the fury of the storm had passed.

Next day, when he came in at noon, there was Hen,

from the Muleshoe, waiting for dinner before he rode back with the mail. Hen's jaw dropped when he saw Bud riding on a Little Lost hay-wagon, and his eyes bulged with what Bud believed was consternation. All through the meal Bud had caught Hen eyeing him miserably, and looking stealthily from him to the others. No one paid any attention, and for that Bud was rather thankful; he did not want the Little Lost fellows to think that perhaps he had done something which he knew would hang him if it were discovered, which, he decided, was the mildest interpretation a keen observer would be apt to make of Hen's behavior.

When he went out, Hen was at his heels, trying to say something in his futile, tongue-tied gobble. Bud stopped and looked at him tolerantly. "Hen, it's no use — you might as well be talking Chinese, for all I know. If it's important, write it down or I'll never know what's on your mind."

He pulled a note-book and a pencil from his vest-pocket and gave them to Hen, who looked at him dumbly, worked his Adam's apple violently and retreated to his horse, fumbled the mail which was tied in the bottom of a flour sack for safe keeping, sought a sheltered place where he could sit down, remained there a few minutes, and then returned to his horse. He beckoned to Bud, who was watching him curiously, and when Bud went over to him said something unintelligible and handed back the note-book, motioning for caution when Bud would have opened the book at once.

So Bud thanked him gravely, but with a twinkle in his eyes, and waited until Hen had gone and he was alone before he read the message. It was mysterious enough, certainly. Hen had written in a fine, cramped, uneven hand:

" You bee carful. bern this up & and dont let on like you no enything but i warn you be shure bern this up."

Bud tore out the page and burned it as requested, and since he was not enlightened by the warning he obeyed Hen's instructions and did not " let on." But he could not help wondering, and was unconsciously prepared to observe little things which ordinarily would have passed unnoticed.

At the dance on Friday night, for instance, there was a good deal of drinking and mighty little hilarity. Bud had been accustomed to loud talk and much horseplay outside among the men on such occasions, and even a fight or two would be accepted as a matter of course. But though several quart bottles were passed around during the night and thrown away empty into the bushes, the men went in and danced and came out again immediately to converse confidentially in small groups, or to smoke without much speech. The men of Burroback Valley were not running true to form.

The women were much like all the women of cow-country: mothers with small children who early became cross and sleepy and were hushed under shawls on the most convenient bed, a piece of cake in their hands; mothers whose faces were lined too soon with work and ill-health, and with untidy hair that became untidier as the dance progressed. There were daughters — shy and giggling to hide their shyness — Bud knew their type very well and made friends with them easily, and immediately became the centre of a clamoring audience after he had sung a song or two.

There was Honey, with her inscrutable half smile and her veiled eyes, condescending to graciousness and quite plainly assuming a proprietary air toward Bud, whom she put through whatever musical paces pleased her fancy. Bud, I may say, was extremely tractable. When Honey said sing, Bud sang; when she said play, Bud sat down to the piano and played until she asked him to do something else. It was all very pleasant for Honey — and Bud ultimately won his point — Honey decided to extend her graciousness a little.

Why had n't Bud danced with Marian? He must go right away and ask her to dance. Just because Lew was gone, Marian need not be slighted — and besides, there were other fellows who might want a little of Honey's time.

So Bud went away and found Marian in the pantry, cutting cakes while the coffee boiled, and asked her to dance. Marian was too tired, and she had not the time to spare; wherefore Bud helped himself to a knife and proceeded to cut cakes with geometrical precision, and ate all the crumbs. With his hands busy, he found the courage to talk to her a little. He made Marian laugh out loud and it was the first time he had ever heard her do that.

Marian disclosed a sense of humor, and even teased Bud a little about Honey. But her teasing lacked that edge of bitterness which Bud had half expected in retaliation for Honey's little air of superiority.

" Your precision in cutting cakes is very much like your accurate fingering of the piano," she observed irrelevantly, surveying his work with her lips pursed. " A pair of calipers would prove every piece exactly the same width; and even when you play a Meditation

I'm sure the metronome would waggle in perfect unison with your tempo. I wonder — " She glanced up at him speculatively. " — I wonder if you think with such mathematical precision. Do you always find that two and two make four?"

"You mean, have I any imagination whatever?" Bud looked away from her eyes — toward the uncurtained, high little window. A face appeared there, as if a tall man had glanced in as he was passing by and halted for a second to look. Bud's eyes met full the eyes of the man outside, who tilted his head backward in a significant movement and passed on. Marian turned her head and caught the signal, looked at Bud quickly, a little flush creeping into her cheeks.

"I hope you have a little imagination," she said, lowering her voice instinctively. "It does n't require much to see that Jerry is right. The conventions are strictly observed at Little Lost — in the kitchen, at least," she added, under her breath, with a flash of resentment. "Run along — and the next time Honey asks you to play the piano, will you please play *Lotusblume?* And when you have thrown open the prison windows with that, will you play Schubert's *Ave Maria* — the way you play it — to send a breath of cool night air in?"

She put out the tips of her fingers and pressed them lightly against Bud's shoulder, turning toward the door. Bud started, stepped into the kitchen, wheeled about and stood regarding her with a stubborn look in his eyes.

"I might kick the door down, too," he said. "I don't like prisons nohow."

"No — just a window, thank you," she laughed.

Bud thought the laugh did not go very deep. " Jerry wants to talk to you. He 's the whitest of the lot, if you can call that — " she stopped abruptly, put out a hand to the door, gave him a moment to look into her deep, troubled eyes, and closed the door gently but inexorably in his face.

Jerry was standing at the corner of the house smoking negligently. He waited until Bud had come close alongside him, then led the way slowly down the path to the corrals.

" I thought I heard the horses fighting," he remarked. " There was a noise down this way."

" Is that why you called me outside? " asked Bud, who scorned subterfuge.

" Yeah. I saw you was n't dancing or singing or playing the piano — and I knew Honey 'd likely be looking you up to do one or the other, in a minute. She sure likes you, Bud. She don't, everybody that comes along."

Bud did not want to discuss Honey, wherefore he made no reply, and they walked along in silence, the cool, heavy darkness grateful after the oil lamps and the heat of crowded rooms. As they neared the corrals a stable door creaked open and shut, yet there was no wind. Jerry halted, one hand going to Bud's arm. They stood for a minute, and heard the swish of the bushes behind the corral, as if a horse were passing through. Jerry turned back, leading Bud by the arm. They were fifty feet away and the bushes were still again before Jerry spoke guardedly.

" I guess I made a mistake. There was n't nothing," he said, and dropped Bud's arm.

Bud stopped. " There was a man riding off in the

brush," he said bluntly, " and all the folks that came to the dance rode in through the front gate. I reckon I'll just take a look where I left my saddle, anyway."

" That might have been some loose stock," Jerry argued, but Bud went back, wondering a little at Jerry's manner.

The saddle was all right, and so was everything else, so far as Bud could determine in the dark, but he was not satisfied. He thought he understood Jerry's reason for bringing him down to the corrals, but he could not understand Jerry's attitude toward an incident which any man would have called suspicious.

Bud quietly counted noses when he returned to the house and found that supper was being served, but he could not recall any man who was missing now. Every guest and every man on the ranch was present except old Pop, who had a little shack to himself and went to bed at dark every night.

Bud was mystified, and he hated mysteries. Moreover, he was working for Dave Truman, and whatever might concern Little Lost concerned him also. But the men had begun to talk openly of their various " running horses ", and to exchange jibes and boasts and to bet a little on Sunday's races. Bud wanted to miss nothing of that, and Jerry's indifference to the incident at the stable served to reassure him for the time being. He edged close to the group where the talk was loudest, and listened.

A man they called Jeff was trying to jeer his neighbors into betting against a horse called Skeeter, and was finding them too cautious for his liking. He laughed and, happening to catch Bud's eyes upon him, strode forward with an empty tin cup in his hand and slapped Bud friendliwise on the shoulder.

"Why, I bet this singin' kid, that don't know what I got ner what you fellers has got, ain't scared to take a chance. Are yuh, kid? What d' yuh think of this pikin' bunch here that has seen Skeeter come in second and third more times 'n what he beat, and yet is afraid to take a chance on losin' two bits? What d' yuh think of 'em? Ain't they an onery bunch?"

"I suppose they hate to lose," Bud grinned.

"That's it — money's more to 'em than the sport of kings, which is runnin' horses. This bunch, kid, belly-ached till Dave took his horse Boise outa the game, and now, by gosh, they're backin' up from my Skeeter, that has been beat more times than he won."

"When you pulled him, Jeff!" a mocking voice drawled. "And that was when you wasn't bettin', yourself."

Jeff turned injuredly to Bud. "Now don't that sound like a piker?" he complained. "It ain't reason to claim I'd pull my own horse. Ain't that the out-doinest way to come back at a man that likes a good race?"

Bud swelled his chest and laid his hand on Jeff's shoulder. "Just to show you I'm not a piker," he cried recklessly, "I'll bet you twenty-five dollars I can beat your Skeeter with my Smoky horse that I rode in here. Is it a go?"

Jeff's jaw dropped a little, with surprise. "What fer horse is this here Smoky horse of yourn?" he wanted to know.

Bud winked at the group, which cackled gleefully. "I love the sport of kings," he said. "I love it so well I don't have to see your Skeeter horse till Sunday. From the way these boys sidestep him, I guess he's a sure-enough running horse. My Smoky's a good little horse, too, but he never scared a bunch till they had cramps in the pockets. Still," he added with a grin, " I 'll try anything once. I bet you twenty-five dollars my Smoky can beat your Skeeter."

" Say, kid, honest I hate to take it away from yuh. Honest, I do. The way you can knock the livin' tar outa that pyanny is a caution to cats. I c'd listen all night. But when it comes to runnin' horses — "

" Are you afraid of your money? " Bud asked him arrogantly. " You called this a bunch of pikers — "

" Well, by golly, it 'll be your own fault, kid. If I take your money away from yuh, don't go and blame it onto me. Mebbe these fellers has got some cause to sidestep — "

" All right, the bet 's on. And I won't blame you if I lose. Smoky 's a good little horse. Don't think for a minute I 'm giving you my hard earned coin. You 'll have to throw up some dust to get it, old-timer. I forgot to say I 'd like to make it a quarter dash."

" A quarter dash it is," Jeff agreed derisively as Bud turned to answer the summons of the music which was beginning again.

The racing enthusiasts lingered outside, and Bud smiled to himself while he whirled Honey twice around in an old-fashioned waltz. He had them talking about him, and wondering about his horse. When they saw Smoky they would perhaps call him a chancey kid. He meant to ask Pop about Skeeter, though Pop seemed confident that Smoky would win against anything in the valley.

But on the other hand, he had seen in his short acquaintance with Little Lost that Pop was considered childish — that comprehensive accusation which belittles the wisdom of age. The boys made it a point to humor him without taking him seriously. Honey pampered him and called him Poppy, while in Marian's chill courtesy, in her averted glances, Bud had read her dislike of Pop. He had seen her hand shrink away from contact with his hand when she set his coffee beside his plate.

But Bud had heard others speak respectfully of Boise, and regret that he was too fast to run. Pop might be childish on some subjects, but Bud rather banked on his judgment of horses — and Pop was penurious and anxious to win money.

"What are you thinking about?" Honey demanded when the music stopped. "Something awful important, I guess, to make you want to keep right on dancing!"

"I was thinking of horse-racing," Bud confessed, glad that he could tell her the truth.

"Ah, you! Don't let them make a fool of you. Some of the fellows would bet the shirt off their backs, on a horse-race! You look out for them, Bud."

"They wouldn't bet any more than I would," Bud boldly declared. "I've bet already against a horse I've never seen. How's that?"

"That's crazy. You'll lose, and serve you right." She went off to dance with someone else, and Bud turned smiling to find a passable partner amongst the older women — for he was inclined to caution where strange girls were concerned. Much trouble could come to a stranger who danced with a girl who happened to have a jealous sweetheart, and Bud did not court trouble of that kind. He much preferred to fight over other things. Besides, he had no wish to antagonize Honey.

But his dance with some faded, heavy-footed woman was not to be. Jerry once more signalled him and drew him outside for a little private conference. Jerry was ill at ease and inclined to be reproachful and even condemnatory.

He wanted first to know why Bud had been such a many kinds of a fool as to make that bet with Jeff Hall. All the fellows were talking about it. "They was asking me what kind of a horse you've got — and I would n't put it past Jeff and his bunch to pull some kind of a dirty trick on you," he complained. "Bud, on the square, I like you a whole lot. You seem kinda innocent, in some ways, and in other ways you don't. I wish you'd tell me just one thing, so I can sleep comfortable. Have you got some scheme of your own? Or what the devil ails you?"

"Well, I've just got a notion," Bud admitted. "I'm going to have some fun watching those fellows perform, whether I win or lose. I've spent as much as twenty-five dollars on a circus, before now, and felt that I got the worth of my money, too. I'm going to enjoy myself real well, next Sunday."

Jerry glanced behind him and lowered his voice, speaking close to Bud's ear. "Well, there's something I'd like to say that it ain't safe to say, Bud. I'd hate like hell to see you get in trouble. Go as far as you like having fun — but — oh, hell! What's the use?" He turned abruptly and went inside, leaving Bud staring after him rather blankly.

Jerry did not strike Bud as being the kind of a man who goes around interfering with every other man's business. He was a quiet, good-natured young fellow with quizzical eyes of that mixed color which we call hazel simply because there is more brown than gray or green. He did not talk much, but he observed much. Bud was strongly inclined to heed Jerry's warning, but it was too vague to have any practical value — "about like Hen's note," Bud concluded. "Well-meaning but hazy. Like a red danger flag on a railroad crossing where the track is torn up and moved. I saw one, once, and my horse threw a fit at it and almost piled me. I figured that the red flag created the danger, where I was concerned. Still, I'd like to oblige Jerry and side-step something or other, but . . ."

His thoughts grew less distinct, merged into word-less rememberings and conjectures, clarified again into terse sentences which never reached the medium of speech.

"Well, I'll just make sure they don't try out Smoke when I'm not looking," he decided, and slipped away in the dark.

By a roundabout way which avoided the trail he managed to reach the pasture fence without being seen. No horses grazed in sight, and he climbed through and went picking his way across the lumpy meadow in the starlight. At the farther side he found the horses standing out on a sandy ridge where the mosquitoes were not quite so pestiferous. The Little Lost horses snorted and took to their heels, his three following for a short distance.

Bud stopped and whistled a peculiar call invented long ago when he was just Buddy, and watched over

the Tomahawk *remuda*. Every horse with the Tomahawk brand knew that summons — though not every
horse would obey it. But these three had come when
they were sucking colts, if Buddy whistled; and in
their breaking and training, in the long trip north, they
had not questioned its authority. They turned and
trotted back to him now and nosed Bud's hands which
he held out to them.

He petted them all and talked to them in an affec-
tionate murmur which they answered by sundry lip-
nibbles and subdued snorts. Smoky he singled out
finally, rubbing his back and sides with the flat of his
hand from shoulder to flank, and so to the rump and
down the thigh to the hock to the scanty fetlock which
told, to those who knew, that here was an aristocrat
among horses.

Smoky stood quiet, and Bud's hand lingered there,
smoothing the slender ankle. Bud's fingers felt the
fine-haired tail, then gave a little twitch. He was busy
for a minute, kneeling in the sand with one knee, his
head bent. Then he stood up, went forward to
Smoky's head, and stood rubbing the horse's nose
thoughtfully.

"I hate to do it, old boy — but I'm working to
make us a home — we've got to work together. And
I'm not asking any more of you than I'd be willing
to do myself, if I were a horse and you were a man."

He gave the three horses a hasty pat apiece and
started back across the meadow to the fence. They
followed him like pet dogs — and when Bud glanced
back over his shoulder he saw in the dim light that
Smoky walked with a slight limp.

CHAPTER TWELVE

SPORT O' KINGS

SUNDAY happened to be fair, with not too strong a wind blowing. Before noon Little Lost ranch was a busy place, and just before dinner it became busier. Horse-racing seemed to be as popular a sport in the valley as dancing. Indeed, men came riding in who had not come to the dance. The dry creek-bed where the horses would run had no road leading to it, so that all vehicles came to Little Lost and remained there while the passengers continued on foot to the races.

At the corral fresh shaven men, in clean shirts to distinguish this as a dress-up occasion, foregathered, looking over the horses and making bets and arguing. Pop shambled here and there, smoking cigarettes furiously and keeping a keen ear toward the loudest betting. He came sidling up to Bud, who was leading Smoky out of the stable, and his sharp eyes took in every inch of the horse and went inquiringly to Bud's face.

"Goin' to run him, young feller — lame as what he is?" he demanded sharply.

"Going to try, anyway," said Bud. "I've got a bet up on him, dad."

"Sho! Fixin' to lose, air ye? You kin call it off,

like as not. Jeff ain't so onreason'ble 't he'd make yuh run a lame horse. Air yuh, Jeff?"

Jeff strolled up and looked Smoky over with critical eyes. "What's the matter? Ain't the kid game to run him? Looks to me like a good little goer."

"He's got a limp — but I'll run him anyway." Bud glanced up. "Maybe when he's warmed up he'll forget about it."

"Seen my Skeeter?"

"Good horse, I should judge," Bud observed indifferently. "But I ain't worrying any."

"Well, neither am I," Jeff grinned.

Pop stood teetering back and forth, plainly uneasy. "I'd rub him right good with liniment," he advised Bud. "I'll git some 't I know ought t' help."

"What's the matter, Pop? You got money up on that cayuse?" Jeff laughed.

Pop whirled on him. "I ain't got money up on him, no. But if he was n't lame I'd have some! I'd show ye 't I admire gameness in a kid. I would so."

Jeff nudged his neighbor into laughter. "There ain't a gamer old bird in the valley than Pop," Jeff cried. "C'm awn, Pop, I'll bet yuh ten dollars the kid beats me!"

Pop was shuffling hurriedly out of the corral after the liniment. To Jeff's challenge he made no reply whatever. The group around Jeff shooed Smoky gently toward the other side of the corral, thereby convincing themselves of the limp in his right hind foot. While not so pronounced as to be crippling, it certainly was no asset to a running horse, and the wise ones conferred together in undertones.

"That there kid's a born fool," Dave Truman stated

positively. " The horse can't run. He's got the look of a speedy little animal — but shucks! The kid don't know anything about running horses. I've been talking to him, and I know. Jeff, you're taking the money away from him if you run that race."

" Well, I'm giving the kid a chance to back out," Jeff hastened to declare. " He can put it off till his horse gits well, if he wants to. I ain't going to hold him to it. I never said I was."

" That's mighty kind of you," Bud said, coming up from behind with a bottle of liniment, and with Pop at his heels. " But I'll run him just the same. Smoky has favored this foot before, and it never seemed to hurt him any. You need n't think I'm going to crawfish. You must think I'm a whining cuss — say! I'll bet another ten dollars that I don't come in more than a neck behind, lame horse or not!"

" Now, kid, don't git chancey," Pop admonished uneasily. " Twenty-five is enough money to donate to Jeff."

" That's right, kid. I like your nerve," Jeff cut in, emphasizing his approval with a slap on Bud's shoulder as he bent to lift Smoky's leg. " I've saw worse horses than this one come in ahead — it would n't be no sport o' kings if nobody took a chance."

" I'm taking chance enough," Bud retorted without looking up. " If I don't win this time I will the next, maybe."

" That's right," Jeff agreed heartily, winking broadly at the others behind Bud's back.

Bud rubbed Smoky's ankle with liniment, listened to various and sundry self-appointed advisers and, without seeming to think how the sums would total, took several other small bets on the race. They were small — Pop began to teeter back and forth and lift his shoulders and pull his beard — sure signs of perturbation.

"By Christmas, I'll just put up ten dollars on the kid," Pop finally cackled. "I ain't got much to lose — but I'll show yuh old Pop ain't going to see the young feller stand alone." He tried to catch Bud's eye, but that young man was busy saddling Smoky and returning jibe for jibe with the men around him, and did not glance toward Pop at all.

"I'll take this bottle in my pocket, Pop," he said with his back toward the old man, and mounted carelessly. "I'll ride him around a little and give him another good rubbing before we run. I'm betting," he added to the others frankly, "on the chance that exercise and the liniment will take the soreness out of that ankle. I don't believe it amounts to anything at all. So if any of you fellows want to bet — "

"Shucks! Don't go 'n — " Pop began, and bit the sentence in two, dropping immediately into a deep study. The kid was getting beyond Pop's understanding.

A crowd of perhaps a hundred men and women — with a generous sprinkling of unruly juveniles — lined the sheer bank of the creek-bed and watched the horses run, and screamed their cheap witticisms at the losers, and their approval of those who won. The youngster with the mysterious past and the foolhardiness to bet on a lame horse they watched and discussed, the women plainly wishing he would win — because he was handsome and young, and such a wonderful musician. The men were more cold-blooded. They could not see that Bud's good looks or the haunting melody of his voice

had any bearing whatever upon his winning a race.
They called him a fool, and either refused to bet at all
on such a freak proposition as a lame horse running
against Skeeter, or bet against him. A few of the
wise ones wondered if Jeff and his bunch were merely
" stringing the kid along "; if they might not let him
win a little, just to make him more " chancey." But
they did not think it wise to bet on that probability.

While three races were being run Bud rode with the
Little Lost men, and Smoky still limped a little. Jerry
Myers, still self-appointed guardian of Bud, herded
him apart and called him a fool and implored him to
call the race off and keep his money in his own pocket.

Bud was thinking just then about a certain little
woman who sat on the creek bank with a wide-brimmed
straw hat shading her wonderful eyes, and a pair of
little, high-arched feet tapping heels absently against
the bank wall. Honey sat beside her, and a couple of
the valley women whom Bud had met at the dance.
He had ridden close and paused for a few friendly
sentences with the quartette, careful to give Honey the
attention she plainly expected. But it was not Honey
who wore the wide hat and owned the pretty little feet.
Bud pulled his thoughts back from a fruitless wish
that he might in some way help that little woman
whose trouble looked from her eyes, and whose lips
smiled so bravely. He did not think of possession
when he thought of her; it was the look in her eyes,
and the slighting tones in which Honey spoke of her.

" Say, come alive! What yuh going off in a trance
for, when I'm talking to yuh for your own good? "
Jerry smiled whimsically, but his eyes were worried.

Bud pulled himself together and reined closer.

" Don't bet anything on this race, Jerry," he advised.
" Or if you do, don't bet on Skeeter. But — well,
I 'll just trade you a little advice for all you 've given
me. *Don't bet!*"

" What the hell!" surprise jolted out of Jerry.

" It 's my funeral," Bud laughed. " I 'm a chancey
kid, you see — but I 'd hate to see you bet on me."
He pulled up to watch the next race — four nervy
little cow-horses of true range breeding, going down
to the quarter post.

" They 're going to make false starts aplenty," Bud
remarked after the first fluke. " Jeff and I have it out
next. I 'll just give Smoke another treatment." He
dismounted, looked at Jerry undecidedly and slapped
him on the knee. " I 'm glad to have a friend like you,"
he said impulsively. " There 's a lot of two-faced sin-
ners around here that would steal a man blind. Don't
think I 'm altogether a fool."

Jerry looked at him queerly, opened his mouth and
shut it again so tightly that his jawbones stood out a
little. He watched Bud bathing Smoky's ankle. When
Bud was through and handed Jerry the bottle to keep
for him, Jerry held him for an instant by the hand.

" Say, for Gawdsake don't talk like that promiscu-
ous, Bud," he begged. " You might hit too close — "

" Say, Jerry! Ever hear that old Armenian proverb,
' He who tells the truth should have one foot in the
stirrup '? I learned that in school."

Jerry let go Bud's hand and took the bottle, Bud's
watch that had his mother's picture pasted in the back,
and his vest, a pocket of which contained a memo-
randum of his wagers. Bud was stepping out of his
chaps, and he looked up and grinned. " Cheer up,

Jerry. You're going to laugh in a minute." When Jerry still remained thoughtful, Bud added soberly, "I appreciate you and old Pop standing by me. I don't know just what you've got on your mind, but the fact that there's *something* is hint enough for me." Whereupon Jerry's eyes lightened a little.

The four horses came thundering down the track, throwing tiny pebbles high into the air as they passed. A trim little sorrel won, and there was the usual confusion of voices upraised in an effort to be heard. When that had subsided, interest once more centered on Skeeter and Smoky, who seemed to have recovered somewhat from his lameness.

Not a man save Pop and Bud had placed a bet on Smoky, yet every man there seemed keenly interested in the race. They joshed Bud, who grinned and took it good-naturedly, and found another five dollars in his pocket to bet — this time with Pop, who kept eyeing him sharply — and it seemed to Bud warningly. But Bud wanted to play his own game, this time, and he avoided Pop's eyes.

The two men rode down the hoof-scored sand to the quarter post, Skeeter dancing sidewise at the prospect of a race, Smoky now and then tentatively against Bud's steady pressure of the bit.

"He's not limping now," Bud gloated as they rode. But Jeff only laughed tolerantly and made no reply.

Dave Truman started them with a pistol shot, and the two horses darted away, Smoky half a jump in the lead. His limp was forgotten, and for half the distance he ran neck and neck with Skeeter. Then he dropped to Skeeter's middle, to his flank — then ran with his black nose even with Skeeter's rump. Even so it was a closer race than the crowd had expected, and all the cowboys began to yell themselves purple.

But when they were yet a few leaps from the wire clothes-line stretched high, from post to post, Bud leaned forward until he lay flat alongside Smoky's neck, and gave a real Indian war-whoop. Smoky lifted and lengthened his stride, came up again to Skeeter's middle, to his shoulder, to his ears — and with the next leap thrust his nose past Skeeter's as they finished.

Well, then there was the usual noise, everyone trying to shout louder than his fellows. Bud rode to where Pop was sitting apart on a pacing gray horse that he always rode, and paused to say guardedly,

"I pulled him, Pop. But at that I won, so if I can pry another race out of this bunch to-day, you can bet all you like. And you owe me five dollars," he added thriftily.

"Sho! Shucks a'mighty!" spluttered Pop, reaching reluctantly into his pocket for the money. "Jeff, he done some pullin' himself — I wish I knowed," he added pettishly, "just how big a fool you air."

"Hey, come over here!" shouted Jeff. "What yuh nagging ole Pop about?"

"Pop lost five dollars on that race," Bud called back, and loped over to the crowd. "But he isn't the only one. Seems to me I've got quite a bunch of money coming to me, from this crowd!"

"Jeff, he'd a beat him a mile if his bridle rein had busted," an arrogant voice shouted recklessly. "Jeff, you old fox, you know damn well you pulled Skeeter. You must love to lose, doggone yuh."

"If you think I didn't run right," Jeff retorted, as

if a little nettled, " someone else can ride the horse.
That is, if the kid here ain't scared off with your talk.
How about it, Bud? Think you won fair? "

Bud was collecting his money, and he did not immediately answer the challenge. When he did it was
to offer them another race. He would not, he said,
back down from anyone. He would bet his last cent
on little Smoky. He became slightly vociferous and
more than a little vain-glorious, and within half an
hour he had once more staked all the money he had in
the world. The number of men who wanted to bet
with him surprised him a little. Also the fact that the
Little Lost men were betting on Smoky.

Honey called him over to the bank and scolded him
in tones much like her name, and finally gave him ten
dollars which she wanted to wager on his winning.
As he whirled away, Marian beckoned impulsively and
leaned forward, stretching out to him her closed hand.

" Here 's ten," she smiled, " just to show that the
Little Lost stands by its men — and horses. Put it on
Smoky, please." When Bud was almost out of easy
hearing, she called to him.   " Oh — was that a five or
a ten dollar bill I gave you? "

Bud turned back, unfolding the banknote. A very
tightly folded scrap of paper slid into his palm.

" Oh, all right — I have the five here in my pocket,"
called Marian, and laughed quite convincingly. " Go
on and run! We won't be able to breathe freely until
the race is over."

Wherefore Bud turned back, puzzled and with his
heart jumping. For some reason Marian had taken
this means of getting a message into his hands. What
it could be he did not conjecture; but he had a vague,

unreasoning hope that she trusted him and was asking him to help her somehow. He did not think that it concerned the race, so he did not risk opening the note then, with so many people about.

A slim, narrow-eyed youth of about Bud's weight was chosen to ride Skeeter, and together they went back over the course to the quarter post, with Dave to start them and two or three others to make sure that the race was fair. Smoky was full now of little prancing steps, and held his neck arched while his nostrils flared in excitement, showing pink within. Skeeter persistently danced sidewise, fighting the bit, crazy to run.

Skeeter made two false starts, and when the pistol was fired, jumped high into the air and forward, shaking his head, impatient against the restraint his rider put upon him. Halfway down the stretch he lunged sidewise toward Smoky, but that level-headed little horse swerved and went on, shoulder to shoulder with the other. At the very last Skeeter rolled a pebble under his foot and stumbled — and again Smoky came in with his slaty nose in the lead.

Pop rode into the centre of the yelling crowd, his whiskers bristling. " Shucks a'mighty! " he cried. " What fer ridin' do yuh call that there? Jeff Hall, that feller held Skeeter in worse 'n what you did yourself! I kin prove it! I got a stop watch, an' I timed 'im, I did. An' I kin tell yuh the time yore horse made when he run agin Dave's Boise. He 's three seconds — yes, by Christmas, he 's *four* seconds slower t'day 'n what he 's ever run before! What fer sport d' you call that? " His voice went up and cracked at the question mark like a boy in his early teens.

Jeff stalked forward to Skeeter's side. "Jake, did
you pull Skeeter?" he demanded sternly. "I'll swan
if this ain't the belly-achinest bunch I ever seen! How
about it, Jake? Did Skeeter do his durndest, or did n't
he?"

"Shore, he did!" Jake testified warmly. "I'd a
beat, too, if he had n't stumbled right at the last.
Did n't yuh see him purty near go down? And was n't
he within six inches of beatin'? I leave it to the
crowd!"

The crowd was full of argument, and some bets
were paid under protest. But they were paid, just the
same. Burroback Valley insisted that the main points
of racing law should be obeyed to the letter. Bud collected his winnings, the Scotch in him overlooking
nothing whatever in the shape of a dollar. Then, under cover of getting his smoking material, he dared
bring out Marian's note. There were two lines in a
fine, even hand on a cigarette paper, and Bud, relieved
at her cleverness, unfolded the paper and read while
he opened his bag of tobacco. The lines were like
those in an old-fashioned copy book:

> "Winners may be losers.
> Empty pockets, safe owner."

And that was all. Bud sifted tobacco into the paper,
rolled it into a cigarette and smoked it to so short a
stub that he burnt his lips. Then he dropped it beside
his foot and ground it into the sand while he talked.

He would run Smoky no more that day, he declared,
but next Sunday he would give them all a chance to
settle their minds and win back their losings, providing his horse's ankle did n't go bad again with to-day's

running. Pop, Dave, Jeff and a few other wise ones examined the weak ankle and disagreed over the exact cause and nature of the weakness. It seemed all right. Smoky did not flinch from rubbing, though he did lift his foot away from strange hands. They questioned Bud, who could offer no positive information on the subject, except that once he and Smoky had rolled down a bluff together, and Smoky had been lame for a while afterwards.

It did not occur to anyone to ask Bud which leg had been lamed, and Bud did not volunteer the detail. An old sprain, they finally decided, and Bud replaced his saddle, got his chaps and coat from Jerry, who was smiling over an extra twenty-five dollars, and rode over to give the girls their winnings.

He stayed for several minutes talking with them and hoping for a chance to thank Marian for her friendly warning. But there was none, and he rode away dissatisfied and wondering uneasily if Marian thought he was really as friendly with Honey as that young lady made him appear to be.

He was one of the first to ride back to the ranch, and he turned Smoky in the pasture and caught up Stopper to ride with Honey, who said she was going for a ride when the races were over, and that if he liked to go along she would show him the Sinks. Bud had professed an eagerness to see the Sinks which he did not feel until Marian had turned her head toward Honey and said in her quiet voice:

"Why the Sinks? You know that is n't safe country to ride in, Honey."

"That's why I want to ride there," Honey retorted flippantly. "I hate safe places and safe things."

Marian had glanced at Bud — and it was that glance which he was remembering now with a puzzled sense that, like the note, it had meant something definite, something vital to his own welfare if he could only find the key. First it was Hen, then Jerry, and now Marian, all warning him vaguely of danger into which he might stumble if he were not careful.

Bud was no fool, but on the other hand he was not one to stampede easily. He had that steadfast courage, perhaps, which could face danger and still maintain his natural calm — just as his mother had corrected grammatical slips in the very sentences which told her of an impending outbreak of Indians long ago.

Bud saddled Stopper and the horse which Honey was to ride, led them to the house and went inside to wait until the girl was ready. While he waited he played — and hoped that Marian, hearing, would know that he played for her; and that she would come and explain the cryptic message. Whether Marian heard and appreciated the music or not, she failed to appear and let him know. It seemed to him that she might easily have come into the room for a minute when she knew he was there, and let him have a chance to thank her and ask her just what she meant.

He was just finishing the *Ave Maria* which Marian had likened to a breath of cool air, when Honey appeared in riding skirt and light shirtwaist. She looked very trim and attractive, and Bud smiled upon her approvingly, and cut short the last strain by four beats, which was one way of letting Marian know that he considered her rather unappreciative.

CHAPTER THIRTEEN

The Sinks

"We can go through the pasture and cut off a couple of miles," said Honey when they were mounted. "I hope you don't think I'm crazy, wanting a ride at this time of day, after all the excitement we've had. But every Sunday is taken up with horse-racing till late in the afternoon, and during the week no one has time to go. And," she added with a sidelong look at him, "there's something about the Sinks that makes me love to go there. Uncle Dave won't let me go alone."

Bud dismounted to pull down the two top bars of the pasture gate so that their horses could step over. A little way down the grassy slope Smoky and Sunfish fed together, the Little Lost horses grouped nearer the creek.

"I love that little horse of yours — why, he's gone lame again!" exclaimed Honey. "Isn't that a shame! You ought n't to run him if it does that to him."

"He likes it," said Bud carelessly as he remounted. "And so do I, when I can clean up the way I did to-day. I'm over three hundred dollars richer right now than I was this morning."

"And next Sunday, maybe you'll be broke," Honey

added significantly. "You never know how you are coming out. I think Jeff let you win to-day on purpose, so you'd bet it all again and lose. He's like that. He don't care how much he loses one day, because he gets it back some other time. I don't like it. Some of the boys never do get ahead, and you'll be in the same fix if you don't look out."

"You did n't bring me along to lecture me, I know," said Bud with a good-natured smile. "What about the Sinks? Is it a dangerous place as — Mrs. Morris says?"

"Oh, Marian? She never does want me to come. She thinks I ought to stay in the house always, the way she does. The Sinks is — is — queer. There are caves, and then again deep holes straight down, and tracks of wildcats and lions. And in some places you can hear gurgles and rumbles. I love to be there just at sundown, because the shadows are spooky and it makes you feel — oh, you know — kind of creepy up your back. You don't know what might happen. I — do you believe in ghosts and haunted places, Bud?"

"I'd need a lot of scaring before I did. Are the Sinks haunted?"

"No-o — but there are funny noises and people have got lost there. Anyway they never showed up afterwards. The Indians claim it's haunted." She smiled that baffling smile of hers. "Do you want to turn around and go back?"

"Sure. After we've had our ride, and seen the sights." And he added with some satisfaction, "The moon's full to-night, and no clouds."

"And I brought sandwiches," Honey threw in as

an especial blessing. "Uncle Dave will be mad, I expect. But I've never seen the Sinks at night, with moonlight."

She was quiet while the horses waded Sunk Creek and picked their way carefully over a particularly rocky stretch beyond. "But what I'd rather do," she said, speaking from her thoughts which had evidently carried forward in the silence, "is explore Catrock Canyon."

"Well, why not, if we have time?" Bud rode up alongside her. "Is it far?"

Honey looked at him searchingly. "You *must* be a stranger to these parts," she said disbelievingly. "Do you think you can make me swallow that?"

Bud looked at her inquiringly, which forced her to go on.

"You must know about Catrock Canyon, Bud Birnie. Don't try to make me believe you don't."

"I don't. I never heard of it before that I remember. What is it makes you want to explore it?"

Honey studied him. "You're the queerest specimen I ever did see," she exclaimed pettishly. "Why, it's not going to hurt you to admit you know Catrock Canyon is — unexplorable."

"Oh. So you want to explore it because it's unexplorable. Well, why is it unexplorable?"

Honey looked around her at the dry sageland they were crossing. "Oh, you make me *tired!*" she said bluntly, with something of the range roughness in her voice. "Because it is, that's all."

"Then I'd like to explore it myself," Bud declared.

"For one thing," Honey dilated, "there's no way to get in there. Up on the ridge this side, where the rock is that throws a shadow like a cat's head on the opposite wall, you can look down a ways. But the two sides come so close together at the top that you can't see the bottom of the canyon at all. I 've been on the ridge where I could see the cat's head."

Bud glanced speculatively up at the sun, and Honey, catching his meaning, shook her head and smiled.

"If we get into the Sinks and back to-day, they will do enough talking about it; or Uncle Dave will, and Marian. I — I thought perhaps you 'd be able to tell me about — Catrock Canyon."

"I 'm able to say I don't know a thing about it. If no one can get into it, I should think that 's about all, is n't it?"

"Yes — you 'd think so," Honey agreed enigmatically, and began to talk of the racing that day, and of the dance, and of other dances and other races yet to come. Bud discussed these subjects for a while and then asked boldly, "When 's Lew coming back?"

"Lew?" Honey shot a swift glance at him. "Why —" She looked ahead at the forbidding, craggy hills toward which she had glanced when she spoke of Catrock. "Why, I don't know. How should I?"

Bud saw that he had spoken unwisely. "I was thinking he 'd maybe hate to miss another running match like to-day," he explained guilelessly. "Everybody and his dog seemed to be there to-day, and everybody had money up. All," he modified, "except the Muleshoe boys. I did n't see any of them."

"You won't," Honey told him with some emphasis. "Uncle Dave and the Muleshoe are on the outs. They never come around except for mail and things from the store. And most always they send Hen. Uncle Dave and Dirk Tracy had an awful row last winter. It was next thing to a killing. So of course the outfits ain't on friendly terms."

This was more than Pop had gossiped to Bud, and since the whole thing was of no concern to him, and Honey plainly objected to talking about Marian's husband, he was quite ready to fix his interest once more upon the Sinks. He was surprised when they emerged from a cluster of small, sage-covered knolls, directly upon the edge of what at first sight seemed to be another dry river bed — sprawled wider, perhaps, with irregular arms thrust back into the less sterile land. They rode down a steep, rocky trail and came out into the Sinks.

It was an odd, forbidding place, and the farther up the gravelly bottom they rode, the more forbidding it became. Bud thought that in the time when Indians were dangerous as she-bears the Sinks would not be a place where a man would want to ride. There were too many jutting crags, too many unsuspected, black holes that led back — no one knew just where.

Honey led the way to an irregular circle of water-washed cobbles and Bud peered down fifty feet to another dry, gravelly bottom seemingly a duplicate of the upper surface. She rode on past other caves, and let him look down into other holes. There were faint rumblings in some of these, but in none was there any water showing save in stagnant pools in the rock where the rain had fallen.

"There's one cave I like to go into," said Honey at last. "It's a little farther on, but we have time enough. There's a spring inside, and we can eat our sandwiches. It is n't dark — there are openings to the top, and lots of funny, winding passages. That," she finished thrillingly, " is the place the Indians claim is haunted."

Bud did not shudder convincingly, and they rode slowly forward, picking their way among the rocks. The cave yawned wide open to the sun, which hung on the top of Catrock Peak. They dismounted, anchored the reins with rocks and went inside.

When Bud had been investigative Buddy, he had explored more caves than he could count. He had filched candles from his mother and had crept back and back until the candle flame flickered warning that he was nearing the " damps." Indians always did believe caves were haunted, probably because they did not understand the " damps ", and thought evil spirits had taken those who went in and never returned. Buddy had once been lost in a cave for four harrowing hours, and had found his way out by sheer luck, passing the skeleton of an Indian and taking the tomahawk as a souvenir.

Wherefore this particular cave, with a spring back fifty feet from the entrance where a shaft of sunlight struck the rock through some obscure slit in the rock, had no thrill for him. But the floor was of fine, white sand, and the ceiling was knobby and grotesque, and he was quite willing to sit there beside the spring and eat two sandwiches and talk foolishness with Honey, using that part of his mind which was not busy with the complexities of winning money on the speed of his horses when three horses represented his entire business capital, and with wondering what was wrong with Burroback Valley, that three persons of widely different viewpoints had felt it necessary to caution him, — and had couched their admonitions in such general terms that he could not feel the force of their warning.

He was thinking back along his life to where false alarms of Indian outbreaks had played a very large part in the Tomahawk's affairs, and how little of the ranch work would ever have been done had they listened to every calamity howler that came along. Honey was talking, and he was answering partly at random, when she suddenly laughed and got up.

"You must be in love, Bud Birnie. You just said 'yes' when I asked you if you didn't think water snakes would be coming out this fall with their stripes running round them instead of lengthwise! You didn't hear a word — now, did you?"

"I heard music," Bud lied gallantly, "and I knew it was your voice. I'd probably say yes if you asked me whether the moon wouldn't look better with a ruffle around it."

"I'll say the moon will be wondering where we are, if we don't start back. The sun's down."

Bud got up from sitting cross-legged like a Turk, helped Honey to her feet — and felt her fingers clinging warmly to his own. He led the way to the cave's mouth, not looking at her. "Great sunset," he observed carelessly, glancing up at the ridge while he held her horse for her to mount.

Honey showed that she was perfectly at home in the saddle. She rode on ahead, leaving Bud to mount and follow. He was just swinging leisurely into the saddle when Stopper threw his head around, glancing back toward the level just beyond the cave. At the same instant Bud heard the familiar, unmistakable swish of a rope headed his way.

He flattened himself along Stopper's left shoulder as the loop settled and tightened on the saddle horn, and dropped on to the ground as Stopper whirled automatically to the right and braced himself against the strain. Bud turned half kneeling, his gun in his hand ready for the shot he expected would follow the rope. But Stopper was in action — the best rope-horse the Tomahawk had ever owned. For a few seconds he stood braced, his neck arched, his eyes bright and watchful. Then he leaped forward, straight at the horse and the rider who was in the act of leveling his gun. The horse hesitated, taken unaware by the onslaught. When he started to run Stopper was already passing him, turning sharply to the right again so that the rope raked the horse's front legs. Two jumps and Stopper had stopped, faced the horse and stood braced again, his ears perked knowingly while he waited for the flop.

It came — just as it always did come when Stopper got action on the end of a rope. Horse and rider came down together. They would not get up until Bud wished it — he could trust Stopper for that — so Bud walked over to the heap, his gun ready for action — and that, too, could be trusted to perform with what speed and precision was necessary. There would be no hasty shooting, however; Buddy had learned to save his bullets for real need when ammunition was not to be had for the asking, and grown-up Bud had never outgrown the habit.

He picked up the fellow's six-shooter which he had dropped when he fell, and stood sizing up the situation.

By the neckerchief drawn across his face it was a straight case of holdup. Bud stooped and yanked off the mask and looked into the glaring eyes of one whom he had never before seen.

"Well, how d' yuh like it, far as you've got?" Bud asked curiously. "Think you were holding up a pilgrim, or what?"

Just then, *ping-gg* sang a rifle bullet from the ridge above the cave. Bud looked that way and spied a man standing half revealed against the rosy clouds that were already dulling as dusk crept up from the low ground. It was a long shot for a six-shooter, but Buddy used to shoot antelope almost that far, so Bud lifted his arm and straightened it, just as if he were pointing a finger at the man, and fired. He had the satisfaction of seeing the figure jerk backward and go off over the ridge in a stooping kind of run.

"He'd better hurry back if he wants another shot at me," Bud grinned. "It'll be so dark down here in a minute he could n't pick me up with his front sight if I was — as big a fool as you are. How about it? I'll just lead you into camp, I think — but you sure as hell could n't get a job roping gateposts, on the strength of this little exhibition."

He went over to Stopper and untied his own rope, giving an approving pat to that business-like animal. "Hope your leg is n't broken or anything," he said to the man when he returned and passed the loop over the fellow's head and shoulders, drawing it rather snugly around his body and pinning his arms at the elbows. "It would be kind of unpleasant if they happen to take a notion to make you walk all the way to jail."

He beckoned Stopper, who immediately moved up, slackening the rope. The thrown horse drew up his knees, gave a preliminary heave and scrambled to his feet, Bud taking care that the man was pulled free and safe. The fellow stood up sulkily defiant, unable to rest much of his weight on his left leg.

Bud had ten busy minutes, and it was not until they were both mounted and headed for Little Lost, the captive with his arms tied behind him, his feet tied together under the horse, which Bud led, that Bud had time to wonder what it was all about. Then he began to look for Honey, who had disappeared. But in the softened light of the rising moon mingling with the afterglow of sunset, he saw the deep imprints of her horse's hoofs where he had galloped homeward. Bud did not think she ran away because she was frightened; she had seemed too sure of herself for that. She had probably gone for help.

A swift suspicion that the attack might have been made from jealousy died when Bud looked again at his prisoner. The man was swarthy, low of brow — part Indian, by the look of him. Honey would never give the fellow a second thought. So that brought him to the supposition that robbery had been intended, and the inference was made more logical when Bud remembered that Marian had warned him against something of the sort. Probably he and Honey had been followed into the Sinks, and even though Bud had not seen this man at the races, his partner up on the ridge might have been there. It was all very simple, and Bud, having arrived at the obvious conclusion, touched Stopper into a lope and arrived at Little Lost just as Dave Truman and three of his men were riding down into Sunk Creek ford on their way to the Sinks. They pulled up, staring hard at Dave and his captive. Dave spoke first.

"Honey said you was waylaid and robbed or killed — both, we took it, from her account. How'd yuh come to get the best of it so quick?"

"Why, his horse got tangled up in the rope and fell down, and I fell on top of him," Bud explained cheerfully. "I was bringing him in. He's a bad citizen, I should judge, but he did n't do me any damage, as it turned out, so I don't know what to do with him. I'll just turn him over to you, I think."

"Hell! *I* don't want him," Dave protested. I'll pass him along to the sheriff — he may know something about him. Nelse and Charlie, you take and run him in to Crater and turn him over to Kline. You tell Kline what he done — or tried to do. Was he alone, Bud?"

"He had a partner up on the ridge, so far off I could n't swear to him if I saw him face to face. I took a shot at him, and I think I nicked him. He ducked, and there were n't any more rifle bullets coming my way."

"You nicked him with your six-shooter? And him so far off you could n't recognize him again?" Dave looked at Bud sharply. "That's purty good shootin', strikes me."

"Well, he stood up against the sky-line, and he was n't more than seventy-five yards," Bud explained. "I've dropped antelope that far, plenty of times. The light was bad, this evening."

"Antelope," Dave repeated meditatively, and winked at his men. "All right, Bud — we'll let it stand at antelope. Boys, you hit for Crater with this fellow. You ought to make it there and back by tomorrow noon, all right."

Nelse took the lead rope from Bud and the two started off up the creek, meaning to strike the road from Little Lost to Crater, the county seat beyond Gold Gap mountains. Bud rode on to the ranch with his boss, and tried to answer Dave's questions satisfactorily without relating his own prowess or divulging too much of Stopper's skill; which was something of a problem for his wits.

Honey ran out to meet him and had to be assured over and over that he was not hurt, and that he had lost nothing but his temper and the ride home with her in the moonlight. She was plainly upset and anxious that he should not think her cowardly, to leave him that way.

"I looked back and saw a man throwing his rope, and you — it looked as if he had dragged you off the horse. I was sure I saw you falling. So I ran my horse all the way home, to get Uncle Dave and the boys," she told him tremulously. And then she added, with her tantalizing half smile, "I believe that horse of mine could beat Smoky or Skeeter, if I was scared that bad at the beginning of a race."

Bud, in sheer gratitude for her anxiety over him, patted Honey's hand and told her she must have broken the record, all right, and that she had done exactly the right thing. And Honey went to bed happy that night.

CHAPTER FOURTEEN

Even Mushrooms Help

Bud wanted to have a little confidential talk with Marian. He hoped that she would be willing to tell him a great deal more than could be written on one side of a cigarette paper, and he was curious to hear what it was. On the other hand, he wanted somehow to let her know that he was anxious to help her in any way possible. She needed help, of that he was sure.

Lew returned on Tuesday, with a vile temper and rheumatism in his left shoulder so that he could not work, but stayed around the house and too evidently made his wife miserable by his presence. On Wednesday morning Marian had her hair dressed so low over her ears that she resembled a lady of old Colonial days — but she did not quite conceal from Bud's keen eyes the ugly bruise on her temple. She was pale and her lips were compressed as if she were afraid to relax lest she burst out in tears or in a violent denunciation of some kind. Bud dared not look at her, nor at Lew, who sat glowering at Bud's right hand. He tried to eat, tried to swallow his coffee, and finally gave up the attempt and left the table.

In getting up he touched Lew's shoulder with his elbow, and Lew let out a bellow of pain and an oath, and leaned away from him, his right hand up to ward off another hurt.

"Pardon me. I forgot your rheumatism," Bud apologized perfunctorily, his face going red at the epithet. Marian, coming toward him with a plate of biscuits, looked him full in the eyes and turned her glance to her husband's back while her lips curled in the bitterest, the most scornful smile Bud had ever seen on a woman's face. She did not speak — speech was impossible before that tableful of men — but Bud went out feeling as though she had told him that her contempt for Lew was beyond words, and that his rheumatism brought no pity whatever.

Wednesday passed, Thursday came, and still there was no chance to speak a word in private. The kitchen drudge was hedged about by open ears and curious eyes, and save at meal-time she was invisible to the men unless they glimpsed her for a moment in the kitchen door.

Thursday brought a thunder storm with plenty of rain, and in the drizzle that held over until Friday noon Bud went out to an old calf shed which he had discovered in the edge of the pasture, and gathered his neckerchief full of mushrooms. Bud hated mushrooms, but he carried them to the machine shed and waited until he was sure that Honey was in the sitting room playing the piano — and hitting what Bud called a blue note now and then — and that Lew was in the bunk-house with the other men, and Dave and old Pop were in Pop's shack. Then, and then only, Bud took long steps to the kitchen door, carrying his mushrooms as tenderly as though they were eggs for hatching.

Marian was up to her dimpled elbows in bread dough when he went in. Honey was still groping her way lumpily through the Blue Danube Waltz, and Bud stood so that he could look out through the white-curtained window over the kitchen table and make sure that no one approached the house unseen.

"Here are some mushrooms," he said guardedly, lest his voice should carry to Honey. "They're just an excuse. Far as I'm concerned you can feed them to the hogs. I like things clean and natural and wholesome, myself. I came to find out what's the matter, Mrs. Morris. Is there anything I can do? I took the hint you gave me in the note, Sunday, and I discovered right away you knew what you were talking about. That was a holdup down in the Sinks. It could n't have been anything else. But they would n't have got anything. I did n't have more than a dollar in my pocket."

Marian turned her head, and listened to the piano, and glanced up at him.

"I also like things clean and natural and whole-some," she said quietly. "That's why I tried to put you on your guard. You don't seem to fit in, some-how, with — the surroundings. I happen to know that the races held here every Sunday are just thinly veiled attempts to cheat the unwary out of every cent they have. I should advise you, Mr. Birnie, to be very careful how you bet on any horses."

"I shall," Bud smiled. "Pop gave me some good advice, too, about running horses. He says, 'It's every fellow for himself, and mercy toward none.' I'm playing by their rule, and Pop expects to make a few dollars, too. He said he'd stand by me."

"Oh! He did?" Marian's voice puzzled Bud. She kneaded the bread vigorously for a minute. "Don't depend too much on Pop. He's — variable. And don't go around with a dollar in your pocket — unless you don't mind losing that dollar. There are men in this country who would willingly dispense with the formality of racing a horse in order to get your money."

"Yes — I've discovered one informal method already. I wish I knew how I could help *you*."

"Help me — in what way?" Marian glanced out of the window again as if that were a habit she had formed.

"I don't know. I wish I did. I thought perhaps you had some trouble that — My mother had the same look in her eyes when we came back to the ranch after some Indian trouble, and found the house burned and everything destroyed but the ground itself. She didn't say anything much. She just began helping father plan how we'd manage until we could get material and build another cabin, and make our supplies hold out. She didn't complain. But her eyes had the same look I've seen in yours, Mrs. Morris. So I feel as if I ought to help you, just as I'd help mother." Bud's face had been red and embarrassed when he began, but his earnestness served to erase his self-consciousness.

"You're different — just like mother," he went on when Marian did not answer. "You don't belong here drudging in this kitchen. I never saw a woman doing a man's work before. They ought to have a man cooking for all these hulking men."

"Oh, the kitchen!" Marian exclaimed impatiently. "I don't mind the cooking. That's the least — "

"It isn't right, just the same. I — I don't suppose

that's it altogether. I'm not trying to find out what the trouble is — but I wish you'd remember that I'm ready to do anything in the world that I can. You won't misunderstand that, I'm sure."

"No-o," said Marian slowly. "But you see, there's nothing that you can do — except, perhaps, make things worse for me." Then, to lighten that statement, she smiled at him. "Just now you can help me very much if you will go in and play something besides the Blue Danube Waltz. I've had to listen to that ever since Honora sent away for the music with the winter's grocery order, last October. Tell Honora you got her some mushrooms. And don't trust anyone. If you must bet on the horses, do so with your eyes open. They're cheats — and worse, some of them."

Bud's glance followed hers through the window that overlooked the corrals and the outbuildings. Lew was coming up to the house with a slicker over his head to keep off the drizzle.

"Well, remember I'd do anything for you that I'd do for my mother or my sister Dulcie. And I wish you'd call on me just as they would, if you get in a pinch and need me. If I know you'll do that I'll feel a lot better satisfied."

"If I need you be sure that I shall let you know. And I'll say that it's a comfort to have met one white man," Marian assured him hurriedly, her anxious eyes on her approaching husband.

She need not have worried over his coming, so far as Bud was concerned. For Bud was in the sitting-room and had picked Honey off the piano stool, had given her a playful shake and was playing the Blue

Danube as its composer intended that it should be played, when Lew entered the kitchen and kicked the door shut behind him.

Bud spent the forenoon conscientiously trying to teach Honey that the rests are quite as important to the tempo of a waltz measure as are the notes. Honey's talent for music did not measure up to her talent for coquetry; she received about five dollars' worth of instruction and no blandishments whatever, and although she no doubt profited thereby, at last she balked and put her lazy white hands over her ears and refused to listen to Bud's inexorable "One, two, three, one, two, three-and one, two, three." Whereupon Bud laughed and returned to the bunk-house.

He arrived in the middle of a heated argument over Jeff Hall's tactics in racing Skeeter, and immediately was called upon for his private, personal opinion of Sunday's race. Bud's private, personal opinion being exceedingly private and personal, he threw out a skirmish line of banter.

Smoky could run circles around that Skeeter horse, he boasted, and Jeff's manner of riding was absolutely unimportant, non-essential and immaterial. He was mighty glad that holdup man had fallen down, last Sunday, before he got his hands on any money, because that money was going to talk long and loud to Jeff Hall next Sunday. Now that Bud had started running his horse for money, working for wages looked foolish and unprofitable. He was now working merely for healthful exercise and to pass the time away between Sundays. His real mission in life, he had discovered, was to teach Jeff's bunch that gambling is a sin.

The talk was carried enthusiastically to the dinner table, where Bud ignored the scowling proximity of Lew and repeated his boasts in a revised form as an indirect means of letting Marian know that he meant to play the Burroback game in the Burroback way — or as nearly as he could — and keep his honesty more or less intact. He did not think she would approve, but he wanted her to know.

Once, when Buddy was fifteen, four thoroughbred cows and four calves disappeared mysteriously from the home ranch just before the calves had reached branding age. Buddy rode the hills and the valleys every spare minute for two weeks in search of them, and finally, away over the ridge where an undesirable neighbor was getting a start in cattle, Buddy found the calves in a fenced field with eight calves belonging — perhaps — to the undesirable neighbor.

Buddy did not ride down to the ranch and accuse the neighbor of stealing the calves. Instead, he painstakingly sought a weak place in the fence, made a very accidental looking hole and drove out the twelve calves, took them over the ridge to Tomahawk and left them in a high, mountain meadow pretty well surrounded by matted thickets. There, because there was good grass and running water, the calves seemed quite as happy as in the field.

Then Buddy hurried home and brought a branding iron and a fresh horse, and by working very hard and fast, he somehow managed to plant a deep tomahawk brand on each one of the twelve calves. He returned home very late and very proud of himself, and met his father face to face as he was putting away the iron. Explanations and a broken harness strap mingled painfully in Buddy's memory for a long time afterwards, but the full effect of the beating was lost because Buddy happened to hear Bob Birnie confide to mother that the lad had served the old cattle-thief right, and that any man who could start with one thoroughbred cow and in four years have sufficient increase from that cow to produce eight calves a season, ought to lose them all.

Buddy had not needed his father's opinion to strengthen his own conviction that he had performed a worthy deed and one of which no man need feel ashamed. Indeed, Buddy considered the painful incident of the buggy strap a parental effort at official discipline, and held no particular grudge against his father after the welts had disappeared from his person.

Wherefore Bud, the man, held unswervingly to the ethical standard of Buddy the boy. If Burroback Valley was scheming to fleece a stranger at their races and rob him by force if he happened to win, then Bud felt justified in getting every dollar possible out of the lot of them. At any rate, he told himself, he would do his darndest. It was plain enough that Pop was trying to make an opportunity to talk confidentially, but with a dozen men on the place it was easy enough to avoid being alone without arousing the old man's suspicions. Marian had told him to trust no one; and Bud, with his usual thoroughness, applied the warning literally.

Sunday morning he caught up Smoky and rode him to the corral. Smoky had recovered from his lameness, and while Bud groomed him for the afternoon's running the men of Little Lost gathered round him and offered advice and encouragement, and even volunteered to lend him money if he needed it. But Bud told them to put up their own bets, and never to worry about him. Their advice and their encouragement, however, he accepted as cheerfully as they were given.

"Think yuh can beat Skeeter, young feller?" Pop shambled up to inquire anxiously, his beard brushing Bud's shoulder while he leaned close. "Remember what I told ye. You stick by me an' I'll stick by you. You shook on it, don't forget that, young feller."

Bud had forgotten, but he made haste to redeem his promise. "Last Sunday, Pop, I had to play it alone. To-day — well, if you want to make an honest dollar, you know what to do, don't you?"

"Sho! I'm bettin' on yore horse t'day, an' mind ye, I want to see my money doubled! But that there lameness in his left hind ankle — I don't see but what that kinda changes my opinion a little mite. You shore he won't quit on ye in the race, now? Don't lie to ole Pop, young feller!"

"Say! He's the gamest little horse in the state, Pop. He never has quit, and he never will." Bud stood up and laid a friendly hand on the old fellow's shoulder. "Pop, I'm running him to-day to *win*. That's the truth. I'm going to put all I've got on him. Is that good enough?"

"Shucks a'mighty! That's good enough fer me, — plenty good fer me," Pop cackled, and trotted off to find someone who had little enough faith in Smoky to wager a two-to-one against him.

It seemed to Bud that the crowd was larger than that of a week ago, and there was no doubt whatever that the betting was more feverish, and that Jeff meant that day to retrieve his losses. Bud passed up a very good chance to win on other races, and centred all his betting on Smoky. He had been throughout the week boastful and full of confidence, and now he swaggered and lifted his voice in arrogant challenge to all and sundry. His three hundred dollars was on the race, and incidentally, he never left Smoky from the time he led him up from pasture until the time came when he and Jeff Hall rode side by side down to the quarter post.

They came up in a small whirlwind of speed and dust, and Smoky was under the wire to his ears when Skeeter's nose showed beyond it. Little Lost was jubilant. Jeff Hall and his backers were not.

Bud's three hundred dollars had in less than a minute increased to a little over nine hundred, though all his bets had been moderate. By the time he had collected, his pockets were full and his cocksureness had increased to such an unbearable crowing that Jeff Hall's eyes were venomous as a snake's. Jeff had been running to win, that day, and he had taken odds on Skeeter that had seemed to him perfectly safe.

" I 'll run yuh horse for horse! " he bellowed and spat out an epithet that sent Bud at him white-lipped.

" Damn yuh, ride down to the quarter post and I 'll show you some running! " Bud yelled back. " And after you 've swallowed dust all the way up the track, you go with me to where the women can't see and I 'll lick the living tar outa you! "

Jeff swore and wheeled Skeeter toward the starting post, beckoning Bud to follow. And Bud, hastily tucking in a flapping bulge of striped shirt, went after him. At that moment he was not Bud, but Buddy in one of his fighting moods, with his plans forgotten while he avenged an insult.

Men lined up at the wire to judge for themselves the finish, and Dave Truman rode alone to start them. No one doubted but that the start would be fair — Jeff and Bud would see to that!

For the first time in months the rein-ends stung Smoky's flanks when he was in his third jump. Just once Bud struck, and was ashamed of the blow as it fell. Smoky did not need that urge, but he flattened his ears and came down the track a full length ahead of Skeeter, and held the pace to the wire and beyond, where he stopped in a swirl of sand and went prancing back, ready for another race if they asked it of him.

"Guess Dave 'll have to bring out Boise and take the swellin' outa that singin' kid's pocket," a hard-faced man shouted as Jeff slid off Skeeter and went over to where his cronies stood bunched and conferring earnestly together.

"Not to-day, he need n't. I 've had all the excitement I want; and I 'd like to have time to count my money before I lose it," Bud retorted. "Next Sunday, if it 's a clear day and the sign is right, I might run against Boise if it 's worth my while. Say, Jeff, seeing you 're playing hard luck, I won't lick you for what you called me. And just to show my heart 's right, I 'll lend you Skeeter to ride home. Or if you want to buy him back, you can have him for sixty dollars or such a matter. He 's a nice little horse, — if you are n't in a hurry!"

CHAPTER FIFTEEN

WHY BUD MISSED A DANCE

"BUD, you're fourteen kinds of a damn fool and I can prove it," Jerry announced without prelude of any kind save, perhaps, the viciousness with which he thrust a pitchfork into a cock of hay. The two were turning over hay-cocks that had been drenched with another unwelcome storm, and they had not been talking much. "Forking" soggy hay when the sun is blistering hot and great, long-billed mosquitoes are boring indefatigably into the back of one's neck is not a pastime conducive to polite and animated conversation.

"Fly at it," Bud invited, resting his fork while he scratched a smarting shoulder. "But you can skip some of the evidence. I know seven of the kinds, and I plead guilty. Any able-bodied man who will deliberately make a barbecue of himself for a gang of blood-thirsty insects ought to be hanged. What's the rest?"

"You can call that mild," Jerry stated severely. "Bud, you're playing to lose the shirt off your back. You've got a hundred dollar forfeit up on next Sunday's running match, so you'll run if you have to race Boise afoot. That's all right if you want the risk — but did it ever occur to you that if all the coin in the neighborhood is collected in one man's pocket, there 'll be about as many fellows as there are losers, that will lay awake till sun-up figuring how to heel him and ride off with the roll? I ain't over-stocked with courage, myself. I'd rather be broke in Burroback Valley than owner of wealth. It's healthier."

He thrust his fork into another settled heap, lifted it clear of the ground with one heave of his muscular shoulders, and heard within a strident buzzing. He held the hay poised until a mottled gray snake writhed into view, its ugly jaws open and its fangs showing malevolently.

"Grab him with your fork, Bud," Jerry said coolly. "A rattler — the valley's full of 'em, — some of 'em's human."

The snake was dispatched and the two went on to the next hay-cock. Bud was turning over more than the hay, and presently he spoke more seriously than was his habit with Jerry.

"You're full enough of warnings, Jerry. What do you want me to do about it?"

"Drift," Jerry advised. "There's moral diseases just as catching as smallpox. This part of the country has been settled up by men that came here first because they wanted to hide out. They've slipped into darn crooked ways, and the rest has either followed suit or quit. All through this rough country it's the same — over in the Black Rim, across Thunder Mountains, and beyond that to the Sawtooth, a man that's honest is a man that's off his range. I'd like to see you pull out — before you're planted."

Bud looked at Jerry, studied him, feature by feature. "Then what are *you* doing here?" he demanded bluntly. "Why have n't you pulled out?"

"Me?" Jerry bit his lip. "Bud, I'm going to take a chance and tell you the God's-truth. I dassent. I'm protected here because I keep my mouth shut, and because they know I've got to or they can hand me over. I had some trouble. I'm on the dodge, and Little Lost is right handy to the Sinks and — Catrock Canyon. There ain't a sheriff in Idaho that would have one chance in a thousand of getting me here. But you — say!" He faced Bud. "*You* ain't on the dodge, too, are yuh?"

"Nope," Bud grinned. "Over at the Muleshoe they seemed to think I was. I just struck out for myself, and I want to show up at home some day with a stake I made myself. It's just a little argument with my dad that I want to settle. And," he added frankly, "I seem to have struck the right place to make money quickly. The very fact that they're a bunch of crooks makes my conscience clear on the point of running my horse. I'm not cheating them out of a cent. If Jeff's horse is faster than Smoky, Jeff is privileged to let him out and win if he can. It is n't my fault if he's playing to let me win from the whole bunch in the hope that he can hold me up afterwards and get the roll. It's straight ' give and take' — and so far I've been taking."

Jerry worked for a while, moodily silent. "What I'd like is to see you take the trail; while the takin's good," he said later. "I've got to keep my mouth shut. But I like yuh, Bud. I hate like hell to see you walking straight into a trap."

"Say, I'm as easily trapped as a mountain lion," Bud told him confidently.

Whereat Jerry looked at him pityingly. "You going to that dance up at Morgan's?"

"Sure! I'm going to take Honey and — I think Mrs. Morris if she decides to go. Honey mentioned it last night. Why?"

"Oh, nothing." Jerry shouldered his fork and went off to where a jug of water was buried in the hay beside a certain boulder which marked the spot. He drank long, stopped for a short gossip with Charley, who strolled over for a drink, and went to work on another row.

Bud watched him, and wondered if Jerry had changed rows to avoid further talk with him; and whether Jerry had merely been trying to get information from him, and had either learned what he wanted to know, or had given up the attempt. Bud reviewed mentally their desultory conversation and decided that he had accidentally been very discreet. The only real bit of information he had given Jerry was the fact that he was not "on the dodge" — a criminal in fear of the law — and that surely could harm no man.

That he intended to run against Boise on Sunday was common knowledge; also that he had a hundred-dollar forfeit up on the race. And that he was going to a dance with Honey was of no consequence that he could see.

Bud was beginning to discount the vague warnings he had received. Unless something definite came within his knowledge he would go about his business exactly as if Burroback Valley were a church-going community. He would not "drift."

But after all he did not go to the dance with Honey, or with anyone. He came to the supper-table freshly shaved and dressed for the occasion, ate hungrily and straightway became a very sick young man. He did not care if there were forty dances in the Valley that night. His head was splitting, his stomach was in a turmoil. He told Jerry to go ahead with Honey, and if he felt better after a while he would follow. Jerry at first was inclined to scepticism, and accused Bud of crawfishing at the last minute. But within ten minutes Bud had convinced him so completely that Jerry insisted upon staying with him. By then Bud was too sick to care what was being done, or who did it. So Jerry stayed.

Honey came to the bunk-house in her dance finery, was met in the doorway by Jerry and was told that this was no place for a lady, and reluctantly consented to go without her escort.

A light shone dimly in the kitchen after the dancers had departed, wherefore Jerry guessed that Marian had not gone with the others, and that he could perhaps get hold of mustard for an emetic or a plaster — Jerry was not sure which remedy would be best, and the patient, wanting to die, would not be finicky. He found Marian measuring something drop by drop into half a glass of water. She turned, saw who had entered, and carefully counted three more drops, corked the bottle tightly and slid it into her apron pocket, and held out the glass to Jerry.

" Give him this," she said in a soft undertone. " I 'm sorry, but I had n't a chance to say a word to the boy, and so I could n't think of any other way of making sure he would not go up to Morgan's. I put something into his coffee to make him sick. You may tell him, Jerry, if you like. I should, if I had the chance. This will counteract the effects of the other so that he will be all right in a couple of hours."

Jerry took the glass and stood looking at her steadily. "That sure was one way to do it," he observed, with a quirk of the lips. "It's none of my business, and I ain't asking any questions, but — "

"Very sensible, I'm sure," Marian interrupted him. "I wish he'd leave the country. Can't you — ?"

"No. I told him to pull out, and he just laughed at me. I knowed they was figuring on ganging together to-night — "

Marian closed her hands together with a gesture of impatience. "Jerry, I wish I knew just how bad you are!" she exclaimed. "Do you dare stand by him? Because this thing is only beginning. I couldn't bear to see him go up there to-night, absolutely unsuspecting — and so I made him sick. Tell that to anyone, and you can make me — "

"Say, I ain't a damned skunk!" Jerry muttered. "I'm bad enough, maybe. At any rate you think so." Then, as usually happened, Jerry decided to hold his tongue. He turned and lifted the latch of the screen door. "You sure made a good job of it," he grinned. "I'll go an' pour this into Bud 'fore he loses his boots!"

He did so, and saved Bud's boots and half a night's sleep besides. Moreover, when Bud, fully recovered, searched his memory of that supper and decided that it was the sliced cucumbers that had disagreed with him, Jerry gravely assured him that it undoubtedly was the combination of cucumber and custard pie, and that Bud was lucky to be alive after such reckless eating.

Having missed the dance altogether, Bud looked forward with impatience to Sunday. It is quite possible that others shared with him that impatience, though we are going to adhere for a while to Bud's point of view and do no more than guess at the thoughts hidden behind the fair words of certain men in the Valley.

Pop's state of mind we are privileged to know, for Pop was seen making daily pilgrimage to the pasture where he could watch Smoky limping desultorily here and there with Stopper and Sunfish. On Saturday afternoon Bud saw Pop trying to get his hands on Smoky, presumably to examine the lame ankle. But three legs were all Smoky needed to keep him out of Pop's reach. Pop forgot his rheumatism and ran pretty fast for a man his age, and when Bud arrived Pop's vocabulary had limbered up to a more surprising activity than his legs.

"Want to bet on yourself, Pop?" Bud called out when Pop was running back and forth, hopefully trying to corner Smoky in a rocky draw. "I'm willing to risk a dollar on you, anyway."

Pop whirled upon him and hurled sentences not written in the book of Parlor Entertainment. The gist of it was that he had been trying all the week to have a talk with Bud, and Bud had plainly avoided him after promising to act upon Pop's advice and run so as to make some money.

"Well, I made some," Bud defended. "If you didn't, it's just because you didn't bet strong enough."

"I want to look at that horse's hind foot," Pop insisted.

"No use. He's too lame to run against Boise. You can see that yourself."

Pop eyed Bud suspiciously, pulling his beard. "Are you fixin' to double-cross me, young feller?" he wanted to know. "I went and made some purty big bets on this race. If you think yo're goin' to fool ole Pop, you'll wish you hadn't. You got enemies already in this valley, lemme tell yuh. The Muleshoe ain't any bunch to fool with, and I'm willing to say 't they're laying fer yuh. They think," he added shrewdly, "'t yo're a spotter, or something. Air yuh?"

"Of course I am, Pop! I've spotted a way to make money and have fun while I do it." Bud looked at the old man, remembered Marian's declaration that Pop was not very reliable, and groped mentally for a way to hearten the old man without revealing anything better kept to himself, such as the immediate effect of a horse hair tied just above a horse's hoof, also the immediate result of removing that hair. Wherefore, he could not think of much to say, except that he would not attempt to run a lame horse against Boise.

"All I can say is, to-morrow morning you keep your eyes open, Pop, and your tongue between your teeth. And no matter what comes up, you use your own judgment."

To-morrow morning Pop showed that he was taking Bud's advice. When the crowd began to gather — much earlier than usual, by the way, and much larger than any crowd Bud had seen in the valley — Pop was trotting here and there, listening and pulling his whiskers and eyeing Bud sharply whenever that young man appeared in his vicinity.

Bud led Smoky up at noon — and Smoky was still lame. Dave looked at him and at Bud, and grinned. "I guess that forfeit money's mine," he said in his laconic way. "No use running that horse. I could beat him afoot."

This was but the beginning. Others began to banter and jeer Bud, Jeff's crowd taunting him with malicious glee. The singin' kid was going to have some of the swelling taken out of his head, they chortled. He had been crazy enough to put up a forfeit on to-day's race, and now his horse had just three legs to run on.

"Git out afoot, kid!" Jeff Hall yelled. "If you kin run half as fast as you kin talk, you'll beat Boise four lengths in the first quarter!"

Bud retorted in kind, and led Smoky around the corral as if he hoped that the horse would recover miraculously just to save his master's pride. The crowd hooted to see how Smoky hobbled along, barely touching the toe of his lame foot to the ground. Bud led him back to the manger piled with new hay, and faced the jeering crowd belligerently. Bud noticed several of the Muleshoe men in the crowd, no doubt drawn to Little Lost by the talk of Bud's spectacular winnings for two Sundays. Hen was there, and Day Masters and Chub. Also there were strangers who had ridden a long way, judging by their sweaty horses. In the midst of the talk and laughter Dave led out Boise freshly curried and brushed and arching his neck proudly.

"No use, Bud," he said tolerantly. "I guess you're

set back that forfeit money — unless you want to go through the motions of running a lame horse."

"No, sir, I 'm not going to hand over any forfeit money without making a fight for it!" Bud told him, anger showing in his voice. "I 'm no such piker as that. I won't run Smoky, lame as he is" — Bud probably nudged his own ribs when he said that! — "but if you 'll make it a mile, I 'll catch up my old buckskin packhorse and run the race with him, by thunder! He 's not the quickest horse in the world, but he sure can run a long while!"

They yelled and slapped one another on the back, and otherwise comported themselves as though a great joke had been told them; never dreaming, poor fools, that a costly joke was being perpetrated.

"Go it, kid. You run your packhorse, and I 'll give yuh five to one on him!" a friend of Jeff Hall's yelled derisively.

"I 'll just take you up on that, and I 'll make it one hundred dollars," Bud shouted back. "I 'd run a turtle for a quarter, at those odds!"

The crowd was having hysterics when Bud straddled a Little Lost horse and, loudly declaring that he would bring back Sunfish, led Smoky limping back to the pasture. He returned soon, leading the buckskin. The crowd surged closer, gave Sunfish a glance and whooped again. Bud's face was red with apparent anger, his eyes snapped. He faced them defiantly, his hand on Sunfish's thin, straggling mane.

"You 're such good sports, you 'll surely appreciate my feelings when I say that this horse is mine, and I 'm going to run him and back him to win!" he cried. "I may be a darn fool, but I 'm no piker. I know what this horse can do when I try to catch him up on a frosty morning — and I'm going to see if he can't go just as fast and just as long when I'm on him as he can when I'm after him."

"We'll go yuh, kid! I'll bet yuh five to one," a man shouted. "You name the amount yourself."

"Fifty," said Bud, and the man nodded and jotted down the amount.

"Bud, you're a damn fool. I'll bet you a hundred and make it ten to one," drawled Dave, stroking Boise's face affectionately while he looked superciliously at Sunfish standing half asleep in the clamor, with his head sagging at the end of his long, ewe neck. "But if you'll take my advice, go turn that fool horse back in the pasture and run the bay if you must run something."

"The bay's a rope horse. I don't want to spoil him by running him. That little horse saved my life, down in the Sinks. No, Sunfish has run times enough *from* me — now he's got to run *for* me, by thunder. I'll bet on him, too!"

Jeff pushed his way through to Bud. He was smiling with that crafty look in his eyes which should have warned a child that the smile went no deeper than his lips.

"Bud, doggone it, I like yore nerve. Besides, you owe me something for the way you trimmed me last Sunday. I'll just give you fifteen to one, and you put up Skeeter at seventy-five, and as much money as yo're a mind to. A pile of it come out of my pocket, so —"

"Well, don't holler your head off, Jeff. How's two hundred?"

"Suits me, kid." He winked at the others, who knew how sure a thing he had to back his wager. "It'll be a lot of money if I should lose —" He turned suddenly to Dave. "How much was that you put up agin the kid, Dave?"

"One hundred dollars, and a ten-to-one shot I win," Dave drawled. "That ought to satisfy yuh it ain't a frame-up. The kid's crazy, that's all."

"Oh! Am I?" Bud turned hotly. "Well, I've bet half of all the money I have in the world. And I'm game for the other half —" He stopped abruptly, cast one look at Sunfish and another at Boise, stepping about uneasily, his shiny coat rippling, beautiful. He turned and combed Sunfish's scanty mane with his gloved fingers. Those nearest saw that his lips were trembling a little and mistook his hidden emotion for anger.

"You got him going," a man whispered in Jeff's ear. "The kid's crazy mad. He'll bet the shirt off his back if yuh egg him on a little more."

Jeff must have decided to "egg" Bud on. By the time the crowd had reached the course, and the first, more commonplace races were over, the other half of his money was in the hands of the stake-holder, who happened on this day to be Jerry. And the odds varied from four to one up to Jeff Hall's scornful fifteen.

"Bet yuh five hundred dollars against your bay horse," Lew offered when Bud confessed that he had not another dollar to bet.

"All right, it's a go with me," Bud answered recklessly. "Get his hundred, Jerry, and put down Stopper."

"What's that saddle worth?" another asked meaningly.

"One hundred dollars," snapped Bud. "And if you want to go further, there are my chaps and spurs and this silver-mounted bridle — and my boots and hat — and I'll throw in Sunfish for whatever you say his hide's worth. Who wants the outfit?"

"I'll take 'em," said Jeff, and permitted Jerry and Dave to appraise the outfit, which Bud piled contemptuously in a heap.

He mounted Sunfish bareback, with a rope halter. Bud was bareheaded and in his sock feet. His eyes were terribly blue and bright, and his face was flushed as a drunken man's. He glanced over to the bank where the women and children were watching. It seemed to him that one woman fluttered her handkerchief, and his heart beat unevenly for a minute.

Then he was riding at a walk down the course to the farthest post, and the crowd was laughing at the contrast between the two horses. Boise stepped springily, tossing his head, his eyes ablaze with ardor for the race. Beside him Sunfish walked steadily as if he were carrying a pack. He was not a pretty horse to look at. His neck was long and thin, his mane and tail scanty and uneven, a nondescript sorrel. His head looked large, set on the end of that neck, his nose was dished in and his eyes had a certain veiled look, as if he were hiding a bad disposition under those droopy lids. Without a saddle he betrayed his high, thin withers, the sway in his back, his high hip bones. His front legs were flat, with long, stringy-looking muscles under his unkempt buckskin hide. Even the women laughed at Sunfish.

Beside them two men rode, — the starter and another to see that the start was fair. So they receded down the flat, yellow course and dwindled to mere miniature figures against the sand, so that one could not tell one horse from another.

The crowd bunched, still laughing at how the singin' kid was going to feel when he rode again to meet them. It would cure him of racing, they said. It would be a good lesson; serve him right for coming in there and thinking, because he had cleaned up once or twice, that he could n't be beaten.

"Here they come," Jeff Hall announced satisfiedly, and spat into the sand as a tiny blue puff of smoke showed beside one of the dots, and two other dots began to grow perceptibly larger within a yellow cloud which rolled along the earth.

Men reined this way and that, or stood on their toes if they were afoot, the better to see the two rolling dots. In a moment one dot seemed larger than the other. One could glimpse the upflinging of knees as two horses leaped closer and closer.

"Well-l — he 's keepin' Dave in sight — that 's more 'n what I expected he 'd do," Jeff observed.

It was Pop who suddenly gave a whoop that cracked and shrilled into falsetto.

"Shucks a'mighty! Dave, he 's a-whippin' up to keep the *kid* in sight!" he quavered. "Shucks — a'*mighty,* he 's a-comin'!"

He was. Lying forward flattened along Sunfish's hard-muscled shoulders, Bud was gaining and gaining — one length, then two lengths as he shot under the wire, slowed and rode back to find a silent crowd watching him.

He was clothed safely again in chaps, boots, spurs, hat — except that I have named the articles backward; cowpuncher that he was, Bud put on his hat before he even reached for his boots — and was collecting his wagers relentlessly as Shylock ever took his toll, before he paid any attention to the atmosphere around him. Then, because someone shouted a question three inches from his ear, Bud turned and laughed as he faced them.

"Why, sure he's from running stock! I never said he was n't — because none of you make-believe horsemen had sense enough to see the speed in him and get curious. You bush-racers never saw a real race-horse before, I guess. They are n't always pretty to look at, you know. Sunfish has all the earmarks of speed if you know how to look for them. He's thoroughbred; sired by Trump, out of Kansas Chippy — if that means anything to you fellows." He looked them over, eyes meeting eyes until his glance rested on Jeff Hall. "I've got his registration papers in my grip, if you are n't convinced. And," he added by way of rubbing it in, "I guess I've got about all the money there is in this valley."

"No, you ain't!" Pop Truman cackled, teetering backward and forward while he counted his winnings. "*I* bet on ye, young feller. Brought me in something, too. It did so!"

CHAPTER SIXTEEN

While the Going's Good

At supper Bud noticed that Marian, standing at his right side, set down his cup of coffee with her right hand, and at the same instant he felt her left hand fumble in his pocket and then touch his elbow. She went on, and Bud in his haste to get outside drank his coffee so hot that it scalded his mouth. Jerry rose up and stepped backward over the bench as Bud passed him, and went out at his heels.

" Go play the piano for half an hour and then meet me where you got them mushrooms. And when you quit playing, duck quick. Tell Honey you 'll be back in a minute. Have her hunt for music for yuh while you 're out — or something like that. Don't let on."

Bud might have questioned Jerry, but that cautious young man was already turning back to call something to Dave, so Bud went around the corner, glancing into the pantry window as he passed. Marian was not in sight, nor was Honey at the moment when he stood beside the step of the post-office.

Boldness carries its own talisman against danger. Bud went in — without slamming the door behind him, you may be sure — and drew his small notebook from his inside pocket. With that to consult frequently, he sat down by the window where the failing light was strongest, and proceeded to jot down imaginary figures on the paper he pulled from his coat pocket and unfolded as if it were of no value whatever to him. The piano playing ordered by Jerry could wait.

What Marian had to say on this occasion could not be written upon a cigarette paper. In effect her note was a preface to Jerry's commands. Bud saw where she had written words and erased them so thoroughly that the cheap paper was almost worn through. She had been afraid, poor lady, but her fear could not prevent the writing.

" You must leave to-night for Crater and cash the checks given you to pay the bets. Go to Crater. If you don't know the way, keep due north after you have crossed Gold Gap. There 's the stage road, but they 'll watch that, I 'm afraid. They mean to stop payment on the checks. But first they will kill you if they can. They say you cheated with that thoroughbred horse. They took their losses so calmly — I knew that they meant to rob you. To show you how I know, it was Lew you shot on the ridge that night. His rheumatism was caused by your bullet that nicked his shoulder. So you see what sort we are — *go*. Don't wait — go now."

Bud looked up, and there was Honey leaning over the counter, smiling at him.

" Well, how much is it? " she teased when she saw he had discovered her.

Bud drew a line across the note and added imaginary columns of figures, his hat-brim hiding his face.

"Over eleven thousand dollars," he announced, and twisted the paper in his fingers while he went over to her. "Almost enough to start housekeeping!"

Honey blushed and leaned to look for something which she pretended to have dropped and Bud seized the opportunity to tuck the paper out of sight. "I feel pretty much intoxicated to-night, Honey," he said. "I think I need soothing, or something — and you know what music does to the savage breast. Let's play."

"All right. You've been staying away lately till I thought you were mad," Honey assented rather eagerly, and opened the little gate in the half partition just as Bud was vaulting the counter, which gave her a great laugh and a chance for playful scuffling. Bud kissed her and immediately regretted the caress.

Jerry had told him to play the piano, but Bud took his mandolin and played that while Honey thumped out chords for him. As he had half expected, most of the men strayed in and perched here and there listening just as if there had not been a most unusual horse-race to discuss before they slept. Indeed, Bud had never seen the Little Lost boys so thoughtful, and this silence struck him all at once as something sinister, like a beast of prey stalking its kill.

Two waltzes he played — and then, in the middle of a favorite two-step, a mandolin string snapped with a sharp twang, and Bud came as close to swearing as a well-behaved young man may come in the presence of a lady.

"Now I'll have to go get a new E string," he complained. "You play the Danube for the boys — the way I taught you — while I get this fixed. I've an extra string down in the bunk-house; it won't take five minutes to get it." He laid the mandolin down on his chair, bolted out through the screen door which he slammed after him to let Jerry know that he was coming, and walked halfway to the bunk-house before he veered off around the corner of the machine shed and ran.

Jerry was waiting by the old shed, and without a word he led Bud behind it where Sunfish was standing saddled and bridled.

"You got to go, Bud, while the going 's good. "I'd go with yuh if I dared," Jerry mumbled guardedly. "You hit for Crater, Bud, and put that money in the bank. You can cut into the stage road where it crosses Oldman Creek, if you go straight up the race track to the far end, and follow the trail from there. You can't miss it — there ain't but one way to go. I got yuh this horse because he 's worth more 'n what the other two are, and he 's faster. And Bud, if anybody rides up on yuh, shoot. Don't monkey around about it. And you *ride!*"

"All right," Bud muttered. "But I 'll have to go down in the pasture and get my money, first. I 've got my own private bank down there, and I have n't enough in my pockets to play penny ante more than one round."

"Hell!" Jerry's hand lifted to Bud's shoulder and gripped it for a minute. "That 's right on the road to the Sinks, man!" He stood biting his lips, thinking deeply, turning his head now and then as little sounds came from the house: the waltz Honey was playing, the post-office door slamming shut.

"You tell me where that money 's cached, Bud,

and I'll go after it. I guess you'll have to trust me — I sure would n't let yuh go down to the pasture yourself right now. Where is it?"

"Look under that flat rock right by the gate post, where the top bars hit the ground. It's wrapped up in a handkerchief, so just bring the package. It's been easy to tuck things under the rock when I was putting up the bars. I'll wait here."

"Good enough — I'd sure have felt easier if I'd known you was n't carrying all that money." Whereupon Jerry disappeared, and his going made no sound.

Bud stood beside Sunfish, wondering if he had been a fool to trust Jerry. By his own admission Jerry was living without the law, and this might easily be a smooth scheme of robbery. He turned and strained his eyes into the dusk, listening, trying to hear some sound that would show which way Jerry had gone. He was on the point of following him — suspicion getting the better of his faith — when Sunfish moved his head abruptly to one side, bumping Bud's head with his cheek. At the same instant a hand touched Bud's arm.

"I saw you from the kitchen window," Marian whispered tensely. "I was afraid you had n't read my note, or perhaps would n't pay any attention to it. I heard you and Jerry — of course he won't dare go with you and show you the short-cut, even if he knows it. There's a quicker way than up the creek-bed. I have Boise out in the bushes, and a saddle. I was afraid to wait at the barn long enough to saddle him. You go — he's behind that great pile of rocks, back of the corrals. I'll wait for Jerry." She gave him a push, and Bud was so astonished that he made no reply whatever, but did exactly as she had told him to do.

Boise was standing behind the peaked outcropping of rock, and beside him was a stock-saddle which must have taxed Marian's strength to carry. Indeed, Bud thought she must have had wings, to do so much in so short a space of time; though when he came to estimate that time he decided that he must have been away from the house ten minutes, at least. If Marian followed him closely enough to see him duck behind the machine shed and meet Jerry, she could run behind the corral and get Boise out by way of the back door of the stable. There was a path, screened from the corral by a fringe of brush, which went that way. The truth flashed upon him that one could ride unseen all around Little Lost.

He was just dropping the stirrup down from the saddle horn when Marian appeared with Jerry and Sunfish close behind her. Jerry held out the package. " She says she 'll show you a short cut," he whispered. " She says I don't know anything about it. I guess she 's right — there 's a lot I don't know. Lew 's gone, and she says she 'll be back before daylight. If they miss Boise they 'll think you stole him. But they won't look. Dave would n't slam around in the night on Boise — he thinks too much of him. Well — beat it, and I sure wish yuh luck. You be careful, Marian. Come back this way, and if you see a man's handkerchief hanging on this bush right here where I 'm standing, it 'll mean you 've been missed."

" Thank you, Jerry," Marian whispered. " I 'll look for it. Come, Bud — keep close behind me, and don't make any noise."

Bud would have protested, but Marian did not give him a chance. She took up the reins, grasped the saddle horn, stuck her slipper toe in the stirrup and mounted Boise as quickly as Bud could have done it — as easily, too, making allowance for the difference in their height. Bud mounted Sunfish and followed her on the trail which led to the race track; but when they had gone through the brush and could see starlight beyond, she turned sharply to the left, let Boise pick his way carefully over a rocky stretch and plunged into the brush again, leaning low in the saddle so that the higher branches would not claw at her hair and face.

When they had once more come into open ground, with a shoulder of Catrock Peak before them, Marian pulled up long enough to untie her apron and bind it over her hair like a peasant woman. She glanced back at Bud, and although darkness hid the expression on her face, he saw her eyes shining in the starlight. She raised her hand and beckoned, and Bud reined Sunfish close alongside.

"We're going into a spooky place now," she leaned toward him to whisper. "Boise knows the way, and your horse will follow."

"All right," Bud whispered back. "But you'd better tell me the way and let me go on alone. I'm pretty good at scouting out new trails. I don't want you to get in trouble — "

She would not listen to more of that, but pushed him back with the flat of her bare hand and rode ahead of him again. Straight at the sheer bluff, that lifted its huge, rocky shape before them, she led the way. So far as Bud could see she was not following any trail, but was aiming at a certain point and was sure enough of the ground to avoid detours.

They came out upon the bank of the dry river-bed. Bud knew it by the flatness of the foreground and the general contour of the mountains beyond. But immediately they turned at a sharp angle, travelled for a few minutes with the river-bed at their backs, and entered a narrow slit in the mountains where two peaks had been rent asunder in some titanic upheaval when the world was young. The horses scrambled along the rocky bottom for a little way, then Boise disappeared.

Sunfish halted, threw his head this way and that, gave a suspicious sniff and turned carefully around the corner of a square-faced boulder. In front was blackness. Bud urged him a little with rein and soft pressure of the spurs, and Sunfish stepped forward. He seemed reassured to find firm, smooth sand under his feet, and hurried a little until Boise was just ahead clicking his feet now and then against a rock.

"Coming?" Marian's voice sounded subdued, muffled by the close walls of the tunnel-like crevice.

"Coming," Bud assured her quietly "At your heels."

"I always used to feel spooky when I was riding through here," Marian said, dropping back so that they rode side by side, stirrups touching. "I was ten when I first made the trip. It was to get away from Indians. They would n't come into these places. Eddie and I found the way through. We were afraid they were after us, and so we kept going, and our horses brought us out. Eddie — is my brother."

"You grew up here?" Bud did not know how

much incredulity was in his voice. "I was raised amongst the Indians in Wyoming. I thought you were from the East."

"I was in Chicago for three years," Marian explained. "I studied every waking minute, I think. I wanted to be a singer. Then — I came home to help bury mother. Father — Lew and father were partners, and I — married Lew. I did n't know — it seemed as though I must. Father put it that way. The old story, Bud. I used to laugh at it in novels, but it does happen. Lew had a hold over father and Eddie, and he wanted me. I married him, but it did no good, for father was killed just a little more than a month afterwards. We had a ranch, up here in the Redwater Valley, about halfway to Crater. But it went — Lew gambled and drank and — so he took me to Little Lost. I 've been there for two years."

The words of pity — and more — that crowded forward for utterance, Bud knew he must not speak. So he said nothing at all.

"Lew has always held Eddie over my head," she went on pouring out her troubles to him. "There 's a gang, called the Catrock Gang, and Lew is one of them. I told you Lew is the man you shot. I think Dave Truman is in with them — at any rate he shuts his eyes to whatever goes on, and gets part of the stealings, I feel sure. That 's why Lew is such a favorite. You see, Eddie is one — I 'm trusting you with my life, almost, when I tell you this.

"But I could n't stand by and not lift a hand to save you. I knew they would kill you. They 'd have to, because I felt that you would fight and never give up. And you are too fine a man for those beasts to murder for the money you have. I knew, the minute I saw Jeff paying you his losings with a check, and some of the others doing the same, just what would happen. Jeff is almost as bad as the Catrockers, except that he is too cowardly to come out into the open. He gave you a check; and everyone who was there knew he would hurry up to Crater and stop payment on it, if he could do it and keep out of your sight. Those cronies of his would do the same — so they paid with checks.

"And the Catrock gang knew that. They mean to get hold of you, rob and — and — kill you, and forge the endorsement on the checks and let one man cash them in Crater before payment can be stopped. Indeed, the gang will see to it that Jeff stays away from Crater. Lew hinted that while they were about it they might as well clean out the bank. It would n't be the first time," she added bitterly.

She stopped then and asked for a match, and when Bud gave her one she lighted a candle and held it up so that she could examine the walls. "It 's a natural tunnel," she volunteered in a different tone. "Somewhere along here there is a branch that goes back into the hill and ends in a blow-hole. But we 're all right so far."

She blew out the candle and urged Boise forward, edging over to the right.

"Was n't that taking quite a chance, making a light?" Bud asked as they went on.

"It was, but not so great a chance as missing the way. Jerry did n't hear anything of them when he went to the pasture gate, and they may not come through this way at all. They may not realize at first that you have left, and even when they did they would not believe at first that you had gone to Crater. You see "— and in the darkness Bud could picture her troubled smile — "they think you are an awful fool, in some ways. The way you bet to-day was pure madness."

"It would have been, except that I knew I could win."

"They never bet like that. They always 'figure', as they call it, that the other fellow is going to play some trick on them. Half the time Jeff bets against his own horse, on the sly. They all do, unless they feel sure that their own trick is best."

"They should have done that to-day," Bud observed dryly. "But you've explained it. They thought I'm an awful fool."

Out of the darkness came Marian's voice. "It's because you're so different. They can't understand you."

Bud was not interested in his own foolishness just then. Something in her voice had thrilled him anew with a desire to help her and with the conviction that she was desperately in need of help. There was a pathetic patience in her tone when she summarized the whole affair in those last two sentences. It was as if she were telling him how her whole life was darkened because she herself was different — because they could not understand a woman so fine, so true and sweet.

"What will happen if you are missed? If you go back and discover Jerry's handkerchief on that bush, what will you do? You can't go back if they find out —" There was no need for him to finish that sentence.

" I don't know," said Marian, " what I shall do.   I
had n't thought much about it."

" I have n't thought much about anything else,"
Bud told her straightforwardly.   " If Jerry flags you,
you 'd better keep going.   Could n't you go to
friends ? "

" I could — if I had any.   Bud, you don't understand.   Eddie is the only relative I have on earth, that
I know at all.   He is — he 's with the Catrockers
and Lew dominates him completely.   Lew has pushed
Ed into doing things so that I must shield both or
neither.   And Eddie 's just a boy.   So I 've no one
at all."

Bud studied this while they rode on through the
defile that was more frequently a tunnel, since the
succession of caves always had an outlet which Marian
found.   She had stopped now and dismounted, and
they were leading their horses down a steep, scrambling place with the stars showing overhead.

" A blowhole," Marian informed him briefly.
" We 'll come into another cave, soon, and while it 's
safe if you know it, I 'll explain now that you must
walk ahead of your horse and keep your right hand
always in touch with the wall until we see the stars
again.   There 's a ledge — five feet wide in the nar-
rowest place, if you are nervous about ledges — and
if you should get off that you 'd have a drop of ten
feet or so.   We found that the ledge makes easier
travelling, because the bottom is full of rocks and
nasty depressions that are noticeable only with lights."

She started off again, and Bud followed her, his
gloved fingers touching the right wall, his soul hum-
bled before the greatness of this little woman with the

deep, troubled eyes. When they came out into the starlight she stopped and listened for what seemed to Bud a very long time.

"If they are coming, they are a long way behind us," she said relievedly, and remounted. "Boise knows this trail and has made good time. And your horse has proven beyond all doubt that he's a thoroughbred. I've seen horses balk at going where we have gone."

"And I've seen men who counted themselves brave as any, who would n't do what you are doing to-night; Jerry, for instance. I wish you'd go back. I can't bear having you take this risk."

"I can't go back, Bud. Not if they find I've gone." Then he heard her laugh quietly. "I can't imagine now why I stayed and endured it all this while. I think I only needed the psychological moment for rebellion, and to-night the moment came. So you see you have really done me a service by getting into this scrape. It's the first time I have been off the ranch in a year."

"If you call that doing you a service, I'm going to ask you to let me do something also for you." Bud half smiled to himself in the darkness, thinking how diplomatic he was. "If you're found out, you'll have to keep on going, and I take it you would n't be particular where you went. So I wish you'd take charge of part of this money for me, and if you leave, go down to my mother, on the Tomahawk ranch, out from Laramie. Anyone can tell you where it is, when you get down that way. If you need any money, use it. And tell mother I sent her the finest cook in the country. Mother, by the way, is a great musician, Marian. She taught me all I know of music. You'd get along just fine with mother. And she needs you, honest. She is n't very strong, yet she can't find anyone to suit, down there — "

"I might not suit, either," said Marian, her voice somewhat muffled.

"Oh, I'm not afraid of that. And — there's a message I want to send — I promised mother I'd — "

"Oh, hush! You're really an awfully poor prevaricator, Bud. This is to help me, you're planning."

"Well — it's to help me that I want you to take part of the money. The gang won't hold *you* up, will they? And I want mother to have it. I want her to have you, too, — to help out when company comes drifting in there, sometimes fifteen or twenty strong. Especially on Sunday. Mother has to wait on them and cook for them, and — as long as you are going to cook for a bunch, you may as well do it where it will be appreciated, and where you 'll be treated like a — like a lady ought to be treated."

"You're even worse — " began Marian, laughing softly, and stopped abruptly, listening, her head turned behind them. "Sh-sh — someone is coming behind us," she whispered. "We're almost through — come on, and don't talk!"

CHAPTER SEVENTEEN

Guardian Angels Are Riding " Point "

THEY plunged into darkness again, rode at a half trot over smooth, hard sand, Bud trusting himself wholly to Marian and to the sagacity of the two horses who could see, he hoped, much better than he himself could. His keen hearing had caught a faint sound from behind them — far back in the crevice-like gorge they had just quitted, he believed. For Marian's sake he stared anxiously ahead, eager for the first faint suggestion of starlight before them. It came, and he breathed freer and felt of his gun in its holster, pulling it forward an inch or two.

" This way, Bud," Marian murmured, and swung Boise to the left, against the mountain under and through which they seemed to have passed. She led him into another small gorge whose extent he could not see, and stopped him with a hand pressed against Sunfish's shoulder.

" We 'd better get down and hold our horses quiet," she cautioned. " Boise may try to whinny, and he must n't."

They stood side by side at their horses' heads, holding the animals close. For a time there were no sounds at all save the breathing of the horses and once a repressed sigh from Marian. Bud remembered suddenly how tired she must be. At six o'clock that morning she had fed twelve men a substantial breakfast. At noon there had been dinner for several more than twelve, and supper again at six — and here she was, risking her life when she should be in bed. He felt for her free hand, found it hanging listlessly by her side and took it in his own and held it there, just as one holds the hand of a timid child. Yet Marian was not timid.

A subdued mutter of voices, the click of hoofs striking against stone, and the pursuers passed within thirty feet of them. Boise had lifted his head to nicker a salute, but Marian's jerk on the reins stopped him. They stood very still, not daring so much as a whisper until the sounds had receded and silence came again.

"They took the side-hill trail," whispered Marian, pushing Boise backward to turn him in the narrow defile. "You'll have to get down the hill into the creek-bed and follow that until you come to the stage road. There may be others coming that way, but they will be two or three miles behind you. This tunnel trail cuts off at least five miles but we had to go slower, you see.

"Right here you can lead Sunfish down the bluff to the creek. It's all dry, and around the first bend you will see where the road crosses. Turn to the left on that and *ride!* This horse of yours will have to show the stuff that's in him. Get to Crater ahead of these men that took the hill trail. They'll not ride fast — they never dreamed you had come through here, but they came to cut off the distance and to head you off. With others behind, you must beat them all in or you'll be trapped between."

She had left Boise tied hastily to a bush and was walking ahead of Bud down the steep, rocky hillside to show him the easiest way amongst the boulders. Halfway down, Bud caught her shoulder and stopped her.

"I'm not a kid," he said firmly. "I can make it from here alone. Not another step, young lady. If you can get back home you'll be doing enough. Take this — it's money, but I don't know how much. And watch your chance and go down to mother with that message. Birnie, of the Tomahawk outfit — you'll find out in Laramie where to go. And tell mother I'm all right, and she'll see me some day — when I've made my stake. God bless you, little woman. You're the truest, sweetest little woman in the world. There's just one more like you — that's mother. Now go back — and for God's sake be careful!"

He pressed money into her two hands, held them tightly together, kissed them both hurriedly and plunged down the hill with Sunfish slipping and sliding after him. For her safety, if not for his own, he meant to get away from there as quickly as possible.

In the creek bed he mounted and rode away at a sharp gallop, glad that Sunfish, thoroughbred though he was, had not been raised tenderly in stall and corral, but had run free with the range horses and had learned to keep his feet under him in rough country or smooth. When he reached the crossing of the stage road he turned to the left as Marian had commanded and put Sunfish to a pace that slid the miles behind him.

With his thoughts clinging to Marian, to the harsh-

ness which life had shown her who was all goodness
and sweetness and courage, Bud forgot to keep careful
watch behind him, or to look for the place where the
hill trail joined the road, as it probably did some
distance from Crater. It would be a blind trail, of
course — since only the Catrock gang and Marian
knew of it.

They came into the road not far behind him, out of
rock-strewn, brushy wilderness that sloped up steeply
to the rugged sides of Gold Gap mountains. Sunfish
discovered them first, and gave Bud warning just before they identified him and began to shoot.

Bud laid himself along the shoulder of his horse
with a handful of mane to steady him while he watched
his chance and fired back at them. There were four,
just the number he had guessed from the sounds as
they came out of the tunnel. A horse ran staggering
toward him with the others, faltered and fell. Bud
was sorry for that. It had been no part of his plan to
shoot down the horses.

The three came on, leaving the fourth to his own
devices — and that, too, was quite in keeping with
the type of human vultures they were. They kept
firing at Bud, and once he felt Sunfish wince and leap
forward as if a spur had raked him. Bud shot again,
and thought he saw one horseman lurch backward.
But he could not be sure — they were going at a
terrific pace now, and Sunfish was leaving them farther and farther behind. They were outclassed, hope-
lessly out of pistol range, and they must have known
it, for although they held to the chase they fired no
more shots.

Then a dog barked, and Bud knew that he was

passing a ranch. He could smell the fresh hay in the stacks, and a moment later he descried the black hulk of ranch buildings. Sunfish was running easily, his breath unlabored. Bud stood in the stirrups and looked back. They were still coming, for he could hear the pound of hoofs.

The ranch was behind him. Clear starlight was all around, and the bulk of near mountains. The road seemed sandy, yielding beneath the pound of Sunfish's hoofs. Bud leaned forward again in the saddle, and planned what he would do when he reached Crater; found time, also, to hope that Marian had gone back, and had not heard the shooting.

Another dog barked, this time on the right. Bud saw that they were passing a picket fence. The barking of this dog started another farther ahead and to the left. Houses so close together could only mean that he was approaching Crater. Bud began to pull Sunfish down to a more conventional pace. He did not particularly want to see heads thrust from windows, and questions shouted to him. The Catrock gang might have friends up this way. It would be strange, Bud thought, if they had n't.

He loped along the road grown broader now and smoother. Many houses he passed, and the mouths of obscure lanes. Dogs ran out at him. Bud slowed to a walk and turned in the saddle, listening. Away back, where he had first met the signs of civilization, the dog he had aroused was barking again, his deep baying blurred by the distance. Bud grinned to himself and rode on at a walk, speaking now and then to an inquiring dog and calling him Purp in a tone that soothed.

Crater, he discovered in a cursory patrol of the place, was no more than an overgrown village. The court-house and jail stood on the main street, and just beyond was the bank. Bud rode here and there, examining closely the fronts of various buildings before he concluded that there was only the one bank in Crater. When he was quite sure of that he chose a place near by the rear of the bank, where one horse and a cow occupied a comfortable corral together, with hay. He unsaddled Sunfish and turned him in there, himself returning to the bank before those other night-riders had more than reached the first straggling suburbs of the town.

On the porch of the court-house, behind a jutting corner pillar that seemed especially designed for the concealment of a man in Bud's situation, he rolled a cigarette which he meant to smoke later on when the way was clear, and waited for the horsemen to appear.

Presently they came, rode to a point opposite the court-house and bank with no more than a careless glance that way, and halted in front of an uninviting hotel across the street. Two remained on their horses while the third pounded on the door and shook it by the knob and finally raised the landlord from his sleep. There was a conference which Bud witnessed with much interest. A lamp had been lighted in the bare office, and against the yellow glow Bud distinctly saw the landlord nod his head twice — which plainly betokened some sort of understanding.

He was glad that he had not stopped at the hotel. He felt much more comfortable on the court-house porch. "Mother's guardian angels must be riding 'point' to-night," he mused.

The horsemen rode back to a livery stable which Bud had observed but had not entered. There they also sought for news of him, it would appear. You will recall, however, that Bud had ridden slowly into the business district of Crater, and his passing had been unmarked except by the barking of dogs that spent their nights in yammering at every sound and so were never taken seriously. The three horsemen were plainly nonplussed and conferred together in low tones before they rode on. It was evident that they meant to find Bud if they could. What they meant to do with him Bud did not attempt to conjecture. He did not intend to be found.

After a while the horsemen rode back to the hotel, got the landlord out with less difficulty than before and had another talk with him.

" He stole a horse from Dave Truman," Bud heard one of the three say distinctly. " That there running horse Dave had."

The landlord tucked in his shirt and exclaimed at the news, and Bud heard him mention the sheriff. But nothing came of that evidently. They talked further and reined their horses to ride back whence they came.

" He likely 's give us the slip outside of town, some place," one man concluded. " We 'll ride back and see. If he shows up, he 'll likely want to eat. . . . And send Dick out to the Stivers place. We 'll come a-running." He had lowered his voice so that Bud could not hear what was to happen before the landlord sent Dick, but he decided he would not pry into the matter and try to fill that gap in the conversation.

He sat where he was until the three had ridden back

down the sandy road which served as a street. Then he slipped behind the court-house and smoked his cigarette, and went and borrowed hay from the cow and the horse in the corral and made himself some sort of bed with his saddle blanket to help out, and slept until morning.

CHAPTER EIGHTEEN

THE CATROCK GANG

A WOMAN with a checkered apron and a motherly look came to let her chickens out and milk the cow, and woke Bud so that she could tell him she believed he had been on a " toot ", or he never would have taken such a liberty with her corral. Bud agreed to the toot, and apologized, and asked for breakfast. And the woman, after one good look at him, handed him the milk bucket and asked him how he liked his eggs.

" All the way from barn to breakfast," Bud grinned, and the woman chuckled and called him Smarty, and told him to come in as soon as the cow was milked.

Bud had a great breakfast with the widow Hanson. She talked, and Bud learned a good deal about Crater and its surroundings, and when he spoke of holdup gangs she seemed to know immediately what he meant, and told him a great deal more about the Catrockers than Marian had done. Everything from murdering and robbing a peddler to looting the banks at Crater and Lava was laid to the Catrockers. They were the human buzzards that watched over the country and swooped down wherever there was money. The sheriff could n't do anything with them, and no one expected him to, so far as Bud could discover.

He hesitated a long time before he asked about
Marian Morris. Mrs. Hanson wept while she related
Marian's history, which in substance was exactly what
Marian herself had told Bud. Mrs. Hanson, however, told how Marian had fought to save her father
and Ed, and how she had married Lew Morris as a
part of her campaign for honesty and goodness. Now
she was down at Little Lost cooking for a gang of
men, said Mrs. Hanson, when she ought to be out in
the world singing for thousands and her in silks and
diamonds instead of gingham dresses and not enough
of them.

" Marian Collier is the sweetest thing that ever
grew up in this country," the old lady sniffled. " She 's
one in a thousand and when she was off to school
she showed that she was n't no common trash. She
wanted to be an opery singer, but then her mother
died and Marian done what looked to be her duty. A
bird in a trap is what I call her."

Bud regretted having opened the subject, and
praised the cooking by way of turning his hostess's
thoughts into a different channel. He asked her if
she would accept him as a boarder while he was in
town, and was promptly accepted.

He did not want to appear in public until the bank
was opened, and he was a bit troubled over identifica-
tion. There could be no harm, he reflected, in con-
fiding to Mrs. Hanson as much as was necessary of
his adventures. Wherefore he dried the dishes for
her and told her his errand in town, and why it was
that he and his horse had slept in her corral instead of
patronizing hotel and livery stable. He showed
her the checks he wanted to cash, and asked her, with

a flattering eagerness for her advice, what he should do. He had been warned, he said, that Jeff and his friends might try to beat him yet by stopping payment, and he knew that he had been followed by them to town.

"What you'll do will be what I tell ye," Mrs. Hanson replied with decision. "The cashier is a friend to me — I was with his wife last month with her first baby, and they swear by me now, for I gave her good care. We'll go over there this minute, and have a talk with him. He'll do what he can for ye, and he'll do it for my sake."

"You don't know me, remember," Bud reminded her honestly.

The widow Hanson gave him a scornful smile and a toss of her head. "And do I not?" she demanded. "Do you think I've buried three husbands and thinking now of the fourth, without knowing what's wrote in a man's face? Three I buried, and only one died in his bed. I can tell if a man's honest or not, without giving him the second look. If you've got them checks you should get the money on them — for I know their stripe. Come on with me to Jimmy Lawton's house. He's likely holding the baby while Minnie does the dishes."

Mrs. Hanson guessed shrewdly. The cashier of the Crater County Bank was doing exactly what she said he would be doing. He was sitting in the kitchen, rocking a pink baby wrapped in white outing flannel with blue border, when Mrs. Hanson, without the formality of more than one warning tap on the screen door, walked in with Bud. She held out her hands for the baby while she introduced the cashier to Bud. In the next breath she was explaining what was wanted of the bank.

"They've done it before, and ye know it's plain thievery and ought to be complained about. So now get your wits to work, Jimmy, for this friend of mine is entitled to his money and should have it if it's there to be had."

"Oh, it's there," said Jimmy. He looked at his watch, looked at the kitchen clock, looked at Bud and winked. "We open at nine, in this town," he said. "It lacks half an hour — but let me see those checks."

Very relievedly Bud produced them, watched the cashier scan each one to make sure that they were right, and quaked when Jimmy scowled at Jeff Hall's signature on the largest check of all. "He had a notion to use the wrong signature, but he may have lost his nerve. It's all right, Mr. Birnie. Just endorse these, and I'll take them into the bank and attend to them the first thing I do after the door is open. You'd better come in when I open up —"

"The gang had some talk about cleaning out the bank while they're about it," Bud remembered suddenly. "Can't you appoint me something, or hire me as a guard and let me help out? How many men do you have here in this bank?"

"Two, except when the president's in his office in the rear. That's fine of you to offer. We've been held up, once — and they cleaned us out of cash." Jimmy turned to Mrs. Hanson. "Mother, can't you run over and have Jess come and swear Mr. Birnie in as a deputy? If I go, or he goes, someone may notice it and tip the gang off."

Mrs. Hanson hastily deposited the baby in its cradle

and went to call "Jess", her face pink with excitement.

"You're lucky you stopped at her house instead of some other place," Jimmy observed. "She's a corking good woman. As a deputy sheriff, you'll come in mighty handy if they do try anything, Mr. Birnie — if you're the kind of a man you look to be. I'll bet you can shoot. Can you?"

"If you scare me badly enough, I might get a cramp in my trigger finger," Bud confessed. Jimmy grinned and went back to considering his own part.

"I'll cash these checks for you the first thing I do. And as deputy you can go with me. I'll have to unlock the door on time, and if they mean to stop payment, and clean the bank too, it will probably be done all at once. It has been a year since they bothered us, so they may need a little change. If Jess isn't busy he may stick around."

"No one expects him to round up the gang, I heard."

"No one expects him to go into Catrock Canyon after them. He'll round them up, quick enough, if he can catch them far enough from their holes."

Jess returned with Mrs. Hanson, swore in a new deputy, eyed Bud curiously, and agreed to remain hidden across the road from the bank with a rifle. He nodded understandingly when Bud warned him that the looting was a matter of hearsay on his part, and departed with an awkward compliment to Mrs. Jim about hoping that the baby was going to look like her.

Jim lived just behind the bank, and a high board fence between the two buildings served to hide his coming and going. But Bud took off his hat and walked stooping, — by special request of Mrs. Hanson — to make sure that he was not observed.

"I think I'll stand out in front of the window," said Bud when they were inside. "It will look more natural, and if any of these fellows show up I'd just as soon not show my brand the first thing."

They showed up, all right, within two minutes of the unlocking of the bank and the rolling up of the shades. Jeff Hall was the first man to walk in, and he stopped short when he saw Bud lounging before the teller's window and the cashier busy within. Other men were straggling up on the porch, and two of them entered. Jeff walked over to Bud, who shifted his position enough to bring him facing Jeff, whom he did not trust at all.

"Mr. Lawton," Jeff began hurriedly, "I want to stop payment on a check this young feller got from me by fraud. It's for five thousand eight hundred dollars, and I notify you — "

"Too late, Mr. Hall. I have already accepted the checks. Where did the fraud come in? You can bring suit, of course, to recover."

"I'll tell you, Jimmy. He bet that my horse could n't beat Dave Truman's Boise. A good many bet on the same thing. But my horse proved to have more speed, so a lot of them are sore." Bud chuckled as other Sunday losers came straggling in.

"Well, it's too late. I have honored the checks," Jimmy said crisply, and turned to hand a sealed manila envelope to the bookkeeper with whispered instructions. The bookkeeper, who had just entered from the rear of the office, turned on his heel and left again.

Jeff muttered something to his friends and went outside as if their business were done for the day.

"I gave you five thousand in currency and the balance in a cashier's check," Jimmy whispered through the wicket. "Sent it to the house. We don't keep a great deal — ten thousand's our limit in cash, and I don't think you want to pack gold or silver — "

"No, I didn't. I'd rather — "

Two men came in, one going over to the desk where he apparently wrote a check, the other came straight to the window. Bud looked into the heavily bearded face of a man who had the eyes of Lew Morris. He shifted his position a little so that he faced the man's right side. The one at the desk was glancing slyly over his shoulder at the bookkeeper, who had just returned to his work.

"Can you change this twenty so I can get seven dollars and a quarter out of it?" asked the man at the window. As he slid the bill through the wicket he started to sneeze, and reached backward — for his handkerchief, apparently.

"Here's one," said Bud. "Don't sneeze too hard, old-timer, or you're liable to sneeze your whiskers all off. It's happened before."

Someone outside fired a shot in at Bud, clipping his hatband in front. At the sound of the shot the whiskered one snatched his gun out, and the cashier shot him. Bud had sent a shot through the outside window and hit somebody — whom, he did not know, for he had no time to look. The young fellow at the desk had whirled, and was pointing a gun shakily, first at the cashier and then at Bud. Bud fired and knocked the gun out of his hand, then stepped over the man he suspected was Lew and caught the young fellow by the wrist.

"You're Ed Collier — by your eyes and your mouth," Bud said in a rapid undertone. "I'm going to get you out of this, if you'll do what I say. Will you?"

"He got me in here, honest," the young fellow quaked. He couldn't be more than nineteen, Bud guessed swiftly.

"Let me through, Jimmy," Bud ordered hurriedly. "You got the man that put up this job. I'll take the kid out the back way, if you don't mind."

Jimmy opened the steel-grilled door and let them through.

"Ed Collier," he said in a tone of recognition. "I heard he was trailing — "

"Forget it, Jimmy. If the sheriff asks about him, say he got out. Now, Ed, I'm going to take you over to Mrs. Hanson's. She'll keep an eye on you for a while."

Eddie was looking at the dead man on the floor, and trembling so that he did not attempt to reply; and by way of Jimmy's back fence and the widow Hanson's barn and corral, Bud got Eddie safe into the kitchen just as that determined lady was leaving home with a shotgun to help defend the honor of the town.

Bud took her by the shoulder and told her what he wanted her to do. "He's Marian's brother, and too young to be with that gang. So keep him here, safe and out of sight, until I come. Then I'll want to borrow your horse. Shall I tie the kid?"

"And me an able-bodied woman that could turn him acrost my knee?" Mrs. Hanson's eyes snapped.

" It 's more likely the boy needs his breakfast. Get along with ye! "

Bud got along, slipping into the bank by the rear door and taking a hand in the desultory firing in the street. The sheriff had a couple of men ironed and one man down and the landlord of the hotel was doing a great deal of explaining that he had never seen the bandits before. Just by way of stimulating his memory Bud threw a bullet close to his heels, and the landlord thereupon grovelled and wept while he protested his innocence.

" He 's a damn liar, sheriff," Bud called across the hoof-scarred road. " He was talking to them about eleven o'clock last night. There were three that chased me into town, and they got him up out of bed to find out whether I 'd stopped there. I had n't, luckily for me. If I had he 'd have showed them the way to my room, and he 'd have had a dead boarder this morning. Keep right on shedding tears, you old cut-throat! I was sitting on the court-house porch, last night, and I heard every word that passed between you and the Catrockers! "

" I 've been suspicioning here was where they got their information right along," the sheriff commented, and slipped the handcuffs on the landlord. Investigation proved that Jeff Hall and his friends had suddenly decided that they had no business with the bank that day, and had mounted and galloped out of town when the first shot was fired. Which simplified matters a bit for Bud.

In Jimmy Lawton's kitchen he received his money, and when the prisoners were locked up he saved himself some trouble with the sheriff by hunting him up and explaining just why he had taken the Collier boy into custody.

"You know yourself he's just a kid, and if you send him over the road he's a criminal for life. I believe I can make a decent man of him. I want to try, anyway. So you just leave me this deputy's badge, and make my commission regular and permanent, and I'll keep an eye on him. Give me a paper so I can get a requisition and bring him back to stand trial, any time he breaks out. I'll be responsible for him, sheriff."

"And who in blazes are you?" the sheriff inquired, with a grin to remove the sting of suspicion. "Name sounded familiar, too!"

"Bud Birnie of the Tomahawk, down near Laramie. Telegraph Laramie if you like and find out about me."

"Good Lord! I know the Tomahawk like a book!" cried the sheriff. "And you're Bob Birnie's boy! Say! D'you remember dragging into camp on the summit one time when you was about twelve years old — been hidin' out from Injuns about three days? Well, say! I'm the feller that packed you into the tent, and fed yuh when yuh come to. Remember the time I rode down and stayed over night at yore place, the time Bill Nye come down from his prospect hole up in the Snowies, bringin' word the Injuns was up again?" The sheriff grabbed Bud's hand and held it, shaking it up and down now and then to emphasize his words.

"Folks called you Buddy, then. I remember yuh, helpin' your mother cook 'n' wash dishes for us fellers. I kinda felt like I had a claim on yuh, Buddy.

" Say, Bill Nye, he 's famous now. Writin' books full of jokes, and all that. He always was a comical cuss. Don't you remember how the bunch of us laughed at him when he drifted in about dark, him and four burros — that one he called Boomerang, that he named his paper after in Laramie? I 've told lots of times what he said when he come stoopin' into the kitchen — how Colorou had sent him word that he 'd give Bill just four sleeps to get outa there. An, ' Hell! ' says Bill. ' I did n't need *any* sleeps! ' An' we all turned to and cooked a hull beef yore dad had butchered that day — and Bill loaded up with the first chunks we had ready, and pulled his freight. He sure *did n't* need any sleeps — "

" Yes, you bet I remember. Jesse Cummings is your name. I sure ought to remember you, for you and your partner saved my life, I expect. I thought I 'd seen you before, when you made me deputy. How about the kid? Can I have him? Lew Morris, the man that kept him on the wrong side of the law, is dead, I heard the doctor say. Jimmy got him when he pulled his gun."

" Why, yes — if the town don't git onto me turnin' him loose, I guess you can have the kid for all I care. He did n't take any part in the holdup, did he, Buddy? "

" He was over by the customers' desk when Lew started to hold up the cashier."

" Well I got enough prisoners so I guess he won't be missed. But you look out how yuh git him outa town. Better wait til kinda late to-night. I sure would like to see him git a show. Them two Collier kids never did have a square deal, far as I 've heard.

But be careful, youngster. I want another term off this county if I can get it. Don't go get me in bad."

"I won't," Bud promised and hurried back to Mrs. Hanson's house.

That estimable lady was patting butter in a wooden bowl when Bud went in. She turned and brushed a wisp of gray hair from her face with her fore arm and sh-shed him into silent stepping, motioning toward an inner room. Bud tiptoed and looked, saw Ed Collier fast asleep, swaddled in a blanket, and grinned his approval.

He made sure that the sleep was genuine, also that the blanket swaddling was efficient. Moreover, he discovered that Mrs. Hanson had very prudently attached a thin wire to the foot of the blanket cocoon, had passed the wire through a knot hole in a cupboard set into the partition, and to a sheep bell which she no doubt expected to ring upon provocation — such as a prisoner struggling to release his feet from a gray blanket fastened with many large safety pins.

"He went right to sleep, the minute I'd fed him and tied him snug," Mrs. Hanson murmured. "He was a sulky divvle and wouldn't give a decent answer to me till he had his stomach filled. From the way he waded into the ham and eggs, I guess a square meal and him has been strangers for a long time."

Sleep and Ed Collier must have been strangers also, for Bud attended the inquest of Lew Morris, visited afterwards with Sheriff Cummings, who was full of reminiscence and wanted to remind Bud of everything that had ever happened within his knowledge during the time when they had been neighbors with no more than forty miles or so between them. The sheriff offered

Bud a horse and saddle, which he promised to deliver to the widow's corral after the citizens of Crater had gone to bed. And while he did not say that it would be Ed's horse, Bud guessed shrewdly that it would. After that, Bud carefully slit the lining of his boots, tucked money and checks into the opening he had made, and did a very neat repair job.

All that while Ed Collier slept. When Bud returned for his supper Ed had evidently just awakened and was lying on his back biting his lip while he eyed the wire that ran from his feet to the parting of a pair of calico curtains. He did not see Bud, who was watching him through a crack in the door at the head of the bed. Ed was plainly puzzled at the wire and a bit resentful. He lifted his feet until the wire was well slackened, held them poised for a minute and deliberately brought them down hard on the floor.

The result was all that he could possibly have expected. Somewhere was a vicious clang, the rattle of a tin pan and the approaching outcry of a woman. Bud retreated to the kitchen to view the devastation and discovered that a sheep bell not too clean had been dislodged from a nail and dragged through one pan of milk into another, where it was rolling on its edge, stirring the cream that had risen. As Mrs. Hanson rushed in from the back yard, Bud returned to the angry captive's side.

"I've got him safe," he soothed Mrs. Hanson and her shotgun. "He just had a nightmare. Perhaps that breakfast you fed him was too hearty. I'll look after him now, Mrs. Hanson. We won't be bothering you long, anyway."

Mrs. Hanson was talking to herself when she went

to her milk pans, and Bud released Eddie Collier, guessing how humiliating it must be to be a young fellow pinned into a blanket with safety pins, and knowing from certain experiences of his own that humiliation is quite as apt to breed trouble as any other emotion.

Eddie sat up on the edge of the bed and stared at Bud. His eyes were like Marian's in shape and color, but their expression was suspicion, defiance, and watchfulness blended into one compelling stare that spelled Fear. Or so Bud read it, having trapped animals of various grades ever since he had caught the " *hawn-toe* ", and seen that look many, many times in the eyes of his catch.

" How'd you like to take a trip with me — as a kind of a partner? " Bud began carelessly, pulling a splinter off the homemade bed for which Mrs. Hanson would not thank him — and beginning to whittle it to a sharp point aimlessly, as men have a way of doing when their minds are at work upon a problem which requires much constructive thinking.

" Pardner in what? " Eddie countered sullenly.

" Pardner in what I am planning to do to make money. I *can* make money, you know — and stay on friendly terms with the sheriff, too. That's better than your bunch has been able to do. I don't mind telling you — it's stale news, I guess — that I cleaned up close to twelve thousand dollars in less than a month, off a working capital of three thoroughbred horses and about sixty dollars cash. And I'll add the knowledge that I was playing against men that would slip a cold deck if they played solitaire, they were so crooked. And if that does n't recommend me sufficiently, I'll say I'm a deputy sheriff of Crater County, and Jesse

Cummings knows my past. I want to hire you to go with me and make some money, and I 'll pay you forty a month and five per cent bonus on my profits at the. end of two years. The first year may not show any profits, but the second year will. How does it sound to you?"

He had been rolling a cigarette, and now he offered the "makings" to Ed, who accepted them mechanically, his eyes still staring hard at Bud. He glanced toward the door and the one little window where wild cucumber vines were thickly matted, and Bud interpreted his glance.

"Lew and another Catrocker — the one that tried to rope me down in the Sinks — are dead, and three more are in jail. Business won't be very brisk with the Catrock gang for a while."

"If you 're trying to bribe me into squealing on the rest, you 're a damn fool," said Eddie harshly. "I ain't the squealing kind. You can lead me over to jail first. I 'd rather take my chances with the others." He was breathing hard when he finished.

"Rather than work for me?" Bud sliced off the sharp point which he had so carefully whittled, and began to sharpen a new one. Eddie watched him fascinatedly.

"Rather than squeal on the bunch. There 's no other reason in God's world why you 'd make me an offer like that. I ain't a fool quite, if my head does run up to a peak."

Bud chewed his lip, whittled, and finally threw the splinter away. When he turned toward Eddie his eyes were shiny.

"Kid, you 're breaking your sister's heart, follow-

ing this trail. I'd like to see you give her a chance
to speak your name without blinking back tears. I'd
like to see her smile all the way from her dimples to
her eyes when she thinks of you. That's why I made
the offer — that and because I think you'd earn your
wages."

Eddie looked at him, looked away, staring vacantly
at the wall. His eyelashes were blinking very fast,
his lip began to tremble. "You — I — I never wanted
to — I ain't worth saving — oh, hell! I never had a
chance before — " He dropped sidewise on the bed,
buried his face in his arms and sobbed hoarsely, like
the boy he was.

CHAPTER NINETEEN

Bud Rides Through Catrock and Loses Marian

"You'll have to show me the trail, pardner," said Bud when they were making their way cautiously out of town by way of the tin can suburbs. "I could figure out the direction all right, and make it by morning; but seeing you grew up here, I'll let you pilot."

"You'll have to tell me where you want to go, first," said Eddie with a good deal of sullenness still in his voice.

"Little Lost." Without intending to do so, Bud put a good deal of meaning in his voice.

Eddie did not say anything, but veered to the right, climbing higher on the slope than Bud would have gone. "We can take the high trail," he volunteered when they stopped to rest the horses. "It takes up over the summit and down Burroback Valley. It's longer, but the stage road edges along the Sinks and — it might be rough going, after we get down a piece."

"How about the side-hill trail, through Catrock Peak?"

Eddie turned sharply. In the starlight Bud was watching him, wondering what he was thinking.

"How'd you get next to any side-hill trail?" Eddie asked after a minute. "You been over it?"

" I surely have. And I expect to go again, to-night. A young fellow about your size is going to act as pilot, and get me to Little Lost as quick as possible. It 'll be daylight at that."

" If you got another day coming, it better be before daylight we get there," Eddie retorted glumly. He hesitated, turned his horse and led the way down the slope, angling down away from the well-travelled trail over the summit of Gold Gap.

That hesitation told Bud, without words, how tenuous was his hold upon Eddie. He possessed sufficient imagination to know that his own carefully disciplined past, sheltered from actual contact with evil, had given him little enough by which to measure the soul of a youth like Eddie Collier.

How long Eddie had supped and slept with thieves and murderers, Bud could only guess. From the little that Marian had told him, Eddie's father had been one of the gang. At least, she had plainly stated that he and Lew had been partners — though Collier might have been ranching innocently enough, and ignorant of Lew's real nature.

At all events, Eddie was a lad well schooled in iniquity such as the wilderness fosters in sturdy fashion. Wide spaces give room for great virtues and great wickedness. Bud felt that he was betting large odds on an unknown quantity. He was placing himself literally in the hands of an acknowledged Catrocker, because of the clean gaze of a pair of eyes, the fine curve of the mouth.

For a long time they rode without speech. Eddie in the lead, Bud following, alert to every little movement in the sage, every little sound of the night. That was what we rather naïvely call "second nature", a habit born of Bud's growing years amongst dangers which every pioneer family knows. Alert he was, yet deeply dreaming; a tenuous dream too sweet to come true, he told himself; a dream which he never dared to dream until the cool stars, and the little night wind began to whisper to him that Marian was free from the brute that had owned her. He scarcely dared think of it yet. Shyly he remembered how he had held her hand to give her courage while they rode in darkness; her poor work-roughened little hand, that had been cold when he took it first, and had warmed in his clasp. He remembered how he had pressed her hands together when they parted — why, surely it was longer ago than last night! — and had kissed them reverently as he would kiss the fingers of a queen.

"Hell's too good for Lew Morris," he blurted unexpectedly, the thought of Marian's bruised cheek coming like a blow.

"Want to go and tell him so? If you don't yuh better shut up," Eddie whispered fierce warning. "You need n't think all the Catrockers are dead or in jail. They's a few left and they'd kill yuh quicker 'n they'd take a drink."

Bud, embarrassed at the emotion behind his statement, rather than ashamed of the remark itself, made no reply.

Much as Eddie desired silence, he himself pulled up and spoke again when Bud had ridden close.

"I guess you come through the Gap," he whispered. "They's a shorter way than that — Sis don't know it. It's one the bunch uses a lot — if they catch us — I can save my hide by makin' out I led you into a trap. You'll get yours, anyway. How much sand you got?"

Bud leaned and spat into the darkness. "Not much. Maybe enough to get through this scary short-cut of yours."

"You tell the truth when you say scary. It's so darn crazy to go down Catrock Canyon maybe they won't think we'd tackle it. And if they catch us, I'll say I led yuh in — and then — say, I'm kinda bettin' on your luck. The way you cleaned up on them horses, maybe luck'll stay with you. And I'll help all I can, honest."

"Fine." Bud reached over and closed his fingers around Eddie's thin, boyish arm. "You didn't tell me yet why the other trail isn't good enough."

"I heard a sound in the Gap tunnel, that's why. You maybe didn't know what it was. I know them echoes to a fare-ye-well. Somebody's there — likely posted waiting." He was motionless for a space, listening.

"Get off — easy. Take off your spurs." Eddie was down, whispering eagerly to Bud. "There's a draft of air from the blow-holes that comes this way. Sound comes outa there a lot easier than it goes in. Sis and I found that out. Lead your horse — if they jump us, give him a lick with the quirt and hide in the brush."

Like Indians the two made their way down a rambling slope not far from where Marian had guided Bud. To-night, however, Eddie led the way to the right instead of the left, which seemed to Bud a direction that would bring them down Oldman creek, that dry river bed, and finally, perhaps, to the race track.

Eddie never did explain just how he made his way through a maze of water-cut pillars and heaps of sandstone so bewildering that Bud afterward swore that in spite of the fact that he was leading Sunfish, he frequently found himself at that patient animal's tail, where they were doubled around some freakish pillar. Frequently Eddie stopped and peered past his horse to make sure that Bud had not lost the trail. And finally, because he was no doubt worried over that possibility, he knotted his rope to his saddle horn, brought back a length that reached a full pace behind the tail of the horse, and placed the end in Bud's hand.

"If yuh lose me you're a goner," he whispered. "So hang onto that, no matter what comes. And don't yuh speak to me. This is hell's corral and we're walking the top rail right now." He made sure that Bud had the loop in his hand, then slipped back past his horse and went on, walking more quickly.

Bud admitted afterwards that he was perfectly willing to be led like a tame squirrel around the top of "hell's corral", whatever that was. All that Bud saw was an intricate assembly of those terrific pillars, whose height he did not know, since he had no time to glance up and estimate the distance. There was no method, no channel worn through in anything that could be called a line. Whatever primeval torrent had honeycombed the ledge had left it so before ever its waters had formed a straight passage through. How Eddie knew the way he could only conjecture, remembering how he himself had ridden devious trails down on the Tomahawk range when he was a boy. It rather hurt his pride to realize that never had he seen anything approaching this madman's trail.

Without warning they plunged into darkness again. Darkness so black that Bud knew they had entered another of those mysterious, subterranean passages which had created such names as abounded in the country: the " Sinks ", " Little Lost ", and Sunk River itself which disappeared mysteriously. He was beginning to wonder with a grim kind of humor if he himself was not about to follow the example of the rivers and disappear, when the soft padding of their footfalls blurred under the whistling of wind. Fine particles of sand stung him, a blast full against him halted him for a second. But the rope pulled steadily and he went on, half dragged into starlight again.

They were in a canyon; deep, sombre in its night shadows, its width made known to him by the strip of starlight overhead. Directly before them, not more than a hundred yards, a light shone through a window.

The rope slackened in his hands, and Eddie slipped back to him shivering a little as Bud discovered when he laid a hand on his arm.

" I guess I better tie yuh — but it won't be so yuh can't shoot. Get on, and let me tie your feet into the stirrups. I — I guess maybe we can get past, all right — I 'll try — I want to go and take that job you said you 'd give me! "

" What 's the matter, son? Is that where the Cat-rockers hang out? " Bud swung into the saddle. " I trust you, kid. You 're her brother."

" I — I want to live like Sis wants me to. But I 've got to tie yuh, Mr. Birnie, and that looks — But they 'd k— you don't know how they kill traitors. I saw one — " He leaned against Bud's leg, one hand reaching up to the saddle horn and gripping it in a passing frenzy. "If you say so," he whispered rapidly, "we 'll sneak up and shoot 'em through the window before they get a chance —"

Bud reached out his hand and patted Eddie on the shoulder. "That job of yours don't call for any killing we can avoid," he said. "Go ahead and tie me. No use of wasting lead on two men when one will do. It 's all right. I trust you, pardner."

Eddie's shoulders stiffened. He stood up, looked toward the light and gripped Bud's hand. "I thought they 'd be asleep — what was home," he said. "We got to ride past the cabin to get out through another water-wash. But you take your coat and tie your horse's feet, and I 'll tie mine. I — can't tie you, Mr. Birnie. We 'll chance it together."

Bud did not say anything at all, for which Eddie seemed grateful. They muffled eight hoofs, rode across the canyon's bottom and passed the cabin so closely that the light of a smoky lantern on a table was plainly visible to Bud, as was the shaggy profile of a man who sat with his arms folded, glowering over a pipe. He heard nothing. Bud halted Sunfish and looked again to make sure, while Eddie beckoned frantically. They went on undisturbed — the Catrockers kept no dogs.

They passed a couple of corrals, rode over springy sod where Bud dimly discerned hay stubble. Eddie let down a set of bars, replaced them carefully, and they crossed another meadow. It struck Bud that the Catrockers were fairly well entrenched in their canyon, with plenty of horse feed at least.

They followed a twisting trail along the canyon's wall, rode into another pit of darkness, came out into

a sandy stretch that seemed hazily familiar to Bud.
They crossed this, dove into the bushes following a
dim trail, and in ten minutes Eddie's horse backed
suddenly against Sunfish's nose. Bud stood in his
stirrups, reins held firmly in his left hand, and in his
right his six-shooter with the hammer lifted, ready to
snap down.

A tall figure stepped away from the peaked rocks and
paused at Bud's side.

"I been waiting for Marian," he said bluntly. "You
know anything about her?"

"She turned back last night after she had shown
me the way." Bud's throat went dry. "Did they
miss her?" He leaned aggressively.

"Not till breakfast time, they did n't. I was waiting here, most all night — except right after you folks
left. She was n't missed, and I never flagged her —
and she ain't showed up yet!"

Bud sat there stunned, trying to think what might
have happened. Those dark passages through the
mountains — the ledge — "Ed, you know that trail
she took me over? She was coming back that way.
She could get lost —"

"No she could n't — not Sis. If her horse did n't
act the fool — what horse was it she rode?" Ed
turned to Jerry as if he would know.

"Boise," Bud spoke quickly, as though seconds were
precious. "She said he knew the way."

"He sure ought to," Eddie replied emphatically.
"Boise belongs to Sis, by rights. The mare got killed
and Dad gave him to Sis when he was a suckin' colt,
and Sis raised him on cow's milk and broke him herself. She rode him all over. Lew took and sold him

to Dave, and gambled the money, and Sis never signed no bill of sale. They could n't make her. Sis has got spunk, once you stir her up. She 'll tackle anything. She 's always claimed Boise is hers. Boise knows the Gap like a book. Sis could n't get off the trail if she rode him."

"Something happened, then," Bud muttered stubbornly. "Four men came through behind us, and we waited out in the dark to let them pass. Then she sent me down to the creek-bottom, and she turned back. If they got her —" He turned Sunfish in the narrow brush trail. "She 's hurt, or they got her — I 'm going back!" he said grimly.

"Hell! you can't do any good alone," Eddie protested, coming after him. "We 'll go look for her, Mr. Birnie, but we 've got to have something so we can see. If Jerry could dig up a couple of lanterns —"

"You wait. I 'm coming along," Jerry called guardedly. "I 'll bring lanterns."

To Bud that time of waiting was torment. He had faced danger and tragedy since he could toddle, and fear had never overridden the titillating sense of adventure. But then the danger had been for himself. Now terror conjured pictures whose horror set him trembling. Twenty-four hours and more had passed since he had kissed Marian's hand and let her go — to what? The inky blackness of those tunnelled caverns in the Gap confronted his mind like a nightmare. He could not speak of it — he dared not think of it, and yet he must.

Jerry came on horseback, with three unlighted lanterns held in a cluster by their wire handles. Eddie immediately urged his horse into the brushy edge of

the trail so that he might pass Bud and take the lead.
"You sure made quick time," he remarked approvingly to Jerry.

"I raided Dave's cache of whiskey or I'd have been here quicker," Jerry explained. "We might need some."

Bud gritted his teeth. "*Ride,* why don't yuh?" he urged Eddie harshly. "What the hell ails that horse of yours? You got him hobbled?"

Eddie glanced back over his bobbing shoulder as his horse trotted along the blind trail through the brush. "This here ain't no race track," he expostulated. "We'll make it quicker without no broken legs."

There was justice in his protest and Bud said nothing. But Sunfish's head bumped the tail of Eddie's horse many times during that ride. Once in the Gap, with a lighted lantern in his rein hand and his six-shooter in the other — because it was ticklish riding, in there with lights revealing them to anyone who might be coming through — he was content to go slowly, peering this way and that as he rode.

Once Eddie halted and turned to speak to them. "I know Boise wouldn't leave the trail. If Sis had to duck off and hide from somebody, he'd come back to the trail. Loose, he'd do that. Sis and I used to explore around in here just for fun, and kept it for our secret till Lew found out. She always rode Boise. I'm dead sure he'd bring her out all right."

"She hasn't come out — yet. Go on," said Bud, and Eddie rode forward obediently.

Three hours it took them to search the various passages where Eddie thought it possible that Marian had turned aside. Bud saw that the trail through was safe as any such trail could be, and he wondered at the nerve and initiative of the girl and the boy who had explored the place and found where certain queer twists and turns would lead. Afterwards he learned that Marian was twelve and Eddie ten when first they had hidden there from Indians, and they had been five years in finding where every passage led. Also, in daytime the place was not so fearsome, since sunlight slanted down into many a passageway through the "blow-holes" high above.

"She ain't here. I knew she wasn't," Eddie announced when the final tunnel let them into the graying light of dawn beyond the Peak.

"In that case — " Bud glanced from him to Jerry, who was blowing out his lantern.

Jerry let down the globe carefully, at the same time glancing soberly at Bud. "The kid knows better than I do what would happen if Lew met up with her and Boise."

Eddie shook his head miserably, his eyes fixed helplessly upon Bud. "Lew never, Mr. Birnie. I was with him every minute from dark till — till the cashier shot him. We come up the way I took you through the canyon. Lew never knew she was gone any more than I did."

Jerry bit his lip. "Kid, what if the gang run acrost her, *knowing* Lew was dead?" he grated. "And her on Boise? The word's out that Bud stole Boise. Dave and the boys rode out to round him up — and they ain't done it, so they're still riding — we'll hope. Kid, you know damn well your gang would double-cross Dave in a minute, now Lew's killed. If they got hold of the horse, do yuh think they 'd turn him over to Dave?"

"No, you bet your life they would n't!" Eddie retorted.

"And what about *her?*" Bud cut in with ominous calm. "She 's your sister, kid. Would you be worried if you knew they had *her* and the horse?"

Eddie gulped and looked away. "They would n't hurt her unless they knew 't Lew was dead," he said. "And them that went to Crater was killed or jailed, so—" He hesitated. "It looked to me like Anse was setting up waiting for the bunch to get back from Crater. He—he 's always jumpy when they go off and stay, and it 'd be just like him to set there and wait till daylight. It looks to me, Mr. Birnie, like him and —and the rest don't know yet that the Crater job was a fizzle. They would n't think of such a thing as taking Sis, or Boise either, unless they knew Lew was dead."

"Are you sure of that?" Bud had him in a grip that widened the boy's eyes with something approaching fear.

"Yes sir, Mr. Birnie, I 'm sure. What did n't go to Crater stayed in camp — or was gone on some other trip. No, I 'm sure!" He jerked away with sudden indignation at Bud's disbelief. "Say! Do you think I 'm bad enough to let my *sister* get into trouble with the Catrockers? I know they never got her. More 'n likely it 's Dave."

"Dave went up Burroback Valley," Jerry stated flatly. "Him and the boys was n't on this side the ridge. They had it sized up that Bud might go from Crater straight across into Black Rim, and they rode up to catch him as he comes back across." Jerry grinned a little. " They wanted that money you peeled off the crowd Sunday, Bud. They was willing you should get to Crater and cash them checks before they overhauled yuh and strung yuh up."

" You don't suppose they 'd hurt Marian if they found her with the horse? She might have followed along to Crater — "

" She never," Eddie contradicted. And Jerry declared in the same breath, " She 'd be too much afraid of Lew. No, if they found her with the horse they 'd take him away from her and send her back on another one to do the kitchen work," he conjectured with some contempt. " If they found *you* without the horse — well — men have been hung on suspicion, Bud. Money 's something everybody wants, and there ain't a man in the valley but what has figured your winnings down to the last two-bit piece. It 's just a runnin' match now to see what bunch gets to yuh first."

" Oh, the money! I 'd give the whole of it to anyone that would tell me Marian 's safe," Bud cried unguardedly in his misery. Whereat Jerry and Ed looked at each other queerly.

CHAPTER TWENTY

"Pick Your Footing!"

THE three sat irresolutely on their horses at the tunnel's end of the Gap, staring out over the valley of the Redwater and at the mountains beyond. Bud's face was haggard and the lines of his mouth were hard. It was so vast a country in which to look for one little woman who had *not* gone back to see Jerry's signal!

"I 'll bet yuh Sis cleared out," Eddie blurted, looking at Bud eagerly, as if he had been searching for some comforting word. "Sis has got lots of sand. She used to call me a 'fraid cat all the time when I did n't want to go where she did. I 'll bet she just took Boise and run off with him. She would, if she made up her mind — and I guess she 'd had about as much as she could stand, cookin' at Little Lost — "

Bud lifted his head and looked at Eddie like a man newly awakened. "I gave her money to take home for me, to my mother, down Laramie way. I begged her to go if she was liable to be in trouble over leaving the ranch. But she said she would n't go — not unless she was missed. She knew I 'd come back to the ranch. I just piled her hands full of bills in the dark and told her to use them if she had to — "

"She might have done it," Jerry hazarded hopefully. "Maybe she did sneak in some other way and get her things. She'd have to take some clothes along. Women folks always have to pack. By gosh, she could hide Boise out somewhere and —"

For a young man in danger of being lynched by his boss for horse stealing and waylaid and robbed by a gang notorious in the country, Bud's appetite for risk seemed insatiable that morning. For he added the extreme possibility of breaking his neck by reckless riding in the next hour.

He swung Sunfish about and jabbed him with the spurs, ducking into the gloom of the Gap as if the two who rode behind were assassins on his trail. Once he spoke, and that was to Sunfish. His tone was savage.

"Damn your lazy hide, you've been through here twice and you've got daylight to help — now pick up your feet and travel!"

Sunfish travelled; and the pace he set sent even Jerry gasping now and then when he came to the worst places, with the sound of galloping hoofs in the distance before him, and Eddie coming along behind and lifting his voice warningly now and then. Even the Catrockers had held the Gap in respect, and had ridden its devious trail cautiously. But caution was a meaningless word to Bud just then while a small flame of hope burned steadily before him.

The last turn, where on the first trip Sunfish lost Boise and balked for a minute, he made so fast that Sunfish left a patch of yellowish hair on a pointed rock and came into the open snorting fire of wrath. He went over the rough ground like a bouncing antelope, simply because he was too mad to care how many legs he broke. At the peak of rocks he showed an inclination to stop, and Bud, who had been thinking and planning while he hoped, pulled him to a stand and waited for the others to come up. They could not go nearer the corrals without incurring the danger of being overheard, and that must not happen.

" You damn fool," gritted Jerry when he came up with Bud. " If I 'd knowed you wanted to commit suicide I 'd a caved your head in with a rock and saved myself the craziest ride I ever took in m' life ! "

" Oh, shut up ! " Bud snapped impatiently. " We 're here, are n't we? Now listen to me, boys. You catch up my horses — Jerry, are you coming along with me? You may as well. I 'm a deputy sheriff, and if anybody stops you for whatever you 've done, I 'll show a warrant for your arrest. And by thunder," he declared with a faint grin, " I 'll serve it if I have to to keep you with me. I don't know what you 've done, and I don't care. I want you. So catch up my horses — and Jerry, you can pack my war-bag and roll your bed and mine, if I 'm too busy while I 'm here."

" You 're liable to be busy, all right," Jerry interpolated grimly.

" Well, they won't bother you. Ed, you better get the horses. Take Sunfish, here, and graze him somewhere outa sight. We 'll keep going, and we might have to start suddenly."

" How about Sis? I thought — "

" I 'm going to turn Little Lost upside down to find her, if she 's here. If she is n't, I 'm kinda hoping she went down to mother. She said there was no other place where she could go. And she 'd feel that she had to deliver the money, perhaps — because I must have given her a couple of thousand dollars. It was quite a roll, mostly in fifties and hundreds, and I'm short that much. I'm just gambling that the size of it made her feel she must go."

"That'd be Sis all over, Mr. Birnie." Eddie glanced around him uneasily. The sun was shining level in his eyes, and sunlight to Eddie had long meant danger. "I guess we better hurry, then. I'll get the horses down outa sight, and come back here afoot and wait."

"Do that, kid," said Bud, slipping wearily off Sunfish. He gave the reins into Eddie's hand, motioned Jerry with his head to follow, and hurried down the winding path to the corrals. The cool brilliance of the morning, the cheerful warbling of little, wild canaries in the bushes as he passed, for once failed to thrill him with joy of life. He was wondering whether to go straight to the house and search it if necessary to make sure that she had not been there, or whether Indian cunning would serve him best. His whole being ached for direct action; his heart trembled with fear lest he should jeopardize Marian's safety by his own impetuous haste to help her.

Pop, coming from the stable just as Bud was crossing the corral, settled the question for him. Pop peered at him sharply, put a hand to the small of his back and came stepping briskly toward him, his jaw working like a sheep eating hay.

"Afoot, air ye?" he exclaimed curiously. "Whatfer idea yuh got in yore head now, young feller? Comin' back here afoot when ye rid two fast horses off? Need n't be afraid of ole Pop — not unless yuh lie to 'im and try to git somethin' fur nothin'. Made off with Lew's wife, too, did n't ye? Oh, there ain't much gits past ole Pop, even if he ain't the man he used to be. I seen yuh lookin' at her when yuh oughta been eatin'. I seen yuh! An' her watchin' you when she thought nobuddy 'd ketch her at it! Sho! Shucks a'mighty! You been playin' hell all around, now, ain't ye? Need n't lie — I know what my own eyes tells me! "

"You know a lot, then, that I wish I knew. I've been in Crater all the time, Pop. Did you know Lew was mixed up in a bank robbery yesterday, and the cashier of the bank shot him? The rest of the gang is dead or in jail. The sheriff did some good work there for a few minutes."

Pop pinched in his lips and stared at Bud unwinkingly for a minute. "Don't lie to me," he warned petulantly. "Went to Crater, did ye? Cashed them checks, I expect."

Bud pulled his mouth into a rueful grin. "Yes, Pop, I cashed the checks, all right — and here 's what 's left of the money. I guess," he went on while he pulled out a small roll of bills and licked his finger preparatory to counting them, "I might better have stuck to running my horses. Poker 's sure a fright. The way it can eat into a man's pocket — "

"Went and lost all that money on poker, did ye?" Pop's voice was shrill. "After me tellin' yuh how to git it — and showin' yuh how yuh could beat Boise —" the old man's rage choked him. He thrust his face close to Bud's and glared venomously.

"Yes, and just to show you I appreciate it, I'm going to give you what 's left after I 've counted off enough to see me through to Spokane. I feel sick,

Pop. I want change of air. And as for riding two fast horses to Crater — " he paused while he counted slowly, Pop licking his lips avidly as he watched, " — why I don't know what you mean. I only ride one horse at a time, Pop, when I'm sober. And I was sober till I hit Crater."

He stopped counting when he reached fifty dollars, and gave the rest to Pop, who thumbed the bank notes in a frenzy of greed until he saw that he had two hundred dollars in his possession. The glee which he tried to hide, the crafty suspicion that this was not all of it, the returning conviction that Bud was actually almost penniless, and the cunning assumption of senility, was pictured in his face. Pop's poor, miserly soul was for a minute shamelessly revealed. Distraught though he was, Bud stared and shuddered a little at the spectacle.

" I always said 't you're a good, honest, well-meaning boy," Pop cackled, slyly putting the money out of sight while he patted Bud on the shoulder. " Dave, he thought mebby you took and stole Boise — and if I was you, Bud, I'd git to Spokane quick as I could, and not let Dave ketch ye. Dave's out now lookin' for ye. If he suspicioned you'd have the gall to come right back to Little Lost, I expect mebby he'd string yuh up, young feller. Dave's got a nasty temper — he has so! "

" There's something else, Pop, that I don't like very well to be accused of. You say Mrs. Morris is gone. I don't know a thing about that, or about the horse being gone. I've been in Crater. I'd just got my money out of the bank when it was held up, and Lew was shot."

Pop teetered and gummed his tobacco and grinned

foxily. " Shucks! *I* don't care nothin' about Lew's wife goin', ner I don't care nothin' much about the horse. They ain't no fun-ral uh mine, Bud. Dave an' Lew, let 'em look after their own belongin's."

" They 'll have to, far as I 'm concerned," said Bud. " What would I want of a horse I can beat any time I want to run mine? Dave must think I 'm scared to ride fast, since Sunday! And Pop, I 've got troubles enough without having a woman on my hands. Are you sure Marian 's gone?"

" *Sure?* " Pop snorted. " Honey, she 's had to do the cookin' for me an' Jerry — and if I ain't sure — "

Bud did not wait to hear him out. There was Honey, whom he would very much like to avoid meeting; so the sooner he made certain of Marian's deliberate flight the better, since Honey was not an early riser. He went to the house and entered by way of the kitchen, feeling perfectly sure all the while that Pop was watching him. The disorder there was sufficiently convincing that Marian was gone, so he tiptoed across the room to a door through which he had never seen any one pass save Lew and Marian.

It was her bedroom, meagrely furnished, but in perfect order. On the goods-box dresser with a wavy-glassed mirror above it, her hair brush, comb and a few cheap toilet necessities lay, with the comb across a nail file as if she had put it down hurriedly before going out to serve supper to the men. Marian, then, had not stolen home to pack things for the journey, as Jerry had declared a woman would do. Bud sent a lingering glance around the room and closed the door. Hope was still with him, but it was darkened now with doubts.

In the kitchen again he hesitated, wanting his guitar and mandolin and yet aware of the foolishness of burdening himself with them now. Food was a different matter, however. Dave owed him for more than three weeks of hard work in the hayfield, so Bud collected from the pantry as much as he could carry, and left the house like a burglar.

Pop was fiddling with the mower that stood in front of the machine shed, plainly waiting for whatever might transpire. And since the bunk-house door was in plain view and not so far away as Bud wished it, he went boldly over to the old man, carrying his plunder on his shoulder.

"Dave owes me for work, Pop, so I took what grub I needed," he explained with elaborate candor. "I'll show you what I've got, so you'll know I'm not taking anything that I've no right to." He set down the sack, opened it and looked up into what appeared to be the largest-muzzled six-shooter he had ever seen in his life. Sheer astonishment held him there gaping, half stooped over the sack.

"No ye don't, young feller!" Pop snarled vindictively. "Yuh think I'd let a horse thief git off 'n this ranch whilst I'm able to pull a trigger? You fork over that money you got on ye, first thing yuh do! It's mine by rights — I told yuh I'd help ye to win money off 'n the valley crowd, and I done it. An' what does you do? Never pay a mite of attention to me after I'd give ye all the inside workin's of the game — never offer to give me my share — no, by Christmas, you go steal a horse of my son's and hide him out somewheres, and go lose mighty near all I helped yuh win, playin' poker! Think I'm goin' to

stand for that? Think two hundred dollars is goin'
to even things up when I helped ye to win a fortune?
Hand over that fifty you got on yuh ! "

Very meekly, his face blank, Bud reached into his
pocket and got the money. Without a word he pulled
two or three dollars in silver from his trousers pockets
and added that to the lot. " Now what? " he wanted
to know.

" Now you 'll wait till Dave gits here to hang yuh
fer horse-stealing ! " shrilled Pop. " Jerry! Oh,
Jerry! Where be yuh? I got 'im, by Christmas — I
got the horse thief — caught him carryin' good grub
right outa the house ! "

" Look out, Jerry! " called Bud, glancing quickly
toward the bunk-house.

Now, Pop had without doubt been a man difficult
to trick in his youth, but he was old, and he was ex-
cited, tickled over his easy triumph. He turned to see
what was wrong with Jerry.

" Look out, Pop, you old fool, you 'll bust a blood-
vessel if you don't quiet down," Bud censured mock-
ingly, wresting the gun from the clawing, struggling
old man in his arms. He was surprised at the strength
and agility of Pop, and though he was forcing him
backward step by step into the machine shed, and
knew that he was master of the situation, he had his
hands full.

" Wildcats is nothing to Pop when he gets riled,"
Jerry grinned, coming up on the run. " I kinda expected something like this. What yuh want done with
him, Bud? "

" Gag him so he can't holler his head off, and then
take him along — when I 've got my money back,"

Bud panted. " Pop, you 're about as appreciative as a buck Injun."

" Going to be hard to pack him so he 'll ride," Jerry observed quizzically when Pop, bound and gagged, lay glaring at them behind the bunk-house. " He don't quite balance your two grips, Bud. And we do need that grub."

" You bring the grub — I 'll take Pop — " Bud stopped in the act of lifting the old man and listened. Honey's voice was calling Pop, with embellishments which Bud would never have believed a part of Honey's vocabulary. From her speech, she was coming after him, and Pop's jaws worked frantically behind Bud's handkerchief.

Jerry tilted his head toward the luggage he had made a second trip for, picked up Pop, clamped his hand over the mouth that was trying to betray them, and slipped away through the brush, glancing once over his shoulder to make sure that Bud was following him.

They reached the safe screen of branches and stopped there for a minute, listening to Honey's vituperations and her threats of what she would do to Pop if he did not come up and start a fire.

She stopped, and hoofbeats sounded from the main road. Dave and his men were coming.

In his heart Bud thanked Little Lost for that hidden path through the bushes. He heard Dave asking Honey what was the matter with her, heard the unwomanly reply of the girl, heard her curse Pop for his neglect of the kitchen stove at that hour of the morning. Heard, too, her questioning of Dave. Had they found Bud, or Marian?

" If you got 'em together, and did n't string 'em both up to the nearest tree — "

Bud bit his lip and went on, his face aflame with rage at the brutishness of a girl he had half respected. " Honey ! " he whispered contemptuously. " What a name for that little beast ! "

At the rocks Eddie was waiting with Stopper, upon whom they hurriedly packed the beds and Bud's luggage. They spoke in whispers when they spoke at all, and to insure the horse's remaining quiet Eddie had tied a cotton rope snugly around its muzzle.

" I 'll take Pop," Bud whispered, but Jerry shook his head and once more shouldered the old fellow as he would carry a bag of grain. So they slipped back down the trail, took a turn which Bud did not know, and presently Bud found that Jerry was keeping straight on. Bud made an Indian sign on the chance that Jerry would understand it, and with his free hand Jerry replied. He was taking Pop somewhere. They were to wait for him when they had reached the horses. So they separated for a space.

" This is sure a great country for hideouts, Mr. Birnie," Eddie ventured when they had put half a mile between themselves and Little Lost, and had come upon Smoky, Sunfish and Eddie's horse feeding quietly in a tiny, spring-watered basin half surrounded with rocks. " If you know the country you can keep dodgin' sheriffs all your life — if you just have grub enough to last."

" Looks to me as if there are n't many wasted opportunities here," Bud answered with some irony. " Is there an honest man in the whole country, Ed ? I 'd just like to know."

Eddie hesitated, his eyes anxiously trying to read Bud's meaning and his mood. "Not right around the Sinks, I guess," he replied truthfully. "Up at Crater there are some, and over to Jumpoff. But I guess this valley would be called pretty tough, all right. It's so full of caves and queer places it kinda attracts the ones that want to hide out." Then he grinned. "It's lucky for you it's like that, Mr. Birnie, or I don't see how you'd get away. Now I can show you how to get clear away from here without getting caught. But I guess we ought to have breakfast first. I'm pretty hungry. Ain't you? I can build a fire against that crack in the ledge over there, and the smoke will go away back underneath so it won't show. There's a blow-hole somewhere that draws smoke like a chimney."

Jerry came after a little, sniffing bacon. He threw himself down beside the fire and drew a long breath. "That old skunk's heavier than what you might think," he observed whimsically. "I packed him down into one of them sink holes and untied his feet and left him to scramble out best way he can. It'll take him longer'n it took me. Having the use of your hands helps quite a lot. And the use of your mouth to cuss a little. But he'll make it in an hour or two — I'm afraid." He looked at Bud, a half-shamed tenderness in his eyes. "It sure was hard to leave him like I did. It was like walking on your toes past a rattler curled up asleep somewhere, afraid you might spoil his nap. Only Pop wasn't asleep." He sat up and reached his hand for a cup of coffee which Eddie was offering. "Anyway, I had the fun of telling the old devil what I thought about him," he added, and blew away the steam and took another satisfying nip.

" He 'll put them on our trail, I suppose," said Bud, biting into a ragged piece of bread with a half-burned slice of hot bacon on it.

" When he gets to the ranch he will. His poison fangs was sure loaded when I left. He said he wanted to cut your heart out for robbing him, and so forth, ad swearum. We 'd best not leave any trail."

" We ain't going to," Eddie assured him eagerly. " I 'm glad being with the Catrockers is going to do some good, Mr. Birnie. It 'll help you git away, and that 'll help find Sis. I guess she hit down where you live, maybe. How far can your horse travel to-day — if he has to? "

Bud looked across to where Sunfish, having rolled in a wet spot near the spring and muddied himself to his satisfaction, was greedily at work upon a patch of grass. " If he has to, till he drops in his tracks. And that won't be for many a mile, kid. He 's thoroughbred; a thoroughbred never knows when to quit."

" Well, there ain't any speedy trail ahead of us to-day," Eddie vouchsafed cheeringly. " There 's half a mile maybe where we can gallop, and the rest is a case of picking your footing."

" Let 's begin picking it, then," said Bud, and got up, reaching for his bridle.

By devious ways it was that Eddie led them out of that sinister country surrounding the Sinks. In the beginning Bud and Jerry exchanged glances, and looked at their guns, believing that it would be through Catrock Canyon they would have to ride. Eddie, riding soberly in the lead, had yet a certain youthful sense of his importance. " They 'll never think of following yuh this way, unless old Pop Truman gits back in time to tell 'em I 'm travelling with yuh," he observed once when they had penetrated beyond the neighborhood of caves and blow-holes and were riding safely down a canyon that offered few chances of their being observed save from the front, which did not concern them.

"I guess you don't know old Pop is about the ringleader of the Catrockers. Er he was, till he began to git kinda childish about hoarding money, and then Dave stepped in. And Mr. Birnie, I guess you 'd have been dead when you first came there, if it had n't been that Dave and Pop wanted to give you a chance to get a lot of money off of Jeff's bunch. Lew was telling how you kept cleaning up, and he said right along that they was taking too much risk having you around. Lew said he bet you was a detective. Are you, Mr. Birnie?"

Bud was riding with his shoulders sagged forward, his thoughts with Marian — wherever she was. He had been convinced that she was not at Little Lost, that she had started for Laramie. But now that he was away from that evil spot his doubts returned. What if she were still in the neighborhood — what if they found her? Memory of Honey's vindictiveness made him shiver, Honey was the kind of woman who would kill.

"I am, from now on, kid," he said despondently. "We 're going to ride till we find your sister. And if those hell-hounds got her — "

"They did n't, from the way Honey talked," Jerry comforted. "We 'll find her at Laramie, don't you ever think we won't!"

CHAPTER TWENTY–ONE

TRAILS END

At the last camp, just north of the Platte, Bud's two black sheep balked. Bud himself, worn by sleepless nights and long hours in the saddle, turned furiously when Jerry announced that he guessed he and Ed would n't go any farther.

"Well, damn you both for ungrateful hounds!" grated Bud, hurt to the quick. "I hope you don't think I brought you this far to help hold me in the saddle; I made it north alone, without any mishap. I think I could have come back all right. But if you want to quit here, all right. You can high-tail it back to your outlaws —"

"Well, if you go 'n put it that way!" Jerry expostulated, lifting both hands high in the air in a vain attempt to pull the situation toward the humorous. "You 're a depity sheriff, and you got the drop." He grinned, saw that Bud's eyes were still hard and his mouth unyielding, and lowered his hands, looking crestfallen as a kicked pup that had tried to be friendly.

"You can see for yourself we ain't fit to go 'n meet your mother and your father like we was — like we 'd went straight," Eddie put in explanatorily. "You 've been raised good, and — say, it makes a man want to *be* good to see how a feller don't have to be no preacher to live right. But it don't seem square to let you take us right home with you, just because you 're so darned kind you 'd do it and never think a thing about it. We ain't ungrateful — I know *I* ain't. But — but — "

" The kid's said it, Bud," Jerry came to the rescue. "We come along because it was a ticklish trip you had ahead. And I 've knowed as good riders as you are, that could stand a little holding in the saddle when some freak had tried to shoot 'em out of it. But you 're close to home now and you don't need us no more, and so we ain't going to horn in on the prodigal calf's milk-bucket. Marian, she 's likely there — "

" If Sis ain't with your folks we 'll hunt her up," Eddie interrupted eagerly. " Sis is your kind — she — she 's good enough for yuh, Bud, and I hope she — if she 's got any sense she 'll — well, if it comes to the marrying point, I — well, darn it, I 'd like to see Sis git as good a man as you are ! " Eddie, having blundered that far, went headlong as if he were afraid to stop. " Sis is educated, and she 's an awful good singer and a fine girl, only I 'm her brother. But I 'm going to live honest from now on, Bud, and I hope you won't hold off on account of me. I ain't going to have Sis feel like cryin' when she thinks about me ! You — you — said something that hurt like a knife, Bud, when you told me that, up in Crater. And she was n't to blame for marryin' Lew — and she done that outa goodness, the kind you showed to Jerry and me. And *we* don't want to go spoilin' everything by letting your folks see what you 're bringin' home with yuh ! And it might hurt Sis with your folks, if they found out that I 'm — "

Bud had been standing by his horse, looking from one to the other, listening, watching their faces, measuring the full depth of their manhood. "Say! you remind me of a story the folks tell on me," he said, his eyes shining, while his voice strove to make light of it all. "Once, when I was a kid in pink aprons, I got lost from the trail-herd my folks were bringing up from Texas. It was comin' dark, and they had the whole outfit out hunting me, and everybody scared to death. When they were all about crazy, they claim I came walking up to the camp-fire dragging a dead snake by the tail, and carrying a horn toad in my shirt, and claiming they were mine because I 'ketched 'em.' I'm not branding that yarn with any moral — but figure it out for yourself, boys."

The two looked at each other and grinned. "I ain't dead yet," Eddie made sheepish comment. "Mebbe you kinda look on me as being a horn toad, Bud."

"When you bear in mind that my folks raised that kid, you'll realize that it takes a good deal to stampede mother." Bud swung into the saddle to avoid subjecting his emotions to the cramped, inadequate limitations of speech. "Let's go, boys. She's a long trail to take the kinks out of before supper-time."

They stood still, making no move to follow. Bud reined Smoky around so that he faced them, reached laboriously into that mysterious pocket of a cow-puncher's trousers which is always held closed by the belt of his chaps, and which invariably holds in its depths the things he wants in a hurry. They watched him curiously, resolutely refusing to interpret his bit of autobiography, wondering perhaps why he did not go.

" Here she is." Bud had disinterred the deputy-sheriff's badge, and began to polish it by the primitive but effectual method of spitting on it and then rubbing it vigorously on his sleeve. " You 're outside of Crater County, but by thunder you 're both guilty of resisting an officer, and county lines don't count!" He had pinned the badge at random on his coat while he was speaking, and now, before the two realized what he was about, he had his six-shooter out and aimed straight at them.

Bud had never lived in fear of the law. Instantly he was sorry when he saw the involuntary stiffening of their muscles, the quick wordless suspicion and defiance that sent their eyes in shifty glances to right and left before their hands lifted a little. Trust him, love him as they might, there was that latent fear of capture driven deep into their souls; so deep that even he had not erased it.

Bud saw — and so he laughed.

" I 've got to show my folks that I 've made a gathering," he said. " You can't quit, boys. And I 'm going to take you to the end of the trail, now you 've started." He eyed them, saw that they were still stubborn, and drew in his breath sharply, manfully meeting the question in their minds.

" We 've left more at the Sinks than the gnashing of teeth," he said whimsically. " A couple of bad names, for instance. You 're two bully good friends of mine, and — damn it, Marian will want to see both of you fellows, if she 's there. If she is n't — we 'll maybe have a big circle to ride, finding her. I 'll need you, no matter what 's ahead." He looked from one to the other, gave a snort and added impatiently, " Aw, fork

your horses and don't stand there looking like a couple
of damn fools!"

Whereupon Jerry shook his head dissentingly,
grinned and gave Eddie so emphatic an impulse toward
his horse that the kid went sprawling.

"Guess we're up against it, all right — but I do wish
you'd lose that badge!" Jerry surrendered, and
flipped the bridle reins over the neck of his horse.
"Horn toad is right, the way you're scabbling around
amongst them rocks," he called light-heartedly to the
kid. "Ever see a purtier sunrise? I never!"

I don't know what they thought of the sunset.
Gorgeous it was, with many soft colors blended into
unnamable tints and translucencies, and the songs of
birds in the thickets as they passed. Smoky, Sunfish and
Stopper walked briskly, ears perked forward, heads
up, eyes eager to catch the familiar landmarks that
meant home. Bud's head was up, also, his eyes went
here and there, resting with a careless affection on those
same landmarks which spelled home. He would have
let Smoky's reins have a bit more slack and would have
led his little convoy to the corrals at a gallop, had not
hope begun to tremble and shrink from meeting certainty face to face. Had you asked him then, I think
Bud would have owned himself a coward. Until he
had speech with home-folk he would merely be hoping
that Marian was there; but until he had speech with
them he need not hear that they knew nothing of her.
Bud-like, however, he tried to cover his trepidation with
a joke.

"We'll sneak up on 'em," he said to Ed and Jerry
when the roofs of house and stables came into view.

" Here 's where I grew up, boys. And in a minute or two more you 'll see the greatest little mother on earth — and the finest dad," he added, swallowing the last of his Scotch stubbornness.

" And Sis, I hope," Eddie said wistfully. " I sure hope she 's here."

Neither Jerry nor Bud answered him at all. Smoky threw up his head suddenly and gave a shrill whinny, and a horse at the corrals answered sonorously.

" Say! That sounds to me like Boise!" Eddie exclaimed, standing up in his stirrups to look.

Bud turned pale, then flushed hotly. " Don't *holler* it!" he muttered, and held Smoky back a little. For just one reason a young man's heart pounds as Bud's heart pounded then. Jerry looked at him, took a deep breath and bit his lip thoughtfully. It may be that Jerry's heartbeats were not quite normal just then, but no one would ever know.

They rode slowly to a point near the corner of the stable, and there Bud halted the two with his lifted hand. Bud was trembling a little — but he was smiling, too. Eddie was frankly grinning, Jerry's face was the face of a good poker-player — it told nothing.

In a group with their backs to them stood three: Marian, Bud's mother and his father. Bob Birnie held Boise by the bridle, and the two women were stroking the brown nose of the horse that moved uneasily, with little impatient head-tossings.

" He does n't behave like a horse that has made the long trip he has made," Bud's mother observed admiringly. " You must be a wonderful little horsewoman, my dear, as well as a wonderful little woman in every other way. Buddy should never have sent you on such

a trip — just to bring home money, like a bank mes-
senger! But I'm glad that he did! And I do wish
you would consent to stay — such an afternoon with
music I have n't had since Buddy left us. You could
stay with me and train for the concert work you intend
doing. I'm only an old ranch woman in a slat sun-
bonnet — but I taught my Buddy — and have you
heard him?"

"An old woman in a slat sunbonnet — oh, how *can*
you? Why, you 're the most wonderful woman in the
whole world!" Marian's voice was almost tearful in
its protest. "Yes — I have heard — your Buddy.
But —"

"'T is the strangest way to go about selling a horse
that I ever saw," Bob Birnie put in dryly, smoothing his
beard while he looked at them. "We 'd be glad to have
you stay, lass. But you 've asked me to place a price
on the horse, and I should like to ask ye a question or
two. How fast did ye say he could run?"

Marian laid an arm around the shoulders of the old
lady in a slat sunbonnet and patted her arm while she
answered.

"Well, he beat everything in the country, so they refused to race against him, until Bud came with his
horses," she replied. "It took Sunfish to outrun him.
He 's terribly fast, Mr. Birnie. I — really, I think he
could beat the world's record — if Bud rode him!"

Just here you should picture Ed and Jerry with their
hands over their mouths, and Bud wanting to hide his
face with his hat.

Bob Birnie's beard behaved oddly for a minute, while
he leaned and stroked Boise's flat forelegs, that told of
speed. "Wee-ll," he hesitated, soft-heartedness bat-

tling with the horse-buyer's keenness, " since Bud isna
here to ride him, he 'll make a good horse for the roundup. I 'll give ye " — more battling — " a hundred and
fifty dollars for him, if ye care to sell — "

" Here, wait a minute before you sell to that old
skinflint ! " Bud shouted exuberantly, dismounting
with a rush. The rush, I may say, carried him to the
little old lady in the slat sunbonnet, and to that other
little lady who was staring at him with wide, bright
eyes. Bud's arms went around his mother. Perhaps
by accident he gathered in Marian also — they were
standing very close, and his arms were very long —
and he was slow to discover his mistake.

" I 'll give you two hundred for Boise, and I 'll
throw in one brother, and one long-legged, good-for-
nothing cowpuncher — "

" Meaning yourself, Buddy ? " came teasingly from
the slat sunbonnet, whose occupant had not been told
just everything. " I 'll be surprised if she 'll have you,
with that dirty face and no shave for a week and more.
But if she does, you 're luckier than you deserve, for
riding up on us like this ! We 've heard all about you,
Buddy — though you were wise to send this lassie to
gild your faults and make a hero of you ! "

Now, you want to know how Marian managed to
live through that. I will say that she discovered how
tenaciously a young man's arms may cling when he
thinks he is embracing *merely* his mother; but she freed
herself and ran to Eddie, fairly pulled him off his horse,
and talked very fast and incoherently to him and Jerry,
asking question after question without waiting for a
reply to any of them. All this, I suppose, in the hope
that they would not hear, or, hearing, would not under-

stand what that terrible, wonderful little woman was saying so innocently.

But you cannot faze youth. Eddie had important news for Sis, and he felt that now was the time to tell it before Marian blushed any redder, so he pulled her face up to his, put his lips so close to her ear that his breath tickled, and whispered — without any preface whatever that she could marry Bud any time now, because she was a widow.

"Here! Somebody — Bud — quick! Sis has fainted! Doggone it, I only told her Lew 's dead and she can marry you — shucks! I thought she 'd be glad!"

Down on the Staked Plains, on an evening much like the evening when Bud came home with his "stake" and his hopes and two black sheep who were becoming white as most of us, a camp-fire began to crackle and wave smoke ribbons this way and that before it burned steadily under the supper pots of a certain hungry, happy group which you know.

"It 's somewhere about here that I got lost from camp when I was a kid," Bud observed, tilting back his hat and lifting a knee to snap a dry stick over it. "Mother 'd know, I bet. I kinda wish we 'd brought her and dad along with us. That 's about eighteen years ago they trailed a herd north — and here we are, taking our trail-herd north on the same trail! I kinda wish now I 'd picked up a bunch of yearling heifers along with our two-year-olds. We could have brought another hundred head just as well as not. They sure drive nice. Mother would have enjoyed this trip."

" You think so, do you? "　Marian gave him a supe-
rior little smile along with the coffee-boiler. " If
you 'd heard her talk about that trip north when there
were n't any men around listening, you 'd change your
mind.　Bud Birnie, you are the *simplest* creature!
You think, because a woman does n't make a fuss over
things, she does n't mind.　Your mother told me that
trip was a perfect nightmare.　She taught you music just
in the hope that you 'd go back to civilization and
live there where there are some modern improvements,
and she could visit you!　And here you are — all
wrapped up in a bunch of young stock, dirty as
a pig and your whiskers — ow!　Bud!　Stop that
immediately, or I 'll go put my face in a cactus just
for relief! "

" Maybe you 're dissatisfied yourself with my bunch
of cattle.　Maybe you did n't go in raptures over our
claim and make more plans in a day than four men
could carry out in a year.　Maybe you wish your husband was a man that was content to pound piano keys
all his life and let his hair grow long instead of his
whiskers.　If you hate this, why did n't you say so,
lady? "

" I was speaking," said Marian as dignifiedly as was
possible, " of your mother.　She was raised in civilization, and she has simply made the best of pioneering all
her married life.　I was born and raised in cow-country
and I love it.　As I said before, you are the *simplest*
creature!　Would you really bring a father and mother
on a honeymoon trail — especially when the bride
did n't want them, and they would much rather stay
at home? "

" Hey! " cried Eddie disgustedly, coming up from a

shallow creek with a bucket of water and a few dry sticks. " The coffee 's upset and putting the fire out! Gee whiz! Can't you folks quit love-makin' and tend to business long enough to cook a meal? "

THE END

Bertha Muzzy Bower, born in Cleveland, Minnesota, in 1871, was the first woman to make a career of writing Western fiction and remains one of the most widely known, having written nearly seventy novels. She became familiar with cowboys and ranch life at sixteen when her family moved to the Big Sandy area of Montana. She was nearly thirty and mother of three before she began writing under the surname of the first of her three husbands. Her first novel, *Chip, of the Flying U,* was initially published as a serial in 1904 and was an immediate success. Bower went on to write more books, fourteen in all, about the Flying U, one of the best being the short story collection, *The Happy Family.* In 1933 she turned to stories set prior to the events described in *Chip, of the Flying U. The Whoop-up* actually begins this saga, recounting Chip Bennett's arrival in Montana and at the Flying U. Much of the appeal of this saga is due to Bower's use of humor, the strong sense of loyalty and family depicted among her characters, as well as the authentic quality of her cowboys. She herself was a maverick who experimented with the Western story, introducing modern technologies and raising unusual social concerns—such as aeroplanes in *Skyrider* or divorce in *Lonesome Land.* She was sensitive to the lives of women on the frontier and created some extraordinary female characters, notably in Vada Williams in *The Haunted Hills,* Georgie Howard in *Good Indian,* Helen in *The Bellehelen Mine,* and Mary Allison in *Trouble Rides the Wind,* another early Chip Bennett story. She was also able to write Western novels memorable for the characterization of setting and dramatization of nature, such as *Van Patten* or *The Swallowfork Bulls.*